PRAISE FOR *CODA*

★ "The story hums with tension. Plot twists and lots of action make for a riveting read . . . The music seems almost alive, as if it were itself a character."

—School Library Journal (starred review)

★ "Atmospheric and emotionally rich, this intense story practically sings with defiance, swaggering like the rock and punk of old. A strong debut from an author to watch."

—Publishers Weekly (starred review)

"Anthem's personal connections to the richly written cast make the character-driven plot sing. Trevayne's debut showcases a creative concept, skillful dialogue and vivid characters."

—Kirkus Reviews

"[S]hould appeal to music-loving teens."*—Booklist*

"[A] dystopian hacker novel sure to hypnotize many readers."

—Shelf Awareness

"The action is engaging and fast-paced, propelled forward by the authentic and sometimes conflicting interests of its likable cast of characters. . . . The ending is tense and sensational, and readers won't feel let down by the action."

—ForeWord Reviews

"*Coda* is a fascinating young adult read for music lovers and science fiction fans, highly recommended."

—Midwest Book Review

CHORUS

Also by Emma Trevayne
Coda

CHORUS

Emma Trevayne

RP|TEENS
PHILADELPHIA · LONDON

Books published by Running Press are available at special discounts for bulk purchases in the United States by corporations, institutions, and other organizations. For more information, please contact the Special Markets Department at the Perseus Books Group, 2300 Chestnut Street, Suite 200, Philadelphia, PA 19103, or call (800) 810-4145, ext. 5000, or e-mail special.markets@perseusbooks.com.

ISBN 978-0-7624-4950-7

Library of Congress Control Number: 2013956688

E-book ISBN 978-0-7624-5201-9

9 8 7 6 5 4 3 2 1
Digit on the right indicates the number of this printing

Cover and interior design by T.L. Bonaddio
Edited by Lisa Cheng
Typography: Cheltenham and OCRA

Published by Running Press Teens
An Imprint of Running Press Book Publishers
A Member of the Perseus Books Group
2300 Chestnut Street
Philadelphia, PA 19103–4371

Visit us on the web!
www.runningpress.com/kids

The days of dedicating a song on the radio might be mostly over, but, Lisa, this one's for you.

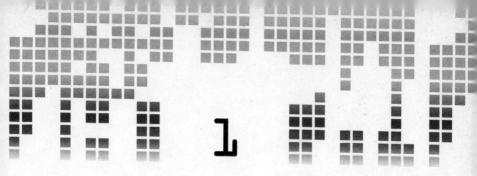

1

It's white, everywhere. Walls, floor, teeth. The woman's smile is the last thing I see before my eyes close, the unbearable sound taking over my ears, my head, the whole world. Unbearable because it's too beautiful, too much. Why wouldn't anyone keep this sound of sunlight and polished wood and a gentle voice to themselves? I know this must be singing, music, and the whispers that I never understood make so much sense now, everything makes sense. Of course, they hide this from us until we can handle it, but it's mine now. I have it and I'm never letting go, the climbing voice is too beautiful and I have to catch it before it runs away. My arms stretch out but something stops me, and the voice is running, fading, too far.

My eyelids flicker against the whiteness and oh, this is music, too, right? Heavier, darker, exciting like being awake in the middle of the night, watching shadows crawl across the floor, knowing I'm supposed to be asleep. Something thumps, like counting seconds. It makes me smile, wider and wider. I'm so happy, everyone should be this happy. The white is blinding, I can't see, but I'm okay. I'll always be okay, because the Corp will look after me and the Corp is eternal, eternal, eternal. . . .

2

Fingers touch my wrist. I'm supposed to be paying attention so that I can make *that* stop happening. One day.

It wasn't a bad one this time; I don't think I was out very long. I blink the room back into focus, the teacher's voice reforming into decipherable words. Bright, blinding sunshine pierces the windows, bleaches every surface white, and even though I know it's the same sun that shines on the Web, it feels more real here. Everything feels more real here. *I* feel more real here. But not real enough. For that, I need to free myself of the poisoned thing in my brain.

The goose bumps on my arms melt back into my skin; my pulse goes back to normal. I'm okay. Fable pulls his hand away from me to make notes, which I'll have to borrow later. He always knows when one's hit me, like he has to take all the responsibility for that because I've never told anyone else about the flashbacks.

Except Omega, obviously. Omega was in the white room, too, but he's not here. He's thousands of miles away, and we don't have that crazy twin thing where we can sense when something's wrong with the other no matter how far apart we are.

On my other side, Jonas's eyes narrow in a way that could be passed off as squinting to anyone who doesn't know him. I nudge his leg with my knee, smile, mouth *tonight* and watch his shoulders relax.

". . . An essay on how psychotherapy has changed as our

understanding of neural pathways has increased."

Pay attention. Right. I need this class to graduate, and I need to graduate to eventually get into medical school, and I need to do that if I want to have a prayer of fixing myself. Of pushing the white room away and into darkness forever.

No one else is going to do it. And this isn't the Web under Corp rule, where they'd pluck me out of school at seventeen or even younger, and train me to be a med-tech while my friends went off to be guards or run clubs. There's none of that anymore.

Everything in Los Angeles takes up so much more space. Sometimes, space and time are the same thing.

We escape five minutes later, into the crazy sprawl that clings with cement hands to the ocean. My ocean. Barely a year here and it's mine, as much a part of me as my pulse, and I cling to the things I know I love, the things I know I despise, the things that define me that aren't a bright, white room.

"Where to?" I ask, as if we don't almost always wind up at the same place after school.

"Actually, I promised I'd go home for dinner," Jonas says. In direct light, his dark hair has little glints of red in it. Natural, in wild contrast to my rainbow mess. "Want to come?"

Fable wanders away to lean against a nearby tree, waiting because he knows what my answer will be. "I should study," I say. Jonas's expression tells me he knew what my answer would be, too.

Jonas's parents don't quite like me. Don't quite trust me. I'm one of *those* people, the refugees from the Web. That it was my older brother who started, and won, a rebellion gets me a little credit, but not enough.

He kisses my nose. My eyes close, fingers twisting into his shirt. "You studied all weekend. You study too much."

I don't, but it's my fault he doesn't get how someone can be so obsessed about going into medical research; that's weird all on its own. How much weirder would it be to tell him it's because the Corp he's heard so many horror stories about performed their last act of sadistic, controlling vengeance on *me*?

The white room flashes across my mind. "Probably," I agree, keeping my voice steady, even. "Part of the deal."

"I know." He smiles back. "Catch up with you later?"

His lips are soft. I feel them on mine even after we've stepped apart and I've turned away. He watches me rejoin Fable before he heads in the opposite direction for a transport stop that will take him to his house out in the foothills.

"I need coffee." Fable pushes himself off the tree.

"Ew. Fine."

"You okay now?"

"Yeah, I've had worse." Much worse.

"Fuck, what did they do to you?" It's not the first time he's asked this, and not the first time I haven't had an answer.

"That's what I'm going to figure out. C'mon." There are still students crowding around outside the school and I don't like talking about it at all, but especially where people can hear.

In the harshness of the summer afternoon, concrete sizzles, mirrored buildings turn to shards of fire stretching to return to the sun. Los Angeles is a blanket flung out over the landscape, wrinkled and lumpy. You can't even tell anymore that it was almost obliterated. It's the only city I've ever seen apart from the Web, and there's only one more out there. Fable and I keep making plans to drive to Seattle, but it hasn't happened yet.

It took a while after the rebellion to discover this place was still here, longer still to uncover how the Corp had kept its existence hidden from us, and ours from it. I wasn't here to see the looks on the faces of the people who met the first visitors from the Web and heard the full story of where they'd come from.

I would've paid good credits for that, or handfuls of the metal money they use here that I'm still getting used to.

Web citizens didn't come here empty-handed, though. We got some things right. I check my tablet as we walk down busy streets, linked across the country to the Web. Nothing. For the first few weeks everyone tabbed every half hour to check on me.

I guess they've gotten used to me not being around now. The thought makes my chest ache, even if the reverse is also true.

"Here?" Fable doesn't wait for an answer, just drops his bag onto a chair and heads inside our usual afternoon spot, with its outdoor tables and an owner who doesn't care how long we linger. Across the street is the intake center, where anyone coming from the Web registers before settling into a new life. A pod full of them has just arrived and I think about waving, but someone might recognize me. Instead, I dump my stuff and slouch in my seat, tipping my face up to the sky. My tablet buzzes against my leg and I grab it quickly. I don't recognize the sender and the message makes even less sense. Someone must've typed in a number wrong.

"You okay?"

"Stop asking."

"Good. He's out of peppermint tea, you get raspberry," Fable says, juggling two cups and his tablet. "Sabine wants to know if you have her leather skirt. She wants it for this weekend."

"At home." I wave vaguely in that direction. "Tell her I'll bring it to practice."

"Cool." He takes a sip of coffee and I wrinkle my nose. I spend my life avoiding things I could get addicted to, which is an addiction of its own, I guess. Everyone has a vice; mine is hatred of what that witch did to me.

Ell. That's what Ant called her, so it'll always be how I think of her, and I think of her far too often. Her sharp Corp suit and that manic smile of the truly devoted. Devoted enough to her precious Corp to kill and maim.

And drug me and Omega in the last hours of the rebellion that erased the Corp from the Web for good.

On the table, my tablet screen is now flat, black, silent. I push it away and pull out my computer.

I like my classes, I like studying, but if it weren't for the flashbacks, I'd be doing something else. School is a means to an end. Maybe it is for other people, too, I haven't asked. Jonas is one of the few I've made an effort to get to know, one of the few who's never looked at me like I was something under a microscope.

Okay, he does, but for a different reason. I could tell, right from our first class together, that his stare was different. That it was the same way I looked at him the moment I saw him come into the room.

"Stop thinking about him and work," Fable teases.

"I—"

"Don't even try it. I know that expression."

"Shut up."

He raises his hands in mock surrender, knowing he's won, and I refocus on Fable's notes. Interesting stuff. Some of it might be useful later, hopefully.

Hope is all I have. I'm feeling in the dark—my own darkness that I carry around with me under the baking sunshine here.

The flashbacks are not normal. The constant push at the edge of my brain, like something trying to find a way in . . . not normal.

And so I have only two options. Give in, or find a cure.

Make a cure.

■

I can give you everything you want._

"Al?" Jonas asks, sleep-fuzzed, one eye open to blink at the clock. "It's three—is everything okay? Is it your brother?"

I love him a little more for the question, but I'll tell him that tomorrow. "Go back to sleep," I whisper, kissing him, willing my pulse to calm. "Everything's fine. I'll be right back."

The living room is dark, quiet except for the sound of the waves beyond the windows and closed curtains. In the kitchen, I drink some water, splash more on my face before I look at my tablet again.

Third one in three days.

Who is this?_ I type back, fingers only a little shaky.

No answer. I stare at the screen for five minutes, ten, jump when the door opens.

"Hey, what are you doing up?" Phoenix's heels click over the floor, Mage's heavy boots a low bass line.

"Just getting some water," I say, pointing to the bottle. "How was the club?"

"Not as good as when you're there," Mage says, smiling. "Back to bed, kiddo."

"You know you're the only one who can get away with calling me that."

"Yup."

"I'm going, I'm going." My fingers curl around my tablet. Still nothing. I crawl back in bed beside Jonas, his arms slipping around me even as he snores. I sleep that crazy half sleep of waiting, garbled dreams chasing each other, one ear listening for a new message.

3

Pay attention.

Jonas teases me about this class, says I've learned more about music already than most people ever will. Says he just wants to feel it, not learn about it. I wince every time, because I know where that road goes, and it's nowhere good. I grew up around people who never asked any questions. I'd still be there with them if I hadn't also grown up with the person who asked the most.

I check my tablet again after class. Maybe whoever it was knows they got the number wrong, so they've finally given up. I step out into the sunshine and see Jonas waiting. I love this, my routine out here. School, studying, Jonas, beach, Fridays. There are always variations on the theme, tiny changes to keep things interesting, but the melody has been the same since the day I first stepped onto the beach, felt the sand between my toes.

"Fable went to meet some girl he met."

"Surprise, surprise. Disappointed?" I know he's not. He knows I know.

"Guess I can handle having you all to myself," he says, shrugging, failing completely at casual. "Do you need to study? Why am I even asking that?"

"You know what? No. Let's go do something."

He doesn't need convincing. We head downtown, where the

sleek, clustered buildings almost make me feel like I'm back in the Web. And make me so fucking glad that I'm not.

"Do you miss it? I mean, other than your family. Obviously you miss them," Jonas says.

I stop, startled. Someone behind us almost runs into me, curses, and Jonas flips him the finger as the guy veers around us. The idea that Jonas can read my mind, even a little, makes my stomach turn over. "The Web?" I ask, stalling, but the part of me that's usually so good at redirecting the conversation when it comes up is as tired as the rest of me today.

"You never talk about it."

I don't, unless he asks, or Sabine does, and even then I avoid it if I can. I understand the curiosity, but there's a lot that's hard to talk about. Some stuff I never will, not to them.

"Let's go sit," I say, moving toward the park on the next corner. It's kind of busy, but also kind of an answer in itself. I miss the park outside our apartment in the Web. We find an empty bench and I sit sideways, facing him. "Every spring, there were these cherry blossoms; they turned half the park pink. They'd be gone by now."

He smiles, the smile that made me notice him in the first place. "What else?"

"That's it. That and my family, my friends who stayed there. Seriously."

"How's Anthem doing? Any better?"

I watch a bird hop between two branches. "He seems fine when he tabs. He hasn't in a couple days. He's not better, but I would've heard if he was worse."

"Will you go back?"

"I'll *have* to go back." For my brother and other reasons I don't want to think about on a beautiful day. "But not yet. You're stuck with me for now."

18

"Damn." His lips quirk, I can't stop myself from leaning in to kiss them until someone yells that we should charge admission to the show. My skin heats from more than the sun and I stand, pulling Jonas down the path and back out onto the street. We wander some more, talking about easier things: school, the band, the gig tomorrow. I get home too exhausted to even eat, and just kick off my boots and fall into bed.

Friday is my day. The moment I wake up, excitement starts to fizz, bubble, crackle under my skin. Fable and Jonas spend the day shooting me knowing grins, and the white room stays away, far in the deepest reaches of my mind. Good. My tablet stays silent. Even better.

Sabine meets the three of us after school, another quickly established tradition, another note in the constant song of my days. Her plastic skirt glistens whenever light touches it, her lips sparkle with pink gloss. We grab an early dinner, head to the club. She drives, so a twenty-minute trip takes us seven and a half. What I think of as pods are a little different here, boxier, closer to what I've read about cars. Bet she'd drive those like a lunatic, too.

"Let's do this thing," she says, flipping the solar battery off and climbing out. Mage and Phoenix's club is a huge, hulking thing, once two buildings at the very edge of downtown.

"Going to let me keep time tonight?" Fable teases her.

"What do you think?"

Jonas grins, I take his hand. The door is thick, hammered steel—not for soundproofing, like the Sky-Clubs back home, but because Phoenix thinks it looks good. She's behind the bar, scowling, though she smiles as soon as we step in.

"What's up?" I ask. My voice echoes, bounces off metal and mirrors.

"Shorthanded tonight."

"Gotcha." It means she'll be serving alcohol, which thrills her about as much as it would thrill me. "Want me to help out after?"

"Nah, you're fine. You guys ready?"

"Aren't we always?"

Her smile widens into a real one. "Just checking."

Our instruments are already onstage, waiting for us to pick them up, to pull out the music they hold inside carved wood and keys and drumsticks. I follow the others through a door at the far end of the massive room, halfway down a hallway, through another. No one uses this dressing room except us. I think half my clothes are here, tossed over every surface except a table Mage keeps clear for snacks and water.

I drop my bag and stare at it, then look at Jonas. "Those from you?" My heart flutters, a little off its usual time. "Where'd you find them?"

"What?" He follows my eyes as they go back to the cherry blossoms in a vase. "No, but . . ."

I step closer, see the edges of a small white card nestled in with the pink.

Bile rises, stings the back of my throat. There's no point in reading it. I already know what it's going to say.

■

"You're not going on tonight," Mage says, throwing the card back on the table. Phoenix flips through my tabs, teeth clenched.

I can give you everything you want.

"The fuck I'm not. So I have a fan, so what?"

"I'm basically up there with a weapon." Sabine points at the bass she grabbed from the stage on our way. She likes to keep it with her in the hours before we go on, absorb its energy. I want to hug her, but I stay close to Jonas instead, my hand on his waist, thumb brushing the inch of skin above his belt. An apology for not telling him—or anyone—before.

"It's not a big deal, okay? A few tabs and some flowers. I thought someone was tabbing me by mistake, that's why I didn't mention it. Please, just let it go. I'll get a new tablet." Please, let's not think about how they knew to send me cherry blossoms in the first place, how they got my tab number, which I don't exactly go around giving everyone. Silently, I appeal to Fable for his agreement. He uncrosses his arms, crosses them again, maybe more offended than Jonas that I didn't say anything. He gives me that look, that *we're gonna talk about this later* look.

"Don't like that someone got in here." Mage moves to check the one window, which probably hasn't been opened since before the war. Any war. Pick one.

"Where does someone even *find* cherry blossoms in July?" Sabine asks.

I have no idea. "People are in and out of here all the time. Deliveries, cleaners, all the staff. No one would notice one more. Can we stop now? I have to rest my voice." A truth, kind of. I tug Jonas over to the old, faded couch, fall onto it, curl against him. "Sorry," I whisper, below the sounds of everyone else now trying to organize my life for me. "I really did think it was just a mistake."

A tiny amount of tension leaves his shoulders. "Okay, but now we know it's not." Around us, Sabine, Fable, Phoenix, and Mage are discussing where I should sleep, where I should go when I'm not at school, whether I should be going to school at all for a while. I let them at it; it's not going to make a difference. This asshole isn't taking tonight from me, or my bed by the ocean, or the things I need to learn to find my cure. When they start talking about telling someone, I lock eyes with Phoenix and shake my head. No.

I remember guards, and uniforms. Pod sirens and stories of Ant in a cell. No police, no matter how unlike the old Web guards they are. *Okay,* she mouths, disappears from the room with the vase in her hand. Eventually Mage gives me a long look and goes to join her, leaving the four of us alone like we usually are at this time on a Friday night.

It's the only thing that feels even a little normal. I might've told them it's not a big deal, but someone fucking followed me. Someone listened while I told Jonas about the park back home.

Home. It's not really, not anymore, but it's still so clear in my memories. All of it, before and after the rebellion. I wasn't so young that it all went over my head.

Nobody was safe. People were watched, tailed, taken, and used. This is different, but the feeling is the same. Eyes in the walls, following my every movement. Ears, listening.

Music begins to thump outside, a song I know as well as my own heartbeat. Old, now, but still awesome. I can hear the happiness in Ant's voice. Joy turned to song, if they're not the same thing. Mage always puts Ant's stuff on while we're waiting; I'm grateful he does it tonight, even if it reminds me every time that I haven't heard this voice in person in almost a year. They all encouraged me to leave, to come here and find myself, but that doesn't help much. Homesickness isn't a thing for me, but people-sickness is, and I can't shrug it off like it's a sweater I can just wear when I'm cold.

"Still with me?" Jonas asks. I nod. Sabine is sitting against the wall, a book open on her lap. Probably something she wants to teach her students on Monday, helping their little hands trace the words as they spell them out. Fable's lying flat on the floor, eyes closed, fingers tapping against his thigh. The adrenaline that took a brief vacation slams back into me, growing with the sound of the club filling up with people. The lights in our room flick off and on, Mage's ten-minutes-to-go signal.

I push myself up, get a bottle of water, stop myself from staring too long at the wet ring where the vase was.

"You sure about this?" Sabine asks, closing her book. I roll my eyes.

"*Yes.* And I have Jonas," I say, catching the tiny smile I get for this. "If the guy's here, Bean, whack him with your bass and I'll buy you a new one. If not, we play and hit the beach, just like always."

"You're the boss," Fable says. Guess I'm mostly forgiven, and it is true. Technically, this is my band. Past the window, night has fully fallen, and as much as I love the sunshine here, this is when I come alive. Nothing is going to ruin this for me.

■

I blink. Breathe. Look away from the bright stage lights.

Screams for encores pick up where the final chords of the last song leave off, but it's the same crowd as always and they know I'm done for tonight. My voice is shot because it's summer and an ocean breeze filtered in from somewhere, down onto the stage. Too perfect not to play too hard, too fast.

No shadowy figures stepped to the front of the stage to grab me. There was a guy who kept moving around, disappearing and reappearing like a ghost, but he left midway through the set. Just some jerk who doesn't know good music when he hears it, not my crazy fan. Still, the idea that someone could've tried something has made me reckless, tuned my senses to perfect pitch. Turned the night to the kind of sharp, crystalline hours that only come after a fucking weird day and nothing can be too loud or too raw. Sweat stings my eyes; strands of hair stick to my face; my lungs are hot lead weights.

A stupid, giddy smile spreads across my face and my blood hammers as I step off the back of the stage, Fable and Jonas shielding me from the crowd on our way back to the dressing room. The DJ starts, the song pounding and furious.

"See?" I say, throwing my arms open. Music out there grants us anonymity in here; they're not listening for me now. "That was the tightest we've ever been, and no one so much as touched me. Everything's fine."

Fable drops his drumsticks to high-five me, and his silver rings bite my hand. Doesn't matter, I can't feel real pain right now.

"It was pretty good." Jonas grins.

"Damn right." Sabine collapses onto the couch; I swipe another bottle of water. "Okay, Al, you win. Beach?"

"Maybe not for Fable. The girl in the front row?"

Sabine glares at me, but hey, if she wants him to know, she has to tell him herself. Or wait for him to realize, and I'm pretty sure he thinks Bean's out of his league.

He's probably right about that.

"C'mon, I'm not leaving you tonight," Fable says.

Jonas puts his arm around me. "We'll be with her."

"And I *don't* need bodyguards. Go. I'll see you tomorrow."

He hugs me, leaves in a swish of black and fishnet. "Poor girl," Sabine says, but she watches him leave, gaze lingering, wincing as the lock snaps. I stare pointedly at her bass until she shifts it off the couch so I can fall onto it. Almost instantly I wind up with a lapful of crazy boots, steel buckles hard and cold against my legs. I check my tablet for the hundred-and-forty-third time today, half relieved, half annoyed at its emptiness. Omega usually asks

24

about the show, even if he's been too busy during the week. I close my eyes and tip my head back. Leather creaks beside me as someone sits on the arm of the couch, a warm hand curling around the back of my neck. I smile, look up at Jonas.

There's a red mark near his hairline from the headlamp he uses to see his electronics onstage. My fingers curl around Sabine's feet instead of reaching up to smooth it away.

"Ready to go?" he asks. Sabine nods, swinging from horizontal to vertical in an easy, graceful movement, then hauls me up.

The main part of the club is louder, darker except for the beams of neon light that spin overhead and paint the crowd. Someone tries to dance with me as we carve our way across the packed floor. A glare from my five-foot-nothing doesn't do much, but Jonas is a good foot taller. The guy backs off, too easily for it to be anyone I'm supposed to worry about. I spot Fable, the girl I noticed during the gig clinging to him like some kind of black lace fungus.

Steel walkways crisscross overhead, filled with people happy that it's the weekend. Girls check themselves out in mirrored walls, pretending not to notice that the guys are doing the same to them. The glass tiles under my feet thump to an unrelenting rhythm.

Phoenix is behind the bar, but she joins us outside, catching up just as we get to Sabine's pod. In the dark, it looks almost black, but I remember commenting on the red color when I first got here: I'd never seen one that wasn't white before. Mage went quiet, then said it reminded him of someone. I had to think longer than I should've, and I went quiet, too. In my memories, Uncle Scope is a big smile and brilliant flashes of scarlet. I can't picture the rest of his face anymore.

"Where're you going?" she asks, shaking her fiery hair out of her eyes so she can pierce me properly with them.

"Same place as always." I don't say *the beach*, just in case. "I'm fine, Aunt Phoenix, and I won't be alone."

She'll never admit she likes it when I call her that. "I promised your brother I'd look after you."

"And you do. You were doing way more dangerous shit than this when you were my age."

That gets her, because I'm right.

"Fine. Stay with them, and tab if anything happens."

"Promise."

Jonas sprawls in the backseat of the pod, I fit myself in between his long legs and I lean over to unlace my boots, tugging them off along with thick socks whose only purpose is to prevent blisters. "You really okay?" he asks, voice low. "You kinda went somewhere else during that last song."

Another flashback. *Eternal, eternal, eternal.* "Yeah, I'm okay." I stare out the window to watch as the city slides quickly past. I love this place even more at night than I do in the daytime. It's a city meant to live in the dark because the people fill it with light, with life. Crowds spill out of bars and restaurants onto the streets; clouds of music billow from open windows. Laughter bounces down the sidewalks. We stop for boxes of spicy noodles that fill the pod with their scent.

My knuckles turn white. The Corp kept us trapped on our island, never knowing this place was here. Even now, it still stings, and it's an easier thing to be mad about than everything that's happened today.

I'm the first out of the pod, sliding open the door even before Sabine cuts the power. Asphalt, cracked and baked and still holding on to the sun's warmth, scrapes at the soles of my feet for a few running steps until I hit sand. It creeps between my wriggling toes as I spread my arms and spin, listen to the breaking waves, gulp the salt-sting of the wind. Jonas catches me around the waist and throws me over his shoulder, ignoring my fists against his back all the way down to the water's edge.

"No!" I scream, trying to squirm from his grip through my laughter, unconvincing because I don't really want him to drop me.

"You sure? Really, really sure?"

"Yes!" They say it's cleaner than it used to be, but I have exactly zero desire to swim in it. Ew. I'm not dunking myself in anything that glows in the dark. "Put me down!"

"O-kay," he says, letting me slide a few inches.

"On the sand, you ass!"

He does, finally, and has the good grace to double over when I elbow him in the stomach. Our fingers twist together on the walk back up the beach to Sabine, who's shaking her head at the pair of us from beside a pile of old scrap wood we've gathered from wherever we could find it. A box of matches rattles, tossed carelessly back and forth between her hands.

"I can't see anyone," she says quietly to Jonas. I hold up my hands.

"New rule. No talking about it any more tonight. Look around. Everything's totally cool." I want the peace I always find here and I'm not going to get it if these two are all jumpy.

It takes a few minutes to build the fire, a few more to settle down with our food and open drinks. Thick, sludgy brown beer for Sabine, water for Jonas and me, though I've told him a zillion times I don't care if he drinks. Then again, I've told him a lot of what really happened in the Web, too. Definitely more than the short, sanitized version everyone apparently got when the first explorers arrived to share our story with a wall of initial disbelief.

The people of Los Angeles apologized for not looking for us, but why would they? Everything they needed was right here, a wasteland beyond. As far as they knew, there was nowhere else to go. Stay with the people, the numbers, food and water, the shelter where it's safe.

We toss our cardboard containers and flimsy wooden forks into the flames to see the grease spit and crackle. Conversation ebbs and flows in sync with the waves and I relax against Jonas.

"What's on for tomorrow?"

I open my eyes to look at Sabine, half in shadow, half in fire-light. "Studying."

"Of course. All day?"

"Yup. Exams next week, and I'm the one who has to tell Ant if I don't pass."

"Yeah, yeah. I'm just saying, when I'm sick, I'm coming to you, not him," she says, pointing to Jonas.

He laughs. "Years away, Bean."

"Are you planning on a brain transplant during those years? No? Then my point stands."

"And she thinks *we* argue," I say, nudging him with my shoulder. He scowls at her, but can't hold it, and they're talking again when I jog back to the pod to grab an old, honey-colored acoustic guitar. The one I learned on, when my fingers were so little I could barely reach the right frets.

Sabine sings to give my voice a break while I play, the music whisper-drifting soft and slow against the backdrop of the ocean and the hum of the city. Jonas stretches out, dark hair spreading like spider legs over the sand.

Sometime around two, the breeze picks up and the remaining embers begin to lose their fight. I shiver, my fingers slipping on the strings.

"Let's go," Jonas says.

"You guys want a ride?" Sabine asks.

If I squint, I can actually see my house from here. When I first decided to come, my only demand was that I be able to see the water. Not the rivers I'd known for sixteen years, but real, open water. The idea felt like freedom. Anthem's demand was that I live with Phoenix and Mage. They moved out of their apartment and the three of us got a house right on the beach. After nearly a year, it *almost* feels like the only home I have.

"Yeah. A ride would be good," I say. "Thanks." We kick sand over the fire and grab our stuff. I look through the final sparks at Jonas. "You coming over?"

He smiles. "If you want me to."

"The blankets aren't going to steal themselves."

A light on the floor of the pod catches my attention as soon as I open the door. My tablet is alive with a message. Fuck, not now. Any more and nobody's going to let me have another night like this one. Carefully, I slide the guitar onto the back row of seats and pick it up, pressing a button to stop the alert, pulsing red like a headache.

Like a warning.

"Al? Al, you okay?" Jonas's voice comes from somewhere far away. The message swims, words bleeding into black spots, but melting them away wouldn't be enough to erase them. Neither is letting the tablet slip from my hands and splinter to pieces on the ground. Hysterical laughter bubbles, unstoppable, because all week I've been thinking some random fucking messages are the worst tabs I could get. Tears scald my cheeks.

"Oh no," Sabine whispers. She knows. They've both guessed. I close my eyes, Haven's words seared into my brain.

Alpha, it's time. Come home._

4

If I don't go, it's not happening.

"I'm coming with you."

Shirts, skirts, pants, a single boot land on top of my back-pack, thrown from my tiny closet without looking. "No," I say through chattering teeth. I *feel* him cross his arms behind me, picture the veins in sharp relief against lean muscles.

"Why not?"

"Your parents would lose their shit. You have exams. *I* have exams."

For a split second, in the middle of packing, I pretend I have a choice. Anthem or me. This is the worst possible time to ditch school. I don't know how long I'll be gone, and I think of the set-back to my cure.

"We can catch up later. My parents will deal."

There's no space in this room for his optimism. And I know what choice Anthem would've made. *Did* make. "You have no clothes or anything, and I'm not waiting."

"I'll buy new ones."

"I want you to come," I whisper. It barely makes any noise, but it makes enough and he touches my face, bringing me stillness for an instant. Since the day I met Jonas, he's been able to dismantle me like this.

"I know."

"Your parents will be really fucking thrilled about you driving across the country with me to go *there*. They've heard the stories." I free myself and walk back to my bed.

"And they know it's not like that anymore. It was already in the past—"

Noise cuts him off. Footsteps. Sabine's boots and two other pairs. "Open the door?" I ask, hurling a toothbrush into my bag. He does, and my room is suddenly crowded. Phoenix is paler than usual, and for once her hair looks less like fire than blood. Mage's knuckles are nearly white. Tangled clothes on the floor trip me up. I crash into Mage's chest, my shoulders shaking. Two pairs of arms wrap around me, tightly enough that I can pretend they're why I can't breathe.

Fingernails click on a tablet screen. "Fable's almost—" Sabine starts.

"Here," Fable finishes, squeezing in. "Al." His voice cracks and he glues it back together. "Want me to come?"

"Yeah."

Jonas flinches at how easily I say it.

"I'll drive," Sabine says. That, I won't argue with at all. She'll probably get us there in half an hour.

"We all going to fit?"

Phoenix shakes her head at Fable, but her eyes are on me. "We've said our good-byes," she says quietly. "He knew we were never coming back. Al, tell him we love him."

I only nod, throat burning. It feels wrong, but if I'd wanted to think about it, I would've guessed this is what they'd do.

"C'mon, guys," Mage says quietly. "I'll give you some stuff to wear for the trip. Bean, Phoenix's stuff'll fit you." Fable follows him out; Phoenix takes Sabine to raid the kitchen for food. Beyond twenty miles outside the city limits, there's nowhere to get anything until we hit Central.

Jonas's strong hands cup my chin, tilt it so I'll look at him. The angles of his face always make him look more intense than he really is, but it's the eyes that get me, Frozen gray. Ant used to take Omega and me down to the edge of the river when we were little, steely ice floating on the black water. I wanted to run across it; he had to grab my hand and pull me back. Tell me it wasn't safe, that there was nothing out there.

We were all so wrong. The Corp wanted it that way.

"You have to remember. . . . When you see for yourself . . . the war, it damaged him. Life there wasn't good, for a long time. What you'll see—" I swallow. I don't know what we'll see. How the months have changed him. "It won't really be *him*." Not the brother I know. "And Haven, they hurt her. People there aren't like people here, not the older ones who went through it. It's different still. It won't just be like meeting someone who has come here. There, they're everywhere."

"Shhh." He touches his lips to mine, gently, the kind of almost-nothing that's exactly enough. "I know. Are you ready?"

"Yeah." No. But yeah.

He leads me down the hallway, into the living room. I glance around, just once, to make sure I can picture it while I'm gone, and move to the window. The crests of the waves beyond the sand glow an iridescent, cobalt blue I know too well. Sabine's a blur in the kitchen, clattering, slamming. I'll never tease her again for doing everything too fast.

"Jonas," Fable calls. Jonas lifts his hands in time to catch a bag that Fable tosses across the room. It's like we all rehearsed this or something, everyone prepared for their assigned task, poised to move the moment word came. I'm not sure whether to be depressed or grateful. Both, maybe, swirled in with the rest of my pulsing emotions.

The pod sits by the curb, right where I jumped out of it less than an hour ago.

But every second we're not on our way east is a second we won't get back. "Let's go," I say, looking in the windows. Someone's moved my guitar. My heart beats too fast until I see it on the floor behind the back row of seats, shifted to make room for a pile of pillows and blankets.

"Your battery okay?" Mage asks.

"Long as we get a little sunlight on the way." Sabine stashes the box of food and jumps in the driver's seat before anyone else can, as if someone is going to fight her for it.

"My tablet's broken," I say. My voice doesn't sound right.

Phoenix touches my face. "It's okay, Al. I'll tell everyone to get you on Fable's. Fable? You've got yours?"

"Right here."

"Be safe, kiddo."

They hug me again, these people who've pretty much adopted me, and nudge me to crawl inside the pod. I curl into a ball. Fable joins Sabine in the front; Jonas stretches out across the middle bench, back to the window, arm draped over the seat to hold my hand.

I want to sleep, if only as a time killer, but I can't. Fable fiddles with something, cursing under his breath. Hooking up a portable console, I realize, when music filters through the speakers. L.A. does those better than we ever did, though theirs have always been normal. Ordinary little boxes that play ordinary music. I lift my free hand, run my finger over the raised patch of skin on my other wrist.

Even before I left, I knew I'd be back. And I knew this would be one of the reasons, the first reason, I had just hoped it wouldn't be soon. None of us were ever sure how much time Anthem had left, and for years he was filled with energy, renewed by the changes he fought for. A year ago he was teaching guitar to kids, recording tunes of his own, helping Haven with her computers as much as he could, which admittedly wasn't a lot.

I wonder if he's let the blue fade from his hair since I last saw him. Always so bright against his natural silver-blond, like a summer sky competing with a sun that hurts to look at, searing your eyelids.

"Morning."

"Huh? Oh." I rub my eyes. Jonas looks down at me, a gentle smile twisting his lips.

"You slept," he says, brushing my hair back from my forehead.

"How long? Is there . . . ? Did I miss anything?" I ask, jerking upright. My throat feels like I've swallowed a mouthful of my beach. He passes me a bottle of water.

"Couple hours, no news," Fable answers. We must have stopped somewhere. Sabine is passed out, and he's carefully steering the pod along the one usable lane of a fractured highway.

"Okay." I relax a tiny bit. Haven would've given us as much warning as she could, but no one there can probably make anything more than a guess. Fable drives as fast as he can, but I wish Sabine didn't need to sleep at all.

Jonas, all arms and legs for a second, folds and unfolds himself until he lands awkwardly beside me, throwing my blanket over the seat in front. "Hungry?"

"Uh-uh."

"You get to see Omega again, and Haven and everyone you've told me about. That's a good thing, right? I mean . . . Shit, Al, I don't know what I mean."

"It's okay." I lean against him. "You're right, that part's good. I don't really know what Omega's been up to since I left. He's always too curious about L.A. when I tab to answer my questions. So, yeah, it'll be nice to catch up."

"Talk to me," Jonas says a few miles later.

"About what?" I say it lightly, as if there isn't anything I haven't told him already.

"Anything. Tell me more about what the Web is like."

Home. Sort of. Maybe. But I don't want to see it again and I wish they'd all moved with me like I begged them to. I wanted us to be together, just not there. Because I'm old enough to remember. I remember my dad; I remember Anthem. I remember hugging Haven and being told she couldn't hear me anymore. I remember the day they took Bee's body away because she got too old and tired and sick. I remember everyone being sad about Scope for so long, and that Pixel never really got better.

I remember the white room, and what that woman did to me that now I need to try and fix.

"Lots of metal," I say. "And glass. Just like L.A."

He raises his eyebrows. I relent.

"It's an island, divided into four quadrants: the top, the bottom, and down each side. In the middle is the Vortex. That's where the Corporation was. Like, they were everywhere, but that's where the headquarters were. The building's still there, but the government uses it now."

"What else?"

"You're never that far from the river, so you can always smell it. Like lightning. There's a huge park in the middle. Animals are kept there for food, but some of it's just a park. That's where . . ." That's where the cherry blossoms are in the spring. "That's where I heard Ant's music for the first time." The lie is easier to tell than the truth. I didn't understand it at the time, but in the years since, I've realized how funny Ell must have thought it was to drug me and Omega with Ant's music. An evil act with all of the sharp symmetry the Corp loved so much.

Sabine wakes up, muttering that she's starving. We stop by the side of the road, accidental specks of dust on a canvas of nothingness. Everything is flat, gray, dead except for the communications mast glinting in the middle distance. I don't know exactly when it was put up, but it's less than eight years old. It didn't take long to start exploring after the rebellion, but it took a while to build pods capable of traveling long distances, and longer still for us to discover there were places to communicate with.

A handful of metal money spills from a pocket of the pants I yank from my bag. I leave the coins gleaming dully on the floor of the pod, change into clothes I haven't slept in, and slide into the driver's seat. I just need something to do with my hands.

Broken trees. Fields vaporized to barrenness. A lake, its surface sickly, slickly orange. Here and there are signs a city once stood against the elements but buckled under the force of what humans could do to one another.

Fable and Jonas talk in low voices behind me, releasing snippets of conversation about Anthem.

". . . Right under the Corp's nose, like it was no big thing . . ."

". . . Punched him square in the face, though if ever a bastard deserved it, that yellow-wearing freak did . . ."

"There, on TV, in front of everyone. The stories are legends. Dude, he had *balls*."

"Has," I snap, leaning on the accelerator.

Sabine puts her hand on my arm.

My eyes start to burn, but I drive for another hour before conceding defeat to Jonas. Anthem sings to me through the speakers as a violent pink light fills the sky. I never should've left Haven to deal with this alone. Omega will be with her, but still.

Right here, almost exactly halfway between the Web and L.A. I feel tugged in two directions and end up belonging nowhere. My beach and—one day—my cure behind me, home, and Anthem up ahead. Whichever city I'm in, there will always be something in the other one, calling, calling.

■

It's fucking freezing out here and I miss my sunshine, my sand.

"Where are we?" I check Fable's tablet, tap out a message to Phoenix that we're okay.

"About an hour outside Central, I think, if the map's right," Fable says. He peers through the windshield into the pitch blackness beyond. "Eat now, or wait?"

"Wait," I say. Everyone agrees.

Central's not much, a blip on the landscape, but after almost two days of blank vastness, even a cluster of steel-sided cubes around a comms relay tower is something to look at. Generators buzz, a hive of malevolent gray bees, and a group of old, white patrol pods sits in the dust, Corp logos erased from the sides.

We head for the nearest cube, its door fogged with steam. Rickety tables and chairs are scattered in front of a long counter. At one, a man is seated, hands wrapped around a mug of something.

"From the Web?" he asks. Old chrome clings to the sagging skin on his cheeks, the metal decoration spiraling from cheekbone to chin.

"Half of us," Jonas says. "We're headed there."

The guy squints, trying to figure that out. Guess he doesn't see many going east. Why would he? No one goes back. Either he decides not to ask or he just doesn't care. "Need beds?"

Sabine shakes her head. "Just food, showers. Can't stop long."

"Coming right up. Hey, Mist! Four plates!"

"Gotcha!" a woman calls from somewhere in the back.

He pushes himself upright, walks over, and presses his hand to a panel on the wall. It pops open, revealing a stack of towels. "Next one over to the left," he says, pulling four from the top.

"Lonely life out here."

The man peers closely at Jonas's flat, unmarred wrist for a long time, then nods. "Someone's gotta be. Only so far you can go before there should be some sign of life. If there isn't, you make one. Besides"—he laughs, showing gapped teeth—"six months of being stationed out here pays enough credits that we can do nothing the other six. No one wants the job."

"Get many people coming through?" Fable asks. Jonas turns slowly, taking in every detail of the room. His eyes linger on the console in the corner.

"Not so much now. Guess everyone who was going to head out west for a while already has, and you're the first I've ever seen come back. Some government repair crews been hanging around recently, upgrading the tower, but that's it."

The shower's basically a trickle of purified water from a tank and it might be the best one I've ever had. I scrub myself with a cracked bar of soap, wash my hair, try not to scream as I rip impatiently through the tangles. A plate of pale, rubbery chicken waits for me; I'm still pushing it around with a fork when Fable comes back. It's the first time we've been alone—effectively—since the whole thing happened at the club.

"Why didn't you tell me, Al?"

"Because I honestly thought it was nothing. I've smashed my tablet and left the city in the middle of the night. Do we have to talk about it? How much safer do you want me to be?" I recoil. "I didn't mean . . . I'm not glad about . . ."

"Holy shit, where's the Alpha who knows she doesn't need to explain that to me? Calm down."

The chicken churns in my stomach. "Don't say anything when we get there; they don't need to hear about it," I say. He nods, chews his food for way longer than it should take. The man, whose name I haven't caught, pushes his chair back. It scrapes on the tiles; his shoes squeak; his fingers tap against the console screen.

I'm not asking now.

"Hey, you okay?" asks Jonas. I push past him in the doorway, Sabine close behind. In the darkness, Jonas's hair is almost black, dripping down a clean shirt two sizes too big.

"I'll wait out here," I say. I don't want to watch the guy track. Couldn't he have waited another twenty fucking minutes? But it's not just that. Reaching this point's made me jumpy. There is nothing else between here and the Web. I can feel its influence in the hard lines of the cubes, see it mirrored back in chrome, hear it from the console, though he had headphones clamped tight over his ears. Tripping, happy, no white rooms for him. It closes in, wiping the color from my mind, and I grit my teeth. Not now.

Fable can pay for the food, because I'm not going back in there. Thinking about it makes my wrist tingle, the tiny chip reawakened.

The pod is a mess. I fold clothes, pick up empty water bottles and dump them in a container for recycling. My hands itch.

"They'll just be another couple minutes," Jonas says softly. I brush harder at the crumbs on the seats. "What's wrong?"

"Stupid question."

He inhales sharply. "No, it's not," he says, reaching for me. "What is it?"

"What if we don't make it in time?"

"We will."

I kick a chunk of rock across the parking area. "You don't know that."

"Al, c'mon." He sighs, slings an arm around my shoulders. "Okay, so I don't, but we know it hasn't happened yet or Haven would've sent a message. So we keep going. We keep going anyway. Fable says it's less than a day from here, right?"

"Yeah." When we moved from the Web our group stopped here, Fable and I sticking together because we didn't know anyone else in the pod. The group filled the dining cube, loud with excitement and fear of the unknown. Sadness was a private thing, though. We all kept memories of good-byes to ourselves so we didn't flood the pod with tears.

Or maybe that was just me. Fable was fine, but he was leaving less behind than me, at least.

Sometimes my head feels so crowded with memories, both multicolored and stark white, that I don't know how there's going to be room for the rest of my life. And right now, the rest of my life starts when we get into the pod and drive the last stretch to where Anthem is dying, the rest of *his* life much shorter than mine. He's probably trying to remember everything, every last moment, and I won't be in any of them unless we get there soon.

"Will there be a funeral?" Jonas asks. I shake my head.

"We don't do that there, not like you guys. We'll just put his memory chip in a locker and visit him whenever we want. You'll see." Only I won't get to visit Ant all the time, I'll leave him behind—again—when I go back to L.A.

"You both ready?"

Jonas nods at Fable. "Want me to drive?"

"Nah, I will. How about some different tunes?"

"No." I yank the miniconsole out of his hand and throw it back inside the pod. Fable's eyes widen, whites gleaming in the lamp overhead.

41

"Sure," Jonas says after a minute, leaning to kiss the top of my head. "No problem."

Restless sleep comes in bursts; mostly I try just so I don't have to talk to anyone. The sun rises, arcs too slowly across the sky, as if it's afraid, too, of what it'll find in the Web when it gets there. I don't eat anything else, and several times Jonas presses his hand to my leg in a silent request to stop twitching.

Fable's tablet never leaves my hand. Twice I ask Sabine and Jonas if they're sure theirs are turned up loud enough, just in case.

It's dark again, but still tinged with the last traces of light, when I climb past the middle bench to wedge myself between the front seats and stare out the windshield. Ahead, distant windows are lit like a galaxy of stars on the horizon, falling to earth but not quite making it.

The Web.

5

There's only time for the briefest impression of too much white and scraps of bright orange before the air's crushed out of me, my feet a few inches off the floor. "Okay," I gasp after a minute. "Put me . . . down. Can't . . . breathe."

"Missed your face, little sister," Omega says, setting me soundlessly on the thick carpet. "Not sure why, come to think of it. I'm definitely the better-looking twin."

I have to reach up to wave my fist an inch from his nose, just above orange lips. "More than happy to fix that for you, if you want."

"And sorry to make a bad first impression, but I'm gonna have to disagree," Jonas says.

Omega glances over and looks back at me. "This him?"

"Yeah. Jonas, Omega. Omega, Jonas."

He nods, shakes Jonas's hand. "Good to meet you, man. Sorry it had to be, you know, like this."

"I'm sorry about your brother."

"Fable's here too, and our friend Sabine. They'll be up in a sec, just putting the pod away. Where is he?"

"Their room. Haven won't leave him, not even to eat or anything. The rest of us are taking care of stuff but . . . I'm glad you're here."

"Me, too."

The place looks exactly the same as always: huge, too much. Blank expanses broken by clusters of dizzying detail. The sofas are new clones of the same white monstrosities that were here when we first moved in. Outside the windows, the park spreads out below. It's night, but I know exactly the way light will shine on the tops of the trees in the morning.

Most of the bedroom doors are open to rooms heavy with silence. Mine looks like I've never left, and I swallow a lump in my throat. Haven turned one room into an office years ago, filling it with computers whose lights wink at me on my way past. The door at the end of the hallway is ajar, a soft glow from inside spilling out onto my boots.

She's in a chair beside the bed, legs curled under, one hand on a book, the other clasped in Anthem's. His skin is wax over bone, eyes closed, hair tousled on the pillow, bright against black sheets. *Still blue.* It's a dumb thought, a focal point so I don't have to look at the rest. He started coloring it like a normal person when Isis forbade him to use his neck jack again for the glowing tubes he used to wear. He's had enough of his energy sucked out through that thing. That's mostly why we're here.

Music—not his—drifts from a box on the nightstand. Small screens display neon numbers; wires connect to sensors on Anthem's wrist and down the neck of his shirt.

"You made it," Haven says, a slow smile growing beneath red-rimmed eyes. She unlinks her fingers from his. There are new lines on her face and she feels like a frail, soft-winged bird when I hug her. I have to remember that she's getting older, too, though she's still as pretty as she was when I was a kid and even smarter now, which is an achievement. I used to want to be her. Now I just want to be me, if I can figure out who that is.

Haven steps back properly to look at me. "The sun suits you."

"It's different, for sure." I'm not ready to talk about it yet, I'm not here for that. And I can't think about what I left behind, postponed. A flashback threatens. Push, push at the edge of my brain. "How is he? How are you?" I keep my words deliberately a little slower than normal, but in the dimness it takes her a second to read my lips and process what I said.

"Isis is doing what she can, but he won't take anything for the pain."

Yeah, that doesn't surprise me. Neither does the fact that she only answered one of my questions.

"Hey, Ant." The mattress gives slightly under me, and his eyelids flutter.

"Al," he whispers. "No crying." My vision blurs, thrown to prisms by the light. In my head, I hear him singing with that voice, strong and powerful. And now he's . . . this.

"I'm not," I lie.

"Tell me about Los Angeles."

"You'd love it. There's so much space, and it's warmer than here. The ocean is . . ." Indescribable. Not the flat black of the one near here. "The city's so clean, and people are so nice. School is good. All the girls think Fable is *exotic* and believe me, he's not pushing them away."

He smiles, grimaces at the effort it takes. "I'm glad you're happy, Al."

Voices swell and fade outside the door, enough to ignite a spark of recognition in filmy blue eyes. "They want to see you." I swallow. "And there are some people I want you to meet."

The closest thing I've seen to a grin yet flickers painfully across his face. "Uh-huh. I wondered . . . when you'd get to that."

Big as the bedroom is, it's really too small for this kind of crowd. In the time I've been in here, Pixel and Isis have turned up, too. I wave at them, and everyone gathers around the bed. There are people missing: Mage, Phoenix, Scope, their absence maybe more obvious because of how full the room is. Half the people who fought to save the Web are gone from it forever, one way or another. But I'm glad Pixel's here, and especially glad Isis is too. The Corp did a good job of training their med-techs, I'll give them that.

I reach for Jonas's hand.

"So you're the one taking care of our Al," Anthem says, blinking, trying to focus on Jonas's face.

He shrugs a lanky shoulder. "Might be the other way around."

"Yeah." Ant laughs. The mood in the room rises and falls, everyone holding their breath until the coughing fit is over and he's sipped some water from the bottle Haven holds for him. The machines stop screaming alarm; the numbers turn from red back to green. "She always was kind of bossy."

"You have no idea," Omega whispers to Jonas.

"Hey!"

"Stop ganging up on her." At least Haven's smiling now. "It's nice to meet you."

"You, too."

"And this is Sabine," I say, pulling her forward. "She plays killer bass."

"Hi," Sabine says, shyer than I've ever seen her. We all fall silent, watching one another.

Jonas's expression is a puzzle for which I've been collecting the pieces for months. Knitted eyebrows, tight mouth. A stare he knows is too intense, so every few seconds he shifts it from the bed to a lamp or a smudge on the wall. I guess it doesn't matter how many times I've described what happened to Anthem, what the music did.

I tighten my fingers around his; he squeezes back. Call, answer. Like we're back home, onstage, just trying to remember the next line.

No one needs to be told Anthem needs to rest, but no one wants to be the first to leave. I let go of Jonas and slip through the room to Haven. She should rest, too, and eat something, but I've never won an argument with her in my life. Now's not the time to try again. I kiss Ant, promise I'll be back soon.

It's actually true, not like the last time I said that.

Omega put my bag in my old room, Sabine's in the one that was so briefly my father's, and Fable's sleeping on one of the couches like he's done a hundred times before.

My room smells the same as it did the day I left, perfume and hair dye and thin metallic threads from open packs of guitar strings. The bed gives as much as I expect it to when I sit, watching Jonas. He knows my room in Los Angeles. Half the mess in there is his, but there's more of the *me* he doesn't know in this one. All the things I shed like a skin too heavy to carry across the country.

Trailing fingers leave marks in the thin sheen of dust, once-white furniture now a slight gray.

"You okay?"

I pluck at the covers. He's leaning against the dresser, arms folded. "Are you?"

"I just . . ." His hands curl to fists. "I don't understand it. I can't. How did they do this to people?"

He doesn't mean *how*. I've explained the mechanics before, as much as I know and understand. He means *why*, and I don't have a better answer to that now than I did when I first told him what happened here.

"Sorry."

"Don't be."

47

"Omega seems cool."

"Uh, yeah. We're twins."

Jonas laughs. "We talked a little. He interrogated me about my, uh, intentions."

"Do those include kissing me?"

His eyebrows lift. I'm not sure what's gotten into me, either. Wrong time, wrong place, but I need to feel something happy, just for a minute.

Strong, wiry, he pins me to the bed, stops a breath away. "I don't know," he muses. "Seems like your brothers might disapprove."

"Bonus."

■

We congregate in the living room, mostly. Omega rummages in the fridge, the same bottomless pit he's been for years. Haven likes to remind him what a picky eater he used to be, but she's still shut away with Anthem.

Pixel stretches out on one of the couches. Isis stands by the window. I don't think she's looking at anything. Night has turned the glass to mirrors, and she's not really the type to stare endlessly at her own reflection. I think she just knows more than the rest of us and doesn't want anyone to see her eyes. Fable takes his old seat. Sabine and Jonas move around, fidgeting.

I wander, picking up things that once held my fingerprints, as if I need to re-mark myself here.

None of us want to be the first to ask, "What now?" We wait, I know, but for how long?

Not long enough. Too long.

"So how's it going out there?" Pixel asks Fable.

Isis half turns, Fable shifts on the couch. "Good, man.

School's good, the weather's fucking perfect. Mage and Phoenix's club is great. You don't miss those days?"

I never got to go to Pixel's club when it was open, never experienced it the way Ant and his friends did. Not that I'm sorry about missing out on the Corp's encoded music, but sometimes I wish I knew firsthand the way it'd been.

Pixel shakes his head. "Not since I got clean. The memories would be too much, you know?"

We fall into silence, mostly comfortable but with an edge, a blanket of it with a fraying seam we can't quite forget about. Now that I'm so close to losing my own brother, I understand about Pixel and Scope more than ever, how much it must have hurt Pixel for his brother to be the rebellion's final, most devastating loss. Killed in the last moments before victory by someone he'd once loved, a guy who worked for the Corp. Who died, too, but I doubt that's ever made Pixel or Anthem feel better about losing a brother and a best friend.

Omega appears in the archway, a chicken leg in each hand, watching us. He catches my eye and grins. Yeah, no crazy twin stuff, but I know he's feeling the same thing I am—that we're both more ourselves when the other one's around.

A lock clicks down the hall and we all look up, at each other, at the direction of the sound, like we've been caught doing something we shouldn't. Haven's footsteps are soft, muffled. I see the pink before I really see her.

"He'll be asleep all night now." She frowns. "Pretty much."

"He still doesn't want anything for the pain?" Isis asks.

Haven eyes Isis's lips carefully, then shakes her head. "You might as well get some sleep."

Pixel and Isis stand, hug her close. Haven's usually sharp fingernails have been filed dull—*so she doesn't hurt him*—and they cling to Isis's shirt for a second before she lets go.

I think I slept too much in the pod. I'm weirdly wired now, energy humming. It'll catch up with me soon and I'll crash where I'm standing, but back home—L.A. home—the sun's only now beginning to set. I'd be finishing dinner, getting ready to study alone, or with Jonas or Fable or both, the ocean outside my window turning to gold, red, a brief few minutes of darkness before it begins to glow blue. I'd watch it, then settle in to cram everything I could learn about the brain into my own. One day, one day.

But now, maybe a later day than I'd hoped.

I'm cramped in this huge apartment, my muscles trying to jump out of my skin, stretching to fill the space.

"You should get some sleep, too," I tell Haven, whose eyebrows knit together in concentration, stay there for a long minute. Shit. I look up, face her properly, repeat myself.

It's so easy to forget about the damage the Corp did to Haven. She's never let it get to her for longer than a moment, at least not where I could see, but I wouldn't cope like she has if someone held me down and turned me into an Exaur. Put headphones over my ears and played a special kind of track that would be the last thing I'd ever hear.

Omega brings her a bottle of water. It sloshes in her hand, betraying the shakes she's trying to control. Grief, exhaustion, hunger, frustration, all of the above. Maybe something worse, but I don't want to think about that. I can only lose one of them at a time. Please, just one.

My eyes turn wet. I squeeze them shut, feel arms around me. "It'll be okay," Haven whispers. "You're here now."

Like that makes a difference. I bury my face in her neck.

"Go sleep," I say when I think I've gathered up all my pieces from where they fell apart. She leaves the room, shutting herself away with Ant. I avoid looking at the others, stand by the window with my feet carefully placed in the impressions left by Isis's boots. For some reason, that feels important. I was right; she was staring at nothing.

"I can stick around, if you guys want to go stretch your legs."

I blink at Fable. "You sure?"

"This place was basically my place, too; I know where the spoons are."

Yeah. Especially after his mom died, he was here more often than not. I give him his tablet back, tell him to tab Omega if anything happens. The Web isn't that big, and we're not going far. Nothing'll happen we can't get back for. If it did, the living room would still be too far.

Sharp pain bites at the back of my neck. "Ass," I say, slapping Omega's hand from the lock of hair he just pulled. No one but him would get away with that shit right now, and even for him it's a close call. In the corner of my eye, Jonas is trying not to laugh. Both of them get the benefit of my middle finger before I slip my arms into the sleeves of the jacket Omega brought me. Sabine shakes her head; she'll just have to get used to the chaos.

We're quiet in the elevator, the hush of the apartment following us down and out, getting stuck in the revolving doors as we step onto the sidewalk.

"Jonas, Sabine," Omega says, spreading his arms, "welcome to the Web."

The park spreads out across the street, the trees just ghostly shapes against the sky, a path bordered by lights disappearing in the distance. We turn left, my hand in Sabine's while the guys walk behind us, heading out of Quadrant One because there's really only one thing to see first. Omega keeps up a steady stream of stories about this stretch or that one—the time we skipped school to camp out in that water bar with our friends, passing a guitar around the group, getting loud and never getting into too much trouble because everyone knew who our brother was.

The glow always comes first. It trickles out from the epicenter for several blocks all around.

"The Vortex," Jonas says, blinking against the initial on-slaught of bright lights, flashing neon, whirring silver. "Wow. You weren't kidding."

"Never needed sunglasses at night before," Sabine says, finding them in her bag. "This is something fucking else."

"It's a little different now," Omega answers. "Solar panels on all the roofs, and there are six hydro power plants around the island. We don't suck the energy out of people like we're fucking vampires anymore."

Jonas raises an eyebrow. "Omega has weird taste in books," I say. Omega and I edge in, slowly, keeping pace with Jonas and Sabine, seeing it with their eyes. They're cautious, like they're about to dive into the sun. Los Angeles has its share of light, but it's all too concentrated here, too intense.

And in the middle, the black hole. It, too, is a little different, but the repairs eight years ago didn't change it all that much. The old Corp building—now government headquarters—is still a giant black glass spider. Two lit windows halfway up are eerie, staring eyes.

Omega squeezes my arm and I look at him. He holds me back as Jonas and Sabine are drawn closer to the building. "How much do they know?"

"Not everything." I swallow, look at my boots.

"Okay. How's it going out there?"

"Going. Don't expect me to find a cure tomorrow, but I'll find one."

"I know you will."

The room had no windows. Buried in the middle. I remember white more blinding than these rainbow flashes: walls, floor, teeth.

A different set of fingers digging into my skin, one hand on my shoulder, one on Omega's. I'm taking you to see your brother, little darlings, *she said.*

I was always jealous of Ant. The console looked like fun and I wanted to try but I wasn't allowed. And I smiled when Ell gave me the headphones, even though I couldn't see Anthem anywhere.

We play in the lights of the Vortex for a while, letting them paint our skin, ducking in and out of the stores that are still open, getting food at a takeout counter. A couple of times Omega's tablet flashes and my heart stops, but it's only relayed messages from Jonas's parents through Fable. Their latest tabs have lost their edge; he's thousands of miles away, so what can they really do? I feel guilty until he puts his arm around me and I think about him not being here.

I'm the first to yawn. Weak. The thought of a bed reminds me what else is waiting back at the apartment. The night turns airless.

"Let's go," Omega says, tossing our containers into a recycling box.

We leave the Vortex by the nearest street, turning and crossing. We're closer to the river now, but not near enough to hear it, and it wouldn't sound like the ocean anyway.

"'Scuse. 'Scuse me," a man mumbles, staggering from the mouth of an alley right into me, an elbow landing in my rib cage.

"Shit," I wheeze. "Watch where you're going, would you?" Sabine is already pushing him away and the guy stumbles back, looks up. Blank. Disoriented. Under the streetlamp, his skin is a faint, sickly yellow.

"Heyyy," he says, a grin spreading. "You guys know where I can get a fix?"

Omega hisses through his teeth. "Console station that way," he spits, jerking his thumb down a side street on the opposite side of the road. "If you've got the credits for it."

The man doesn't answer. We watch him go, tripping his way roughly in the direction Omega pointed. I glare at my brother, but don't say what I'm thinking.

He got used to our big apartment and unlimited credits pretty fast. He likes to forget it wasn't always that way for us.

"So that was . . . ," Jonas begins.

"Everyone had to make a choice," I tell him. "Forcing withdrawal on people wasn't fair, and lots of them might've died. You didn't notice that dude at Central?"

"Yeah, but he wasn't like that."

"Well, welcome to the Web," I answer, echoing Omega's earlier words.

"Was everyone like that before?"

"No, it was more regulated, I guess. People tracked when they weren't working; the clubs were only open at certain times."

"Isn't that better, though?"

"Depends on your point of view," Omega says, starting to walk again. "Sure, you didn't have people getting completely wrecked all the time. Most of them were pretty functional. But then again, it wasn't exactly an option. Now it's just the ones who want to, most of them were already addicted when the Corp fell. New uptake is pretty low, but for the ones who were . . . it's harder to get a job if you're an addict, so they don't do much except get fucked up all the time."

"I'll never understand this," Jonas mutters.

In a lot of ways, neither will I. I know where every console station is on this island, spent years carefully skirting them.

Because I feel it. Deep inside, an itch. If I scratch it once, that'll be it. The end. Bye, Alpha. I'll never stop. And that's why I won't tell Jonas what that bitch Ell did to me and Omega, because I'm a ticking time bomb, and on the other side of the country, I'm safe. I can learn and research without temptation, without giving in to what I'm trying to cure. There's no one there to offer what a tiny—or not so tiny—corner of my mind desperately wants. But here . . .

Here is a different story.

6

I turn into an alley, scanning for a neon sign halfway up a slimy brick wall. It's lit, a beacon that quickens my steps. No one knows where I am. The others went out before me, tour guides and tourists, and Anthem and Haven were sleeping when I left. Down here in the seedy streets of Quadrant Two, where I was born and spent the first nine years of my life, my home in the Upper Web seems as far away as my house on the beach. Trash rots and rusts in the gutters, barbed wire curtains blow from windows on lower floors.

My stomach twists.

The door hinges creak, and inside is just a tiny room, big enough for half a dozen tables and some chairs. Bottles of water line a bar at the back.

Only one of the tables is taken.

"No way," says a guy sitting at it, raising eyebrows drawn on with black eyeliner that contrasts against his silver-blond hair and grabbing the hand of the guy next to him. "Lynx, I think I'm hallucinating."

"Ditto. Do you think we're seeing the same thing?"

"It must be because you love me. It's like we share a brain."

"You're both fucking hilarious, and if you're high right now I'm leaving again," I tell them, relaxing. They haven't changed a bit. Lynx and his boyfriend, Spectrum, stand, flinging their arms

57

around me, squeezing me from both sides.

"She came back to us," Spectrum says with a sniff. "She must've missed us too much. Wasn't Los Angeles the great promised land we've heard so much about?"

I turn my face into Lynx's chest. He smells the same as he did back in school, when I had the most pointless crush on him.

"Wait." He pulls back just enough to look at me. "Why *are* you back?"

"Ant—" I start. Can't finish.

"Oh, Al," Spectrum whispers, kissing my forehead. "When?"

"Not yet. But, you know, soon. We think. Isis thinks."

"Sit." Lynx grabs me some water. "You okay? Is Haven okay?"

It's not a stupid question, not from someone who knows me as well as he does.

"Yeah. I mean, no, but there's nothing I can do about it except be here. Haven . . . You can imagine, I guess."

"Yeah," Spectrum agrees. "Want to talk about it?"

"No."

"Fine. So, the Web's been super fun since you left." Lynx toys with his hair. Purple spikes. He's had them as long as I've known him, when we wound up in the same class a couple years after Omega and I moved to our new school up in One. "Lock's still an asshole. Not an old-days kind of asshole, but he's carving out a special niche for himself. Definitely has potential. Keeps tossing up more of those antitracking signs, because *obviously* reminding everyone all the time is a good way to get them to stay clean."

I laugh. I've never liked the mayor either, though I agree with Ant and Haven and everyone that he's harmless, just an idiot. A slimy one. And in a twisted way, I can see why no one wanted to elect anyone too smart. We've been there before. "Might help if the two of you didn't get your kicks breaking every law we have left."

"Valid point." Spectrum shrugs. "But that'd be boring, and life's an adventure. How's things out there? We know nothing, since you and Omega both abandoned us."

"You haven't seen him?"

"Not since about a week after you left."

"She doesn't need to worry about that," Lynx says, shooting Spectrum a dark look. "It's good to see *you* again."

I make a mental note to yell at Omega later. For now, I give Lynx and Spectrum the usual edited version—minus what I'm actually doing at school and in every second of my spare time not spent with Jonas or at the club. I know what they'd say, that if I wanted to study tracks it'd be better to do it here. But they wouldn't understand. Neither one of them has ever resisted a console when the mood struck. I tell them about the ocean, the band, Sabine, Fable and his countless girlfriends.

My heart aches and I drink more water to soothe the burn in my throat. I don't know how I can miss L.A. already, how I missed it the minute we left, especially when I *should* be here right now.

"I do need something from you," I say. "A new tablet."

Lynx stands, goes behind the counter and through a door.

"You up to something?" Spectrum asks. There aren't many legitimate reasons why someone would need a tablet from them and not any of the countless stores that sell them.

As it happens, though, I have one. "There were some issues just before I left, some asshole got my number. No big thing, but I don't really want one that can be traced to me."

"Fair enough. Everything's okay?"

"On that front, yeah."

Lynx returns, hands me my new toy. It's a little depressing how much better I feel just holding one of my own again. "I need to get back." My chair scrapes against cheap tiles.

"Come and visit again before you leave?" Lynx asks. "Bring that . . . what's his name?"

"Jonas. Okay. Do me a favor? Don't tell anyone about Ant?"

"'Course not."

I know they won't. These two are better at gathering than giving. Seeing them gives me the strength for what I have to do next.

Quadrant Two's Citizen Remembrance Center is mostly empty in the middle of the day. A young couple, holding hands, keeps the door open for me as I enter and they leave, but after that I don't see anyone. The floors echo and, when I look down, beam back a faint rainbow reflection from my hair.

Soft music plays from speakers in the corners of the room.

"Hi, Mom. Hi, Dad," I whisper, swiping my wrist over the lock. The small black chips we're all reduced to in the end say nothing, of course. We all have them, or all of us from the Web do. Implanted into our brains, ticking away, logging the memories that will be all that's left of any of us when our bodies are gone. I walk to one of the viewers and put Mom's chip in first, waiting for the menu to flicker to life on the touch screen.

All of it's here, waiting to show me a person I don't really remember. I select a scene at random, and the circle of lights overhead flicker and burst to life, painting a hologram on thin air.

I can see now why Ant says I look like her. It's harder to tell from the later files when she was dying, blonde hair turned sickness-gray, but in the earlier ones, yeah. Streaks of that same violet she wore when she was young run through my unruly mass. My eyes are the same blue as hers. For a while I watch. I've seen her holding me and Omega before, as well as every recording of the precious few years we had with her before she died. But I'm not here for her, and leaving her locked in the cabinet while I see my dad seems cruel somehow.

Not that we had all that much more time with our father. He

started going downhill pretty soon after she died, though I don't think I got that at the time. No, I know I didn't. Ant just took over as whatever kind of parent Omega and I had.

Actually, a better one.

"Hi," I say again, exchanging one chip for the other. This I remember, not from having seen it on a viewer a hundred times, but living it. A hand on my back as he guides me across the street to my first day of school, Omega a mirror image of nervous excitement on his other side.

Ghost fingers warm the spot between my shoulder blades. I shiver. I don't know if I'm glad or not that he didn't live to see me now. I think about my school in L.A., picture him—however improbably—walking me to the corner.

I flick the image. Ant stumbles through the door while Omega and I eat oatmeal, trying not to drop sticky lumps on our school clothes. Dad doesn't say anything except to tell Ant not to be late for work.

Then, soon after, the long months on the couch in our old, tiny living room. Corp news playing on an endless cycle to unseeing eyes. Headphones put over his ears and left there to dull the pain.

"He's going to be here with you soon," I say. I'm not crying. *Not. Crying.* "Take care of him, okay?"

My father's image rolls over on a translucent pillow and looks straight at me.

Good enough. I wipe my eyes.

■

Haven and I sit, hands wrapped around mugs of tea, breathing in steam more than drinking. On the bed, Anthem drifts in and out, eyelids occasionally fluttering open enough to focus on one or both of us. He'll reach toward her or smile at me before sleep takes him again.

We've been here for hours, sun arcing across a pale, hazy sky. We're not waiting. No, we're just sitting the same way we used to when I was younger. She'd listen to me complain about teachers or boys or Anthem pushing me too hard with music lessons and then we'd chill, drink tea, somewhere in a cross between friends, sisters, and mother and child.

The weight of every role she's played pulls at her skin, dragging it into fine lines.

"So," she says, tucking her legs under her. "You're really happy out there?"

"I told you, yes."

"I know. Just weird not having you around."

"Weird not being here," I admit. "Weird to be back. Weird to be showing it to people who've never seen it before."

"I like your friend Sabine."

"Everyone does."

"*She* likes Fable."

My lips twist. "Everyone does." But I'm more amused because Haven never misses anything.

"Tell me more about Jonas."

I shift. This is always so completely awkward, and yet I want her to ask. "You know everything."

"Middle name?"

She's been doing her research. Things are different there. "Alexander."

"Favorite color?"

"Red."

"Is he good to you?"

62

"He's here," I say, because that should be enough of an explanation for anyone, and it is for her.

"Is he good in—"

"Don't you dare answer that," Ant whispers from the pillow. I arch an eyebrow and snicker at him. Haven laughs, wicked and free, her old self for a second. I smile. Maybe everything will be okay.

From my spot at the end of the bed, I hear her stomach growl. "You have to eat," I tell her. Pink streaks ripple as she shakes her head, but I learned stubbornness from her. Maybe it's selfish that she needs her strength because all of us need her strength, but I don't care. "Everyone's out. Go. I'll sit with him."

Slowly, she nods, pushes herself from the chair. I take her place, look down at Anthem's face, which has relaxed into calmness again. My mind drifts, wondering what parts of the Web Omega and Fable are showing Jonas and Sabine. Whether Mage and Phoenix regret not coming, though if I have to guess, probably not. When Pixel and Isis will come over.

"Don't worry so much, little sister," Ant says. His fingers twitch; I still them with my own. "Everyone's moping around, like"—he draws a labored breath—"like this is the most terrible thing in the world. It's . . . it's not. My life's been good."

I open my mouth, unsure of what to say. Even I know "What, seriously?" isn't the most appropriate thing.

"I mean it. I made a difference, I think. I had Haven, and you. Omega. It's cool, little one. I'm ready, almost."

A sudden downpour of tears spills over my cheeks. Part of me begs to argue, part warms in agreement. All the things he's seen, done, fought for and against. And so many of them were for me, Omega, other people. We can give him this. "Almost?" I ask.

He nods, a tiny movement. "I want to hear how good you've gotten."

Haven smiles from the couch when I go into the living room,

chrome eyebrows raised above heavy, tired lids. If she notices that I've been crying, she doesn't comment, just watches as I grab my guitar from where Fable stashed it in the corner.

I hold it up, and her plate clinks against the glass table. Anthem's propped himself up, more awake, when Haven and I come back into the room. The bed sinks beneath me, then Haven, her arms reaching out, my fingers poised over the strings.

She never let becoming an Exaur destroy her love of music, especially Anthem's. Night after night, she'd press her hands to whatever he was playing, letting the vibrations creep across her skin, the sound light up the implants on her hands.

Slow, soft is right for this room, this place. Different to the harsh thumps, the heavy bass of the band at the club. Faltering, stupid, irrationally nervous, it takes me a few tries to get started, to let the melody suffuse my brain and then my bones, for the lyrics to come back to me. This is what I play by firelight with sand between my toes, a soundtrack to hours quiet, sincere in their happiness.

I play the ocean's gentle creep up the beach, the moon's swaying light over the breaks, the sparks that pop and fly into the air.

My fingers speed up, a new set of tears coats my lashes. I blink, focus on Haven's implants swimming with color. Blue, green, pink. Ebbing, flowing, brightening and fading as the song drifts to a close.

"Encore," Anthem whispers. I laugh, bizarrely relieved. It's not like he hasn't heard me play before, more often than pretty much anyone else. But none of those times were the last time, or I never thought of them that way.

I'm in the middle of a tricky chord when the others get back, so I don't see the door open, the room fill.

Omega's words stop me, though. "We've got company."

"There's cameras and shit all over the place on the street," Sabine fills in. "They tried to push in behind us when Fable used that chip thing in his wrist." The TV flickers to life and I see footage of the revolving door playing across the screen, lenses blooming like mechanical flowers on human stalks.

"What the fuck," I say to no one in particular. That's not even news. As Jonas puts his hand on my shoulder, the camera pans to a young, pretty reporter, blonde hair streaked with metallic bronze.

"In just a few moments, Mayor Lock will be arriving to pay his respects to Citizen N4003, more popularly known, of course, as Anthem. The force behind the changes that put an end to the Corp's tyranny eight years ago." Behind her, a sleek black pod pulls up to the curb beside the park.

"We shouldn't let him in," Omega says.

Yeah, that. Except I don't think we have a choice. The Web might be a democracy now, the mayor our fairly elected leader— our second one—but we can't pretend Ant's anyone else, someone nameless and faceless, dying an anonymous death.

Much as we might want to.

"We have to," Haven says, sighing in resignation. She doesn't like him, but I don't think she'd like anyone ruling this place, even her mother. President Z had groomed her only daughter to take over the Corp, but she'd only succeeded in making Haven hate the Corp more than anyone.

"Ready?" she asks. Anthem nods, exhausted, a stark contrast to the relative energy he had while I was playing.

I brush past Jonas, down the hallway to the front door, stand an inch from it, steadying my breath, listening. The elevator beeps and I pull open the door before the mayor can push the button that'll make a red light flash in every room. For Haven.

"You have ten minutes," I say before he has a chance to speak. "He's tired."

I get an oily smile. "Alpha, so good to have you back. Enjoying Los Angeles?"

"It's fine."

"Glad to hear it, but I've missed you. No one else speaks to me like you do."

"I'm special. Ten minutes."

He's already heading down the hallway, past the others who've come into the living room, leaving only Haven and Ant in the bedroom. Haven can hold her own, and Anthem's.

"Wow. You really do not like him."

I shake my head at Sabine. "He's not here because he gives a fuck; he's here so he can look like he does. I guarantee he's the one who told the reporters to be downstairs, or got someone to tell them."

"He's always been like that," Omega says. "Trying to hold Anthem up as some kind of treasure. Anthem never wanted that, but it never stopped the guy from trying. The Corp tried to use Anthem, he's been there before. Twenty credits says Lock finds a way to use this to make himself look good. Claim that Anthem said on his deathbed that we should elect him again, or something."

Deathbed. I wince, but Omega's not wrong.

"Charming," Jonas says. I move to his side.

"Plus, he hit on Haven once," Fable says. "At this party we all had to go to."

That was almost funny. Haven can definitely hold her own, but it was proof, if anyone needed it, that he really didn't care about Anthem, only what Anthem represents.

The front door opens again. I flinch until I see Isis with Pixel following. "We saw," Isis says. "I'll go in in a sec and tell them my

66

patient has to rest. Not every day I get to tell the mayor what to do. Fun times."

I smile gratefully at her. Ant still credits her with saving his broken hand, meaning he could play again. And she took care of me and Omega, after . . .

The witch. A pod. My own traitorous excitement because we were going on an adventure, being taken to see Ant at work.

White, so much white. Walls, floor, teeth. The music swirls in my head and it is beautiful, the most beautiful thing I've ever known. Lilting, then loud, soft building to thunder. I feel strange but don't care that my skin is crackling with electricity and my mind is swathed in fog. My arms and legs fill with hot lead and I see, I think . . .

"Al?"

"Yeah. Sorry. Headache." I squeeze Jonas's arm, ignoring Sabine's curious look, Fable's and Omega's knowing ones. It's the only time I'm relieved to see Lock coming toward us.

"You're done with him now," I say. "This is time for his family."

"Family." He looks at the strange faces, at wrists free of the telltale bump. "Of course. Let me know if there's anything I can do." His hand jerks as if he wants to touch me, but he catches himself and bunches it into a fist he presses to his lips, as if he meant to do that all along.

"Don't count on it."

7

At first the sounds are warm, gentle. There's a voice and something else I don't know, something that's like sunshine and a good dream in my ears. I know this must be singing, music, and the gibberish whispers I've never understood make so much sense now. Everything makes sense. Of course they keep this perfection from us until we can handle it. It's right that they do, but it's mine now. I have it and I'm never letting go, the climbing voice is too beautiful. I have to catch it before it runs away. My arms stretch out but something stops me and the voice is disappearing, fading, too far. I'll never find it and I want to cry.

But oh, this is music, too, this noise that pulses through my head, loops and whorls of sound and high, hard beeps. I want to dance but I can't move, hands holding me down, fingers digging into my scalp to keep the headphones in place. But why would I want to take them off? White spins into clouds around me and it's perfect. Why has Ant kept this from us? The woman doesn't need to trap me. I'll stay here forever, letting the music climb into my brain.

More, please.

"Can I borrow one of your computers?"

I should've brought my own, but maybe this is better, at least for a little while. Before the itch gets too much to handle. Communications, connections between here and Los Angeles are good, but I'll have access to different information here.

There's some stuff L.A. didn't want. Some stuff I wouldn't have been allowed to bring with me, even in harmless code form.

Harmless. Ha. It's never that.

"Uh, sure. Just let me . . ." Haven doesn't finish, just stands and leaves the bedroom. By the time I've joined her in her office, all but one of the screens are blank, flat gray.

"Sorry," she says. "Boring crap. Go ahead."

She's never been interested in anything boring. "Thanks." I watch her go, back to Anthem's side.

I log into the mainframe, start reading.

How to encode a song into a drug, a track, isn't as much of a secret as it used to be. It's not public, but it's there if you know where to look.

Sometimes I imagine the flashbacks as a cluster of tiny insects, crawling along the pathways in my brain. Tracking would make them breed, multiply, take over more than they already do.

I'm trying to find what will kill them. Not just kill them, but clear my mind so it'll be like they were never there.

Some of the meds to help with overdoses are closest to what I need, but none of them go nearly far enough.

I read, type, squint, curse at the monitor. Fuck, it would help if I knew what Ell made us listen to, but too much happened that day. No one thought to look, maybe no one thought it would've been anything unusual, even if they had thought to dig in the damaged systems.

Bad dreams, Omega and I told Anthem and Haven. They'd frowned and hugged us. Of course, we'd seen a lot, no matter how much they tried to protect our eyes.

And our ears.

"Hey."

I press the button so the screen matches the others. "Hey," I say, turning to Jonas. "I thought you were out."

"I was." He smiles. "But Fable and Sabine went off somewhere and your brother had plans. Thought I'd come see if I could steal my girlfriend for a while."

I glance at the computer. I'm not making much progress. "Okay."

"It's kind of hard to get around without one of those chips."

I hadn't thought about it, but yeah, I guess it would be. I grab his hand, run my thumb over the spot where it would be, glad of what the absence means.

We head to the park. I can see Ant's bedroom window if I peer through the trees, and I guess Omega's been showing him the more exciting parts of the city because Jonas hasn't come in here yet. I'm not sure why I'm surprised that it's exactly the same; I haven't been gone that long.

"You holding up?"

We're on the path, under solar lamps hoarding light for later.

"Yeah," I say. "Yeah, I am. And in case I forgot to say it before, thanks for coming with me."

His eyes soften. "I'm glad I did. And it's cool to see this place, where you grew up and everything."

"It has its good points." And it does. The park. The feeling that the buildings cup me like a hand. The constant life of the Vortex.

They just don't outweigh the bad parts. I look across the park, in the direction of a console station I can't see but I know is there. The knowledge that at any moment, the hand can curl to a fist and crush me.

We pass a well-dressed woman, maybe Haven's age, sitting on one of the benches. Headphones cover her ears. Portable consoles—for both encoded music and not—became more common after the war. I pay too much attention to her skin, the whites of her eyes, but she doesn't see.

She's tracking. I walk faster. Jonas's long legs keep easy pace with mine. "Have you been having fun with Omega?"

"It's weird." Jonas laughs, startling a bird in a tree overhead. "He's so exactly like you. It's fucked up. If guys were my thing—"

"Stop right there." I hold up my hand. Giggles start in my belly and burst upward until I'm doubled over, laughing so hard I can't breathe, stumbling until I hit soft grass. "Please, for the love of . . . anything, do not ever even hint at that again." Tears—good ones this time—form in my eyes. I sink to my knees, hysterical for no good reason because it's not that funny, but tension melts from my muscles. "I so did not need that visual."

"Sorry," he says, though I can tell he isn't and I'm not really either. He joins me on the grass, arm around my shoulders while I gradually calm myself.

"I need to wash my brain."

"Made you laugh, though."

"True."

"What were you up to before?"

The last of my smile fades. I focus my eyes on the middle distance. "Stuff for school."

"Here? Now?"

"Why not?"

He shrugs. "No reason."

I lean against him, realizing how much I would've just told him if he knew how to understand. I need to wash my brain.

■

Haven's office hums, a low buzz that would be comforting if I was getting anywhere. The break in the park with Jonas put me in a better mood, but that's not enough to unlock carefully hidden secrets.

I don't even know enough to know where to look. I wasn't expecting to have to do this yet, I thought I'd be better prepared, have some idea of what I was hunting for, of what might help me. I went out west to learn about myself, my mind, away from this place where the siren call makes it hard to think about anything else.

Encased in my warm little bubble out in Los Angeles, I'd been telling myself ever since I arrived that I'd come back here when I chose, when I was ready to take the final steps.

Now, my steps are disjointed. A dancer who doesn't quite feel the rhythm. The white text blurs on the black screen, the familiar pounding starting at the base of my skull. Pain ricochets around my head, cold sweat beads on the back of my neck, and my hands curl around the sharp edge of the desk. Stay here. *Stay here.* I focus on the hum. Breathe, too quickly, manage to slow down.

I pull away from the keyboard to tap on my tablet instead. Where are you?_ It stays silent too long, as empty of answers as the monitor in front of me.

Buzz. Finally.

Just heading back with Bean_ Fable answers.

Can you meet me?_ I type back.

Both of us?_

Just you._

Sabine won't be offended, I hope. It's not like her, and she's never wondered about my friendship with Fable the way Jonas sometimes does. Fable's just like another brother to me, as if I needed one of those, and he knows everything. Other than Omega, he's the only person who can say that.

My tablet buzzes twice more and I stand, stretch, lean over to erase everything I was working on. I doubt Haven's in the mood to snoop, but I don't want to make it easy for her. Jonas is in the living room, a book open on his lap, the cover hidden.

"I'm going out," I say, leaning over the back of the couch to kiss him. His fingers grip my sleeve as he tries to pull me over, onto him, another temptation that's so hard to resist. I dig my boots into the carpet.

"Want me to come with?" he asks, giving up.

I shake my head. "Stay here in case Haven needs anything? Tell her I'll be back soon, if she asks."

"Okay."

"Thank you." I do mean that, kiss him again to show it.

It's a beautiful day, prettier than it has a right to be. Almost as warm as L.A. The buildings sparkle and I turn my face to the sun, walking south. Fable's already waiting on the corner we agreed, alone. Before I can open my mouth, he tells me Sabine's

75

gone to check out a music store he told her about over in Three to see what instruments they have. She's missing her bass.

I'll take her back later if she finds anything, will swipe my wrist to buy her anything she wants.

"What's up?"

Fable raises his eyebrows, grins slightly. "You're asking me?"

"Just trying to beat you to it." Ahead, the Vortex spins and flashes.

"I'll play along. Nothing. Just showing Bean around, trying to stay out of your way. I've known Anthem my whole life, but I'm not family. Not my place to be there unless you need me."

"Yeah, it is," I say quietly. "You are. But thanks."

He's silent for half a block, relaxed, waiting for me to say whatever's on my mind. It's not that easy. "They're worse here." *They.* Our code for the flashbacks so I don't have to say it.

"I figured."

"And I don't know what to do about it. I can't leave again, not now. Not until . . . after." The thought punches me. "I've been try-ing to make the most of it, working while we're here, but I'm not finding anything. I can't . . . Do you even know what this is like, having something in your head and not knowing what it is or how to get it out?" My peripheral vision fuzzes, sparks of pain scat-tering behind my eyes.

"Hey, calm down." Fable stops, turns, puts both hands on my shoulders. "You know I don't, but we're going to figure it out, okay? Tell me what you've been looking up so far."

I do, about the digging into the mainframe to find some record of this happening to anyone before, records I know aren't there because it's not the first time I've looked. Or if they are there, someone's hidden them where I can't get access. Same with any trace of exactly what Ell made Omega and me listen to. Thanks to school, I'm a little further along in understanding how brains work, but I don't know anywhere near enough yet. And I can't find enough info on how to build a track from scratch to figure that out.

The problem with being one of only two people alive in need of a cure is there's no room for error. And no way to test anything. When I do it, I need to be fucking sure I have it right.

"You still sure about not telling Haven and Anthem? Haven could help. There's nothing anywhere in the system she wouldn't be able to uncover."

"Asking them to save me now means telling them they didn't completely save me the first time," I say.

"Yeah, I know." He sighs. "Okay. Lynx and Spectrum?"

"I went to see them a couple days ago, but not about this. No. They're better with hardware, anyway." We're within the bounds of the Vortex now, packed with people and energy.

"You know who you could . . ."

My stomach turns over. We both look at the glass spider in front of us. A line of government pods pulls out, heads in the direction of the river behind us. "I know."

■

Getting into the government offices is easy. We just walk in, wave at the receptionist behind the desk, who smiles at us, a mix of surprise and recognition.

The huge computers behind the curved wall still make the whole place hum, but it's not comforting like it is in Haven's office.

Because I remember. Walking into this place for the first time, a hand holding mine so tightly its pointed fingernails made marks in my skin. Stepping into this glass and marble lobby, a different receptionist by the desk. And then I heard the hum.

Fable moves toward one of the elevators; I shake my head. Not that one. I can see him mentally curse himself for forgetting, but why should he remember? Every time we've been here together in the past I've done a good job of steering us to a different one, avoiding actually saying it out loud. I know exactly which one Ell pushed me into with Omega a few inches behind, and I haven't set foot in it since.

Part of me thinks it's stupid that it matters so much. Even when we step into one of the others, I pray nobody makes it stop on the floor Ell and Omega and I stopped on that day. I've never gone back to look at that room. Not when I can see it any time I close my eyes or any time they're open when a flashback hits.

Lots of people thought it was in bad taste for the mayor—and his predecessor—to take over President Z's old office, but it's hard to deny that it's the nicest, at least of all the ones I've ever visited. Ant refused to meet with either of them in it, making them come to him in the studio or at the apartment instead.

Now another desk greets anyone who steps off the elevator. A perky, green-haired guy sits behind it. "Good afternoon"—he squints at me—"Alpha? Whoa. We're all so sorry about Anthem."

"Thanks, Pax." I don't know what else to say.

"Well, uh. Welcome back. Hey, Fable."

Fable nods beside me. "Is he in?" I ask.

A shadow of doubt darkens Pax's eyes; his hair ripples like grass in a breeze when he shakes it away. "Said he didn't want interruptions, but I'm sure he didn't mean you. Let me go check. Is this a social call, or do you need something?" His eyes widen. "Wait, Anthem's not—"

"No. No. I just have a favor to ask."

Leather creaks as Pax pushes his chair away, walks to a door that looks like all the others.

I try to remember what the word *sorry* tastes like. One look at Fable tells me he's thinking of Lock's appearance at the apartment, too, and he's trying not to laugh.

"Stop," I hiss. Fable's mouth twitches harder.

Minutes slide by, stretching out. In my pocket, my tablet buzzes.

`Are you ready to give in, Alpha? I can give you anything. Everything you want._`

My curse when I see the screen echoes around us. I pass it to Fable.

Fable's mouth tugs back down into a straight line and he's about to say something when the door opens again, a welcome distraction. Pax's too-thin body slips through a gap just wide enough before he pulls it closed behind him.

Shit. I should've been nicer to Lock. Pax's hands open and close, reach for a tablet sitting on his desk. "He's busy, but told me to give you whatever you need." He doesn't look at either of us and turns the tablet over and over between his fingers. "Or you can come back in a few hours."

Fable and I glance at each other. Maybe this is better since I have such a hard time not being rude to the mayor. "No," Fable says, "we just need access to some computer files. We're doing a research project at school out in—"

"Fine," Pax interrupts. "No problem." He leans forward, tablet clattering back onto the desk. Keys click. "There's an office on the second floor, fourth door on the left. It'll open to your chip, and I've logged you into the system."

"Thanks, Pax," I say, pulling Fable back to the elevator, determined to get downstairs and into that office before it dawns on anyone except the two of us that we didn't have to give any kind of real explanation for what we wanted. Hey, if this is what I get for insulting Lock, I'll do it more often. And if Pax is pissed at me for being a bitch to his boss, then tough.

The hum gets louder with every floor we descend, like we're falling into it. The second floor is deserted, scented with flowers in ugly vases dotted at intervals around the curving hallway. This wasn't *my* floor; we were higher up that day. A red light blinks on the scanner outside the fourth door on the left, turning green the second I hold up my wrist. Inside, the room is blinding white.

My breath catches.

"You're fine," Fable whispers. Or maybe yells. This whole building does weird shit with sound. "Al, you're fine. I'm here. You're here, with me."

But who am I?

"Just try to tell me if it starts," he says.

If. "Yeah. Yeah, I will."

Huge touch screens make up the wall opposite the door. Our footsteps make no noise on the tiles. I step right up, close enough for the static to raise the hairs on my arms, and I see Fable do the same to another screen out of the corner of my eye.

Ask a hundred people in the Web to think of a random date, ninety-nine of them would say the one I tap into the search field—the date of the rebellion, when everything changed. I'm sure what I'm looking for isn't going to be there. I've already combed these files, but it can't hurt to look.

But I'm right, there's nothing there I haven't seen before. I dig deeper, searching corners that would be neglected and dusty if they were real, physical things. Whatever Ell gave us wouldn't have been in public circulation, or Omega and I wouldn't be the only ones suffering, and I'm as sure as I can be that we are.

Lynx and Spectrum are *very* good at gathering information.

Nobody in their network of med-techs, friends, and addicts had ever heard of anything like what I described. I don't think they ever believed my question was theoretical, but I got a pass on their prying, and if they assumed anything, it was that it was happening to Ant, not me.

So it was something hidden, secret.

It's a lot easier to feel around in the dark if you know the shape of the thing you're looking for.

"Al?"

"Mmm?"

"C'mere for a sec?"

"Hold on." I reach for my tablet, which is still buzzing when I grab it from my pocket. A wash of déjà vu threatens to drown me. The only difference is that this time, it's from Omega.

`Where are you? Get back here, quick._`

9

"Omega, Jonas, hold him *still!*"

I run down the hall, following Isis's voice. It took longer than it should've to get here, even with convincing the receptionist in the lobby of the spider that I needed a pod *right now.*

Anthem's body is shaking, jerking like my pulse. Sheer panic transforms Haven's face into something almost grotesque. Isis reads the glowing numbers and flashing lines that mean nothing to me but obviously translate to danger. Tragedy. Conclusions.

I can't breathe. He can't leave me, us. Not yet. He's wrong. He's not ready. Jonas and Omega pin down his arms as Isis pulls something from a bag—a glass vial. And a needle.

No. No.

I move, meaning to stop Isis's arm but grab Haven instead. Fable joins the others at the bed to help. Haven's tears soak my thin shirt and chill my skin. Inhuman sounds grate from between Ant's whitened lips. Omega loses his grip on one of his legs and Ant thrashes wildly, nearly kicking the syringe from Isis's hand. She tugs the cap off with her teeth, fills it, jabs it into the crook of his elbow before he can break free again.

It's like we all feel it, imagine it. The whole room. Cold steel piercing tender flesh. The struggling stops, muscle by muscle, against his human shackles and it's as if she drugged every one of us, the panic draining into stillness. Red digits stop flashing, turn to green on little monitors. Ant's chest rises and falls with easy breaths. Hand by hand, Omega and Jonas let go but don't move away. A door opens, footsteps thump toward us, louder, louder.

"Got lost," Sabine pants. "Is . . . ?"

"He's stable now," Isis says. The warring thoughts in my brain bare their teeth, clench their fists, prepare to draw blood.

"He didn't want this," I say. Haven, her face buried against me, can't read my lips. When she feels the vibrations and raises her head, I don't repeat myself.

Isis gives me a long, measured look. Nods.

Next time. And there will be one, I know. Next time she won't save him and I'll be here, holding my mother-sister-friend while the life leaves Anthem for good.

■

He's fucking insane. Haven stares at Ant. Ant's eyes are pleading, flicking between her and Isis.

"What's it going to do?" he asks, voice stronger than it's been since I got here. "Kill me?"

"That's not funny." Haven's eyes flash.

"It wasn't supposed to be. Please."

Isis hesitates. "I have to come with you. Everyone does. If something happens like the other day . . ."

"I want everyone there."

He's insane, but if I wanted something like this, I'd be pissed if people didn't let me. Haven looks panicked, knuckles white and eyes wide. Her mouth opens and closes until finally the last argument fades, unspoken, from her lips.

"Get him ready," Isis says. "I'll be back in a couple of hours."

We even re-dye his hair.

Black clothes hang loosely from limbs frightening in their thinness, pooling around him in the wheelchair. Isis has borrowed a med-pod, too, a new kind that's more like a mobile hospital, and I don't ask just how loosely we're using the term *borrowed* here. It's big enough to fit all of us, which is the only thing I care about.

"I'll drive," Sabine says, catching my expression. "Slowly, I swear." Fable climbs into the front with her. Pixel pushes Ant up a ramp. Isis, Haven, Omega, Jonas, and I climb in after them and take seats on benches that run the length of the pod.

Every bump and pothole makes Ant wince. His teeth dig into his lips and his skeleton-bone fingers curl around the arms of the chair. A sheen of sweat breaks out on his skin. But if he complains now, Isis will make Sabine turn the pod around.

"He okay?" Jonas whispers in my ear. I nod.

No. He's never going to be okay again. But he needs this.

Anthem's insistence that the warehouse be kept just as it was screws us. We all stare at the small gap in the barbed wire. Isis rummages inside the pod until she comes up with a pair of brutal shears. I don't want to know what those are used for, but they cut a hole big enough for us to wheel Ant through, gravel and grit crunching under the tires.

The carpet that hid the trapdoor is long gone, probably stolen as a trophy by some kid. Omega grabs the handle and flips it open, the sound ringing around us.

The chair shakes. Anthem's breath immediately strains with his efforts to push himself out of it.

"No way," Haven says. This time, Ant doesn't fight her.

"Go look if you want," I tell Jonas. I know he's curious. Sabine follows. The rest of us can probably picture every dripping pipe, every filthy wall.

"Remember?" Ant asks, but there's nobody here who played

with him down there and nothing else to say.

When Jonas and Sabine climb out, we drive a little way back up the Web. I raise my eyebrows at Isis and she nods. At Pixel's old club, the old scanner is on, blinking. A pass of my wrist and the doors part. We've always had as much access here as we wanted.

"Damn it. Pixel, where are the lights?" Fable fumbles around, hands slapping the wall near the door.

Pixel laughs; it echoes around the cavernous dark. I hear his boots fade away and the lights flare—not overhead fluorescents, but neon beams that paint us all with rainbows. We stand in the middle of the dance floor, filled with first- and secondhand recollections. Where the stage was, where they all used to dance.

"I see where Mage and Phoenix got their design ideas," Sabine says. "Add a few mirrors . . . It's like they brought the place with them."

"They kind of did," I say. And I knew that, but like Sabine, I'm struck by it now.

"C'mon," Omega says to Jonas, pointing to the stairs.

I move to follow and Jonas shakes his head. "Be right back."

With furniture. They carry two of the old sofas down from the balcony, crunchy with dust, choked with clouds of decay that waft up as soon as we sit down. Isis rests her hand on Ant's arm, casually, like she's not checking his pulse.

"I kissed you for the first time here," Ant says to Haven. The rest of us find interesting patches on the walls to stare at.

"You did." She smiles. "Looking back, I'd give it a solid seven out of ten. Maybe an eight."

"Hey."

Everyone laughs. I curl into Jonas's side, let their stories drift over me. Sabine asks all the right questions about the original band, the gigs here, the rebellion. Jonas listens intently, tucking these new details around the broad strokes I've painted for him. Anthem's voice cracks when he talks about Scope, and none of them will call *that yellow-wearing asshole* by his actual name. Come to think of it, I'm not sure I've ever heard it, and I don't want to.

"Time to go," Isis says, soft but firm. Ant's eyes are drooping, his voice slow and thick. We leave the club exactly how we found it and lock the doors behind us.

Bye.

■

No one goes anywhere. We all walk around the apartment in silence, as if we're the ghosts and Ant's the one being haunted. Haven barely leaves him, but once when I come out of the hygiene cube in my room, I see her closing the door to her office, computer lights winking.

Ant doesn't wake up again. The real Anthem is still hidden in there, somewhere. I know his chip's still there, recording away, but the force of personality that made my brother everything he was is smothered by the weight of his failing body.

It takes two days after we get back from the club. Almost to the minute, I think. I stare blankly at the clock, wondering what woke me. There's no beeping, no noise at all. I check my tablet, and anger rises. For fuck's sake, not now.

I can give you everything you want, Alpha. You have no idea how close it is._

Careful not to wake Jonas, I slip from between the sheets and pad, barefoot and dizzy, from our room. In the hall, I stop, breathe until everything stops spinning. The door to Anthem and Haven's is closed. Years ago, I never would've gone in without knocking, but I won't be interrupting anything now.

It takes me a second to realize I don't just need to switch on the lights. It's *completely* dark. The monitors beside the bed are flat black screens, melting into the room around them. My heart beating just a little faster, I find a switch. I am relieved to see Ant's closed eyes and his hair spread across the pillow, but it's just temporary.

"Jonas?" I call, I hope loud enough that he'll hear me, but not loud enough to wake the others. "Jonas? Come here?"

He must've only been half asleep; maybe I did wake him when I got up. He stumbles through the door, rubbing his eyes. "You okay?" he asks, husky and raw, and I don't have time to think about what I've put him through since asking him to come.

"Get Haven. Her office."

He leaves, and slowly I approach the bed. Slowly, because I'm already sure of what I'll find. I already feel the chill on my fingertips before I touch his cheek.

Cold. I'm not thinking fast enough. Why didn't the alarms go off and wake Isis even if Haven couldn't hear them? My eyes go to the wall, a few inches above the floor. Cables snake and tangle, their plugs haphazard on the carpet.

"She's not there." I spin to stare at Jonas, barely seeing him.

"Al? Where's Haven?" Isis pushes past him, hurries to the bed. Her fingers reach for Ant's pulse but, like me, she knows the moment she sees him. I want to collapse, but I don't think I can yet.

"Turn his head," I whisper. A wave of nausea rolls through me at the thought of doing it myself. Isis is as gentle as she can be, but Anthem's muscles have already begun to stiffen. She shifts her hands to get a better grip.

"What?" she asks herself, pulling one hand back. Under the

lights the blood is stark and vivid on her skin, even brighter on Anthem's hair behind his ear. The black sheets have swallowed the rest of the stain, left where Haven removed his memory chip.

"He bled," I say dumbly. Bled. He was alive when she did it. Maybe he couldn't feel anything, but still alive, breathing, blood pumping—however sluggishly—through his veins. "I'm going to . . ."

I need to find her, and I'm all too fucking sure I know exactly where she is.

"What is it, Al?" Jonas crosses the room, but I shrug his hand away. I feel flayed, open, and even his soft touch seems hard enough to bruise. Isis raises her eyes to mine, guessing the same thing I have.

"I need you to drive," I tell him. "Isis, please, stay here. Tell Omega and everyone . . . I don't know. Shut the door. Don't let them see." In my room, I find shoes and pull them on with the clothes I slept in. I don't know how much of a head start she had or if I can stop her and *he didn't want this*. He wanted to die. I don't even know *how* she did it, but I know she's had years to perfect the technology she invented in the first place. "Jonas, come *on*."

We're downstairs and in the pod in minutes. I use giving directions as an excuse for not saying anything else. Left and right make sense when nothing else does. The streets are quiet, the clubs closed, dawn an hour away. Lonely neon flickers, a beacon to no one. I shake in my seat, teeth chattering, Anthem's blood glistening on Isis's hands every time I blink. Jonas bites his lips against the thousand questions I know he has and drives as fast as the pod will go until I point through the windshield, tell him to stop.

This building isn't like any of the other Citizen Remembrance Centers. Already empty, Haven had it renovated to her specifications after the war. When it was ready, the Board members were moved away from people's families. Now the only family in there is hers.

She better not have locked me out. I jump from the pod, Jonas close behind, and run to the scanner to swipe my wrist. Something unlocks inside me as the doors slide open. I pause when I'm in the lobby, and then only for a second before I head for the stairs. She wouldn't put him with the others.

Would she? I didn't think she'd do this. I didn't think about it at all.

I pass the door on the first floor, where the Board and Haven's mother float eternally on their viewers, not alive, not dead, crowned by halos of light.

On the second, I reach for the handle. Jonas's breath is hot on my neck, humming like a tune. Haven's inside, waiting, and she almost smiles as I run into the room.

But it's not her I'm looking at.

Ant doesn't smile, but he waves as I near him, translucent body upright and tall, back straight, no trace of the sickness that wasted him in this likeness rendered in binary and glow.

"Hey, Al," he says.

10

Did Ant know all along, and they just didn't tell me in case it didn't work?

No. I saw his eyes at the club. I saw them before that, when he told me he was ready to go. He's never been that good a liar, not to me and not even when he thought he was.

"I knew it would be you. Who came to find us, I mean." Haven stands from a chair behind a table full of computers, lines of code scrolling across the screens.

"What have you *done*?" My eyes refocus on Ant and he flinches a little at my anger. The ribbons of colored light that form his body flicker, like a glitch, and go still again.

"Al," Jonas says, touching my neck. I shake him off, overwhelmed, overloaded. *He's not gone. I never have to let him go, he never has to die for real now. He didn't want this, he was ready to die. It's really him, watching us. It's not him at all.*

"I couldn't do it," Haven says, stepping around him, toward me, her eyes wet. "I couldn't let him leave." I hold up my hands, not sure whether to hate her or hug her. Wanting to be sure before I do either.

"This is like what you told me about—"

"About the Board and President Z," I say, finishing Jonas's sentence, not missing the visceral, disgusted reaction Haven always has when someone mentions her mother. "Only Haven

91

made it better." If *better* is the right word, but my brain's too frozen to think of another one. "She had to take his chip while he was alive. Didn't you?"

"It was the only way to make it work, to keep him thinking for himself. He was still in there, Al. Trapped, but still there."

I hate that I know what she means, that I had the same thought hours ago. "He said good-bye."

"Not to me."

My mouth opens and closes again. Did she really take that as permission to do this without asking him? "Are *you* okay with this?" I ask, as if it's my brother right there. As if his body isn't back in the apartment, flesh and bones cold, blood all over the sheets, and he can answer my questions like he always has. Patient and generous. Protective.

"Alpha," he says. My breath catches. It really sounds *exactly* like him, the voice coming from the speakers at the base of the viewer. Who built that? They've never had speakers before, never needed them. "Alpha," he says again. I meet his eyes. She got them the right shade of blue—the same as mine, but mine burn with tears. "It's done."

That's not an answer. He knows it. Haven knows it, too, and she turns away. I wonder if she and this Anthem can fight. Maybe they already have. I don't know long she—they—have been here, and they've always done their best to keep that from Omega and me. They didn't even fight over the stupid shit in front of us, like who would go to the depot for more food or do laundry.

"This is crazy. *How?* No, you know what? I don't care." I pace in a circle around the viewer, inspecting the hologram. It's fucking perfect and for some reason that only makes the simmering anger in the pit of my stomach burn hotter. "You killed him. He was breathing. Did you feel his heartbeat when you did it?"

"That's enough, Al," Ant says. I bite my tongue against words that surprise even me.

"I saved him," Haven whispers, the words punctuated by tears.

Killed. Saved. Both those things are true. We're going to need bigger Remembrance Centers. As I watch Ant move around his limited little circle, I picture entire farms of glowing ghosts, entire families. Haven will have to teach the rest of us how she did it. Someone's going to find out Haven did this. Follow her—if she ever leaves—and wonder why she's spending all her time here. People know her face, love her face, but have never completely trusted her because of who her parents were. Because maybe the need for power runs in her blood and in the chip implanted in her brain.

The walls shimmer, close in, crushing my chest, my lungs. Haven says something to Jonas that I don't hear over the buzzing in my ears as I stumble to the door, downstairs, outside to gulp the air. On the street, I'm totally alone. Peace. Quiet. My thoughts whir and spin like strobes, refusing to stay in one place. I drop to the curb near the pod, my head on my knees.

Footsteps. "Hey," Jonas says. And that's all he says. Just lets me know he's there.

"Keys."

He drops them into my hand, wordlessly follows me to the pod. I'm fine. I'm not going to explode or break down.

So much of me is still here, in the Web, and all the parts of myself I've reclaimed since coming back are the parts he doesn't know.

Isis and Omega are at the kitchen table, the others apparently still asleep. "Go see for yourself," I tell them. "They're at the CRC where the . . . you know." I explain as best as I can.

"Holy shit. *Awesome.*" In the harsh kitchen light, Omega's skin is blanched, that sour-milk shade that's almost blue. He pushes himself up, seconds later the front door slams.

"Everything except the awesome," I say, too late.

"It worked," Isis says.

My eyes narrow. "Did you know she was going to try?"

She shakes her head. "No, but I'm not surprised. Are you?"

The question stops me. Angry, yes. Confused, definitely. Haven's ten times smarter than any of us, and stubborn, and has always done stuff just to see if she could. There is more to it than that, but no, I'm not surprised.

"You're not happy," Isis says.

Happy. I think I left *happy* under my bed in Los Angeles, tangled with books and socks. "I'm tired. Is his . . . Is he . . ."

"I'm taking care of it." She comes over to give me a hug and I can tell how exhausted she is, arms slack and leaden. Part of Isis must be relieved it's over, one way or another. She's been patching my brother up since the day they met. "Go to sleep."

Ha. But it's dark and quiet in my bedroom, the different rhythm of Jonas's breath harmonizing with mine.

"Want to talk about it?"

Talk. "No."

"Okay," he says, because he knows this isn't the right time to pluck experimentally at my strings.

I feel his surprise as I find him, hip and shoulder, sense his hesitancy. I need to feel real, alive, tangible, all the things Ant isn't anymore, and I know the moment my desperation wins Jonas over. Mouth softening under mine, he smiles my favorite smile, the one that doesn't care about anything except loving me. I try to say the same, but those words are stuck with all the others in the back of my throat, bottlenecked.

I wish Jonas could strip my worries from me as easily as he does my clothes. After, I lay awake, his arm slung over my shoulder, drifting in and out of strange half dreams, lit with neon, alive with sound.

■

Black water churns underneath us, tinged on the surface by golden-pink light. The pod wheels squeal toward the bridge. I'd tried to sleep until I couldn't anymore, left the rest of the apartment in an uneasy hush with Sabine.

"Fable and Jonas are still back there," Sabine says.

"I know."

"Okay."

We lurch over the seam where the bridge rejoins land, the Web behind us, vastness and Los Angeles ahead, buildings and an ocean I can see if I close my eyes.

"Stop. Stop."

Sabine spins the wheel, hits the brakes. Gravel sprays around us, pinging off the windows. It crunches under my feet when I get out and walk right to the edge of the river. The smell whips around me on the wind, that metal-thunderstorm scent I'd recognize anywhere. The sun's almost finished rising over the Web, touching the pointed tips of the skyline. I shiver, the only warmth coming off Sabine's skin a few inches away.

I could leave, right now. She'd keep driving if I asked her to. It's why I picked Sabine. Jonas would have tried to talk me out of leaving angry. Fable would've known how to succeed.

"Start talking."

"I just don't know how she could do that."

"I'm still not totally clear on what she did, exactly," Sabine says, shielding her eyes from the glare off the water, hair tangling around her face.

"Okay." I try to arrange what happened into something that will make sense to someone from L.A. "We all have these memory chips, right? I've told you that." She'd tried to feel for my scar, faded to nothing because the Corp always thought it was a good idea to do it when we were young. I was three.

"Yeah."

"They record all kinds of things, memories and I don't even know what. Ask Haven, she's the expert. Which is the point. When the rebellion happened, Haven figured out that if they killed her mom—the President—and the Board, which her dad was on, it would do something bad. Shut down the Web's whole computer system, or something. They had to keep them alive. Or *close* to alive."

"So she used these chips to turn them into holograms?"

"Right. Not as good as what she's done with Ant, though." I guess Haven's had time to refine her technique.

"So we get you guys and none of this cool shit?" Sabine asks.

"You think this is *cool*?"

"I think you're pissed at having to be back here, for reasons that are your own business. I'm not prying. But you're taking it out on this woman who practically raised you for doing exactly what I would've done in her shoes, if I knew how. What anyone would do."

I kick a pebble, watch it splash. "I'm not. He wanted to die! She took that from him."

"And leaving helps that . . . how? Look, okay, the reason we had to come sucks. It really does, but it actually has been kind of cool seeing this place. Different. Fable's shown me all this stuff that's nothing like what we have back home. Don't look at me like that, I'm not finished. It's been cool, but I'm not blind. Obviously I've seen what happens here, what's still happening here."

"So?" My vision blurs.

"So you spent the entire trip here worrying we wouldn't make it in time, that you wouldn't get to say good-bye. How much worse is it going to be if next time, it's not just the chance to say good-bye, but the chance to say you're sorry."

"That would involve *being* sorry!"

"Okay." She holds up her hands, and I squeeze my eyes shut. She's right, even if I'm still so angry with Haven I can feel my veins boiling. I can leave, or I can stay and try to convince Haven to unplug him.

When I can stand to look at her again.

I'm not sure I've ever seen the Web look so bright, so fresh as it does through the windshield when Sabine turns the pod toward it. It doesn't fit, at all. It should be dull, bleak, the gray of my memories. Too soon, it catches us in its sticky streets, swallowing us whole.

"Let me out here," I say as soon as the park is in sight.

"You sure?"

"I'll be back soon." I take only my guitar from the backseat, put there an hour ago with a lot more care than the rest of my stuff.

Ant always loved the park. Actually, I think he always loved the park with Haven in it, but he used to bring Omega and me here, too, on nice days. When we got too old to think of it as a treat, he still used to come up with excuses for us all to hang out under the trees.

This is where he taught me to play. Right here. I pull out my tablet first, sending a message to Mage and Phoenix, though I'm sure Isis already has, and probably Pixel, too. It's still early there;

I envy them their last few hours of ignorance before they wake up and learn about everything that's happened since midnight.

It feels like days.

The stretch of grass where Ant first played for us, the day the war ended, is summer-scorched, crackling a little under my boots and my guitar case. People pass by, steps slowing a little, speeding up again as they pass the corner and disappear from earshot.

I miss my stage. Ant would get it, which is why I don't go talk to him now. That and Haven's probably there, but it's mostly because I know he'd tell me I don't need to stay and I do. Haven will see unplugging him as murder. I see it as mercy. My stomach knots at this silent war between me and someone I love so much.

"Thought I'd find you here."

Omega blocks out the sun. "Hey," I say. "Can you sense my presence now or something?"

"No." He laughs. "But you're not my twin for nothing."

"Then you can guess I don't want to talk."

"Good, me neither."

I pluck idly at the strings again. Omega lies back on the grass, listening. Honestly, I want to be pissed at him, too, but I only have so much energy.

"Al." Omega nudges my shin with the toe of his boot and nods at my bag. "Tablet."

"Probably Jonas." I set my guitar on the grass. Guilt floods my stomach. I asked him to come and I've barely spent any time with him since we got here, but it's not like I could spend the whole time showing him the place. Omega's done that for me, Omega who got all that time with Ant that I didn't.

Forget that it was my own choice, that I had reasons. Have reasons. I guess now that I don't need to grieve, things can go back to whatever passes for normal.

Somehow, my tablet always winds up underneath everything else. I finish digging it out and tap the screen.

The world shrinks.

"Al?"

I think Omega is touching my shoulder. It's hard to tell. "Are you okay? Having another one?"

"N-No." No. I'm not in the white room. I'm not there. I'm here.

One breath. Two. The leaves pull back into a thousand things, separate but joined.

Omega and I have talked about this a lot. His flashbacks don't sound like mine. We might be twins, but I guess our brains aren't wired exactly the same, even if it's just that maybe he uses different words to describe the same thing. I shove my tablet away before he can read the message.

It's almost time, Alpha. I can give you everything you want._

"I have to go. Can you go make sure Jonas is okay?" I've been such an idiot since last night, not seeing the bigger picture of what Haven did.

"Yeah, sure." He stands with me. "What is it?"

"I need to go see Ant. Don't, no, I'm not going to fight with her. I need to talk to him." I can tell Omega knows already, but I don't want to give him hope until I'm sure. The flashbacks don't bother him as much as they do me, which is why I'm the one looking for a cure, but I'm doing this as much for him as for myself. I run out of the park, head north, shedding exhaustion with every step.

■

Haven's asleep in a chair, Ant hovers on the viewer in front of her, his eyes open. I guess he doesn't need to sleep anymore, ever. A shiver tingles over my skin; it's not normal that he can see me, wave at me like that. I touch Haven's shoulder, gently, the way we were taught to so we don't scare her.

"Al," she says, hoarse, blinking at the morning though there's no sunlight here, nothing to disturb the glowing lines of Ant's silhouette. I hand her a bottle of water from my bag, check the scarf around my neck. I don't want her questions.

I don't want her sympathy.

"Tell me how it works, again," I say, breath still uneven. "What can he . . . see?" *See* maybe isn't the right word, but it's as close as I can get.

"It helps if you think of him"—she gives Ant's hologram an apologetic look—"a little like a virus. He can get everywhere, but some places might take longer than others. Or like you're in a huge building. You find the big rooms before the closets. Locked files and stuff. Why?"

"I need to talk to him. Alone."

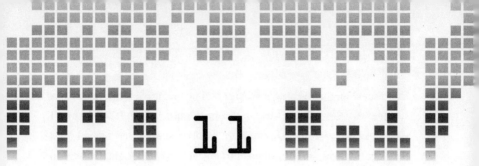

11

"She hates that you're mad at her," Anthem says. "She loves you, Al."

"You're *not* mad?"

I swear he sighs. "I don't know. Kind of, yeah. Some of that's not for the reason she thinks. Or you think."

"Then why?" I take her chair and watch him. He fidgets just like he did in life, running fingers through his hair, tapping soundless rhythms against his thigh. The neon lines blur whenever they meet each other, ripples on water disturbed by a pebble.

"Because I'm useless," he says. "I can't touch her. I can't hug you and tell you to go back to Los Angeles, where I know you want to be. I'm not *living* with the rest of you, so there's no point seeing it. And sure, she's here all the time now, but that won't last forever. So I just chill here, alone, until someone feels like coming to say hi?"

I swallow, afraid of what his answer to my next question will be. "Do you want me to unplug you?" Would it be that simple?

It hits me again, how perfectly blue his eyes are. It must have taken her years, and I almost have to admire the skill at keeping something like that for so long from him, from all of us. For several seconds he stares at me with those intense eyes and finally shakes his head.

"This is what it is. I'm okay, little sister."

"What does it feel like?"

"Floating. Everything's so much clearer than it's been for . . . a while. I can see everything, the whole mainframe. It's . . . I can't describe it. So much information, but I can think just as fast."

It's as good an opening as I'm going to get. I inhale. "I need to tell you something."

I last told this story to Fable, four years ago. It was either that or let him call for a med-pod when a flashback hit on our way home from school. I remember my knees stinging from the scrapes where they hit the sidewalk when I collapsed.

Ant knows the beginning—that Ell came and got me and Omega, promised to take us to Anthem. We knew enough to be aware that Ant worked for her, but too little to realize she couldn't be trusted.

Describing the music I heard that day is easy in theory, if not in reality. I stumble over the words, painting the picture I see in my head too often. The energy in the room shifts when I move on to everything that's happened since that day, shock and sadness radiating off Anthem like static. We didn't want him to know, I explain, as if it is an explanation. Didn't want him to know he hadn't saved us, protected us the way he thought he had.

He started a rebellion for us. The least we could do was let him think he'd won, what with everything else he'd lost.

That was mostly the reason, anyway. The other one sounds ridiculous and juvenile to my ears as I say it: that Omega and I liked having a secret which was only ours. We were good at keeping it.

I still am.

I wipe the tears from my cheeks.

"That's why I left." Why is this so difficult? "I'm trying to find a cure for me and Omega, and I just couldn't do it here. I couldn't stay here."

"How do we know it's only the two of you?" he asks, and it's the *we* that hurts, because he's standing there on a fucking viewer and I can tell from his flickering expression just what learning this is doing to him, and he's thinking of me and Omega. Just like always.

"I had Lynx and Spectrum ask around," I say. "Didn't tell them everything, but enough that they could find out for me. I had to leave, Ant. I feel it when I'm here." Fresh tears sting my eyes. "I want to track. It got so bad before I went."

"Is it bad now?"

It's a whisper. I can't summon any more volume. I nod.

"What you're learning out there, do you think it's going to help?" The hope and pain in his voice are equally evident. I think about my classes, pictures of brains lit from behind.

"I think so?" I say. He can probably hear the hope in my voice, too. "If I track now, whatever damage it does . . . might make it impossible to fix myself. When I do it, I have to know it's going to work. A track I make. I need to go back to the beginning, the first days of the Web, figure out how they did it. Start from scratch."

"Alpha." He doesn't say anything else for a stretched minute. "I wish you'd told me, but that doesn't matter. Fuck knows I hid enough from you for the same reason."

To shield us. Yeah. He can't exactly be mad about that.

"I need you now," I whisper. "I've done some digging around since I got here, but it kind of got interrupted."

"Anything, Al," he says. I wish I knew how my brother became the person he is, always has been. "It'll go faster if we tell Haven."

I look away. Nod.

"Will you try to forgive her? I have," Ant says.

It's selfish that my anger has faded a little because I can use him. I'll just have to live with that if it means not living with the flashbacks anymore. "I'm trying."

He smiles a little. Ripple, ripple. "Have you heard from Phoenix and Mage?"

"Not since I told them about . . . this. You."

"You didn't have to stay."

"Yeah, I did."

Haven knocks on the door, more of a warning since she wouldn't be able to hear my answer. Nervousness tightens her steps but her back is straight, her own body undecided about what she did.

"I have to go meet Jonas," I say. Hurt flashes in her eyes, but I just don't want to see her face when she learns what I've hidden from her. All our long talks, the closeness. I face Ant again. "The first one, that's what I need. My first one." Haven steps around, trying to read my lips, but she's too late. Her fingers curl in frustration.

"Okay," he says.

Only when I'm outside do I let myself consider the possibility that he'll actually find it. Reach into the secret depths of the system, pluck out what I need like an apple from a tree in one of the Hydro-Farms. I can't remember when I last slept, or when I last felt less like I needed to.

It's dark. The Web is alive with lights and so am I.

"Let's go out," I say when I run into the apartment. Jonas, Fable, and Sabine look up. "Come on, let's go have some fun."

"What's gotten into you?" Fable asks. They're all eyeing me warily and I don't care.

"Nothing. Everything's fine. Come on, get ready."

"Okay." Jonas's smile is real. "Where?"

"Anywhere."

I change into a skirt, pull on my boots, line my eyes with black. Jonas mock-twirls for me and I shake my head at him. He looks good, he always does. Fable and Sabine join us and I start to laugh.

"You do that on purpose?" I ask, pointing at their outfits, matching leather and fishnet.

Sabine crosses her arms and tries not to smile. "No."

The nearest console station is a few minutes away, down toward the swirling Vortex. Plate glass windows reflect a thousand points of light onto the street. I slow my steps, enough to see that every console inside is being used. A bored, underpaid receptionist, there to call med-techs or break up fights if anyone has a bad reaction, sits with her feet up on another chair, a book on her lap. Past her, bright hair stands out, bruise-livid, against dull skin. Headphones are clamped tight over a few dozen pairs of ears, each blasting the addict's particular sound of choice. It's Saturday night. If they're going to be busy anytime, it's now.

For once, I don't feel the pull.

We pass the station, skirt the edge of ever-daylight surrounding the black glass spider past a club that does things the old way. No chance I'm going inside, but I'm relieved it doesn't seem too busy. No lines, no gathered clusters of people dressed in black and neon waiting for one last friend to join them before they go in.

"There," I say to Jonas, pointing a block away, where the top floor of a skyscraper is alive above rows of darkened windows. He grins, and the four of us almost run the rest of the way. I haven't been in a Sky-Club in over a year, but the plastic-clad doorman recognizes me instantly. The velvet rope hisses aside with a whisper I can hear because there's never been a point in de-soundproofing these places, even if they don't need the protection anymore. Jonas scans the windows that offer a perfect view of the Web, lit like a circuit board, the spinning dance floor, the speakers lining the ceiling and walls.

No drugs, just music pulsing so loud I can feel it in my teeth.

Sound-responsive implants flash, set into bare, hot skin. Bands of chrome around arms and necks catch the strobes. No drugs, but there's an energy here that doesn't exist anywhere else, built by rhythm and movement and sheer abandon, by noise encompassing enough to erase my thoughts for as long as I want to stay. Sabine heads for the bar, Fable for a group of girls near it. Laughing, I pull Jonas by the hand into the middle of the crowd, let the music—just music—take over.

■

Warm sunlight pierces the windows. Jonas's skin is soft against mine, his breath even with sleep.

We got in late. I'm kind of amazed I'm already awake. My tablet on the bedside table holds no messages from Haven, or my admirer, but there are a bunch from Phoenix. I climb from the bed and slip out into the living room so I can read them without waking Jonas.

The first must've come in while we were out last night, a reply to the last one I sent her.

```
We're fine, pretty much. Is everything
okay there?_
```

Better than they were, much better. But I hold off on answering until I've read the rest.

```
Seriously, how are things?_
Something weird's happening here._
```

I walk into the kitchen, get some water, eyes glued to the screen.

```
Like, I wouldn't even think it was possible,
but I know the signs, Al. Tracks. Lots of
```

106

them. Police came to ask us about it
because they're asking everyone from the
Web._

I can only imagine Phoenix's reaction to that, police coming into her club.

Los Angeles has done a good job of keeping tracks out, making it clear that anyone who wanted to try them could come here to do it. Some have, because people are curious. Mostly it's been easy to keep L.A clean—everyone who went there was trying to escape, and everyone who didn't quit wouldn't leave the source of their fix.

There's no one out there to fix a portable console if it breaks, but I guess someone decided it was worth the risk. Easy to pack full of drugs, small enough to hide.

Things are fine here._ I type back. As fine as they can be, but she'll know what I mean. That nothing's changed since I walked into that CRC. It's four in the morning there, but I get an answer after my next sip.

Good. Keep me posted?_
Yeah. You too?_
Of course._

I dress, every movement seeming too loud because I want to be quiet. Down on the street and in the park, the Web is as slow to wake as everyone else in the apartment.

But it's not completely quiet.

Distantly, someone shouts, breaking through the morning. I don't find her right away, have to scan through the trees and along the winding paths. A girl hardly any older than me, if at all, with her mouth open in a ceaseless scream. She runs, kicks over a recycling container, a hundred water bottles spilling out onto the grass.

Doesn't take a genius to know what's wrong. This happens. Rarely. Still too often.

I drop my bag and step closer, slowly. "Are you okay?" I ask. She's not, obviously, but it's somewhere to start, or would be if she could hear me.

Her eyes are wild, skin sallow.

"Hey!" I yell. The few people around are putting as much distance between themselves and her—us, now—as they can. "Calm down, please?" I'm almost close enough to reach her now, though what I'll do when I get there, I'm still not sure. I only know someone has to help her.

A glimmer of lucidity flashes and snaps in her eyes. Then it is gone. Along with everyone else—cowards, running away from the reminder. It's just her and me, green hair the same shade as her eyes stuck to spit-slick lips stretched over bared teeth.

"Hey—"

I can breathe, and then I can't.

Strong fingers wrap around my throat. Gasping, I throw out my arms, try to push her away, and I don't think she even feels it, she's that far gone. Her grip tightens, and an inky blackness draws around the edges of my vision. Pain sears down my neck; my eardrums feel like they're about to burst. My hand finds her hair and pulls, turning up the volume on her screams.

The ground knocks the wind from both of us, loosens her hold on me enough to steal a breath that pushes the darkness away a fraction. Anger makes her alien, inhuman.

There's a person in there. Buried, not knowing what she's doing, probably not where she is, but there.

"Stop," I beg, my head knocking against a rock as I struggle to keep away from her biting mouth. "Going to help you."

Nothing. Blood drips hotly over my throat, pointed finger-nails digging deeper. It's my turn to scream, twist her hair around my fist, tug as hard as I can. I'm not dying for this girl.

She rolls away, helped by my other hand on her shoulder, and I don't let go, don't give her a chance to move any more before I push her onto her stomach, scramble onto her back, her screams muffled by the grass. Leather creaks under the knee I have right between her shoulder blades.

My stuff is out of reach, tablet buried in the bottom of my bag. Shit. There's no way I'm getting up to grab it. Every turn of my head up and down the path feels like her fingers squeezing again, but I think the bleeding's almost stopped, at least.

Finally. I wave at the man rounding the corner on the path. "Excuse me?" I have to say it again so it makes a sound. The girl thrashes under me and I press down a little harder. "Can you tab for a med-pod?"

He looks between me and the girl, lips twisted, suspicious, like I've just beaten up this chick for stealing my boyfriend or some other pointless crap, and now I'm regretting it.

"Please."

He nods, stands there and does it in front of me before walking away. I spend a few minutes hoping he actually sent it and fighting to keep her under control. I don't think I've ever been so relieved to hear sirens.

The techs approach, carefully pin down her arms before telling me to move. They don't need to say it twice.

"Know her?" one of them asks when they have her strapped to a stretcher and I'm still folded on the earth, adrenaline humming now that it's safe.

"No. No."

The other kneels in front of me, reaches for my neck. I flinch. "It's nothing."

"Sure?"

"Positive. Just go take care of her."

I know how they will. Special tracks are still the best way of curing bad reactions to normal ones. I've done a lot of research into that. I wonder what she was thinking, feeling in those seconds before I went up to her. What she was seeing in her head. Whether she was seeing anything, or if it was just a swirling, burning pit of rage.

Or a white room. A blank slate marred only by Omega and that woman and me. My neck throbs; my pulse burns in the tiny cuts.

This girl. The guy that first night, when Omega and I took Jonas and Sabine to show them the Web. Med-pod sirens.

I want to tell myself I'm just noticing it more because it's so different here from Los Angeles, that the contrast makes everything lurid, overexposed.

But if Phoenix is right, the differences between here and my home on the beach aren't what they were.

Aimless, sore, I head back to the apartment.

"It's nothing," I say before Jonas can freak about the marks on my neck. "Wrong place, wrong time. Everyone else still asleep?"

Gentle fingertips trace the bruises, the spots of dried blood. "Yeah."

"This fucking place does bad things to people. Like, there's sunlight again, and stuff will grow, but it doesn't matter because the ground's still poisoned." It does bad things to *me*.

"I like it. Not why we had to come," he adds, seeing my face, "but the place. It's different."

Different. There's a word. "You don't know the half of it."

"I want to." His eyes fix on a nothing-point in midair. "I want to try it, Al," he says. And it's so out of nowhere that I can't figure what he means at first, and when I think I can, I pretend I still don't understand.

"What?"

"Tracking."

I stand too quickly. This room is a mess. Too many of us were holed up in here for too long, caring about other things. I carry glasses into the kitchen and toss boots into a pile by the door, metal spikes catching on the tender spots between my fingers.

"Why?" I ask, carefully focusing on wiping a smudge from the coffee table with my sleeve.

"To see what the big deal is? To understand? I don't know, it sounds like an experience."

Oh, it's that, for sure.

"I can't stop you," I say, hoping the coldness in my voice covers the searing panic in my chest. "Go right ahead. There are console stations. There are clubs that still do it. Not hard to find. Go to the Vortex and ask around."

"Weren't you ever curious? I mean, Omega's been telling me how Anthem used to leave you two so he could go out every night because he just couldn't stop himself. Didn't you ever wonder what it was like, when you were old enough? What would last night have been like? Or our club back home, if it had—"

"Curious?" I spit, scrubbing harder at the table. "Every fucking day." It's not a lie, not really. I've always wondered what it was like to do it somewhere fun, not the white room with its brightness and pain. "And that's *why* I never . . . went to the clubs or anything. I've seen what happens."

"Al." He slips from the sofa to the floor, kneeling beside me. "Obviously it's bad if you do it all the time." He blinks and I know he's thinking of Ant. "But how much could once hurt? Seriously?"

I open my mouth. It's right there, right on the tip of my tongue, exactly how much just once could hurt. That's why I don't tell him—because I am tempted, and I can picture it so clearly, the two of us dancing, lost, flying, and if I tell him, he'll drop the idea.

I look straight at him, his outline blurred by tears I'm trying to hold back but it's like I'm seeing him for the first time in weeks. "This place does bad things to people," I say again, standing, backing toward the hall, my hand going to the purple bruises. "I never should've let you come."

I should have protected him. But here, I can't even protect myself, and I have to stay. "You want tracks? L.A. has them now. Go home," I say.

12

I barely hear the door slam. Tears gather, blur the room. The familiar pounding starts at the base of my skull.

Oh, for fuck's sake, not now. But I'm powerless against it this time, have no choice but to let it pull me under, into the glare, suffocating as the music blasts in my head. When I come to again, I kick off puke-covered shoes and drag myself to the shower, wondering how I made such a fucking mess of everything.

Wondering what *everything* even is. There are too many threads, too many notes in this melody, my life a discordant mess of sound. My cure. Jonas. Ant on his viewer, digging back eight years to find me the tiniest scrap of information. Tracks in Los Angeles and more people tracking here. Taunting messages on my tablet.

I told Jonas to go home because part of me wishes I could. A bigger part wants to stay—a feeling I've never had about the Web before. For once, the tiniest pinprick of light gleams in the darkness. I touch the bruises on my throat.

Beads of rainbow-tinted water drip down my neck and onto the back of the couch. A door opens down the hall and I jump; I'd forgotten anyone was still here. I'd forgotten Fable was supposed to be sleeping where I'm sitting, not coming out of Sabine's bedroom with her. I raise an eyebrow and get two sheepish grins in response.

"Finally," I say, but it hurts. Hurts because Jonas isn't here and

I have no idea where he is. Hurts because I haven't smiled in hours.

"We heard shouting," Sabine says.

"Jonas and I had a fight."

Fable steps to the edge of the couch and tilts my chin, grin turning to angry grimace. "Did he do this? That mother—"

"What? No, of course not. Come on. I had an . . . incident . . . in the park earlier. It's nothing."

Sabine moves to get a closer look. "Sweet fuck, Al. Doesn't look like nothing."

"It is," I insist. Thinking about it makes my neck throb. "You guys have spent a lot of time out"—I wave in the direction of the windows—"there. Have you noticed more addicts than usual?"

Of course, Sabine wouldn't know what *usual* is here, but Fable does. "I've been waiting to talk to you about this, among other things," he says. "First, yeah. Definitely noticed more addicts."

I hand my tablet from the table to him, Phoenix's tab about Los Angeles open on the screen. His expression barely changes, just the slightest widening of his eyes before he hands it to Sabine.

"I was thinking maybe we should try talking to Lock again," I say. "See if he has any idea what's going on."

Fable shifts. "That's the second thing. When we were there, after he wouldn't talk to us?"

A chill passes over my still damp skin. The day Ant nearly died. *One* of the days Ant nearly died. "Yeah?"

"Well." He clears his throat. "I'm pretty sure Lock was tracking that day. That's what I was looking at on the system. Pax was acting too weird."

What.

No.

I stare at Fable. Stand. Look for my boots and remember I

can't wear them. "And you were going to tell me this when exactly?" I can't believe he didn't. Not like it's relevant information or anything. Of course not.

"There was kind of some other important stuff happening, Al. And so what? We knew he was a creep. Now we know he's a *lying* creep, with all of his *drugs are bad* bullshit, but he's not busy getting people hooked again or sending tracks out west. One, he's not that smart. Two, he's going to a lot of effort to hide what he's doing, and not running around telling everyone to start hitting the console stations. That shit wasn't easy to find. I didn't mention it because who cares? So he's an addict. Lots of people still are. What could you do about it? Nothing. It's none of our business."

"You want this place run by someone who thinks tracks are good?" I ask. "You think that's a good road to go down?"

"I think I don't give enough of a damn about Lock to worry about what he gets up to in his spare time."

"I still can't believe you waited this long to tell me."

"So, what? Secrets are only fine when they're yours?" he mutters. Sabine's head turns back and forth between us, like she's watching two of her students play catch.

"I—"

Fuck.

I disappear into my room, come back wearing an old pair of boots I didn't take with me when I moved. Sabine's taken my spot on the couch; Fable's arm is around her. Envy flares. "I have to go," I tell them, because obviously they didn't guess.

Los Angeles was an oasis, a bubble in which I could hide, but the bubble's popped. Everything's mixed, tainted. If someone had asked me in L.A. which I'd choose, Jonas or my cure, I would've picked the cure every time.

Nobody's asking. But maybe I don't have to make the choice.

■

We approach each other like frightened animals, slow and careful under the trees. This isn't my park, just a tiny square of grass down in Two, near where Omega said they were when I tabbed him. My bag is heavy with water bottles I swiped from Lynx and Spectrum on the way, promising—again—to come back and see them for longer next time. And to bring Jonas. Jonas doesn't touch me, and I don't touch him. I need to earn that back.

Maybe I knew, somewhere out beyond where the white room lives in my brain, that if we came here I'd have to tell him, and that's why I fought him coming with me at all.

And that's why I gave in.

Easy isn't the word, but *easier* might be. Easier here than under the baking sun, or next to a phosphorescent ocean. Maybe easier because for once the whole story is in my immediate memory, still stored there from telling Ant yesterday. My secrets probably seem bigger to me than they should, but they're *mine*, and I've kept them, cultivated them for so long that they've grown, flourished in places that get no sunlight.

I just let the whole thing come out, talking until I can't anymore, gulping some water, talking some more. I sense Jonas going from shock to sadness to anger and back again but can't bear to look at his face.

"So that's it," I say. "That's what I'm studying for, why I can't ever track, why I sometimes seem to space out."

"Fable knows, doesn't he?"

I almost laugh. "That's what you focus on?"

"It's the easiest thing," he says, and I see his point. All the rest of it is too unwieldy, too unbelievable. "I was always worried you

116

two were, you know. Going off together all the time."

"He knows, I had to tell him years ago. But trust me, you don't need to worry about that, especially not after last night. Sabine," I clarify at his raised eyebrow.

The momentary lightness dissolves. A few drops of rain start to fall. He plucks a blade of grass and twirls it between his fingers. "Did you really think it would change how I feel about you?"

My heart pangs. "I'm crazy. You said so yourself."

He reaches out, one of his strong hands tucking a fuchsia strand of hair behind my ear. "I'm sorry," he whispers in the space between our lips, which slowly shrinks to nothing. It's been hours but it feels like days, and I kiss him back as if it really was that long. The heaviness that began to leave my muscles in the CRC yesterday evaporates completely through my skin. I'd never realized how much of it was there, how much it weighed me down.

"What does it feel like?" Jonas asks, tender but with an edge. I'm not sure if it's anger on my behalf or a test to see if I'll tell him.

I focus on my hands. "Like I'm back there, in that room. I'm little and I'm excited to be there. I think it's so cool. I think I'm going to see Ant. Everything's white, and this woman puts head-phones on my ears, on Omega's ears. It's the most amazing thing I've ever heard. I'm *happy*. I don't know how much it's going to hurt later. The headaches and cravings are so bad it feels like my bones are breaking. I'm *happy and I don't fight*. And now I don't know which parts of me are *me* and which parts are whatever they put in my head."

His thumbs catch my tears. "You're Al, my Al. And you're more of a fighter than anyone I know."

"Am I?" My voice shakes.

"Yes."

"There's more. I'm pretty sure this"—I point at my head—"is just Omega and me, but we're not the only ones who have been badly affected, have weird reactions. I'm thinking, I don't know. If I can come up with a cure for that, maybe it's just the first step to curing everyone. Heal addictions completely, repair people, let them lead long lives, like the people I see sometimes walking on the beach, stooped and gray-haired, sun soaking into their wrinkles."

"So now we need to find you a cure."

"We?" My voice shakes.

He meets my eyes. "We. Has Anthem found anything yet?"

"Not yet. I was hoping to hear from him—or Haven, I guess—today, but not so far." I'm kind of glad about that, actually. I didn't have to decide whether to run to the CRC or run here to Jonas.

He cups my face and smiles. "Want to go ask Ant and Haven about that?"

"No. Haven's eating there, sleeping there. I'm sure they're doing everything they can." And I don't want to hear them tell me not to get my hopes up. I want to hold on to this weightless feeling from having told Jonas as much as I can. His smile fades slightly as I tell him about Phoenix's tabs, what Fable said about Lock, my creeping fear that the Web's returning to its former self.

In some ways, this is almost worse. At least under the Corp, people were ordered to track; they had no choice. Now they've had eight years of freedom, clear heads, control over their own lives, and yet they're choosing to track. I wish I could shake every one of them, tell them what those years have been like for me. I've never had that freedom, never had that clear head, not completely. I'm searching for my cure because I'd give anything to have it and they're throwing it away like it means nothing.

Rain begins to fall a little harder. I get up, hold out my hand with one final spark of fear that Jonas won't take it, exhaling when he does. "I really am sorry," I tell him, looking at his boots.

"When I first saw you, you were like . . ." He shakes his head, tugs gently on my hair. "A rainbow. I always knew you came with a storm."

I don't know what to say to that, so I just kiss him again, our clothes soaking through as we stand there. Strange, how history repeats itself. A chorus of secrets and conversations, lies and truths. Haven told me long ago about almost everything that happened between her and Ant, the things they hid from each other. Maybe in some ways I am my brother's sister. Jonas and I run to the nearest trans-pod stop, my feet light, quicker than his.

Maybe I learned faster than Anthem did.

■

Fable and Sabine stand in the living room, bags packed, the first light brightening the windows.

"Sure you're not coming with us?" Sabine teases Jonas, picking up her stuff. He grins, shrugs.

"Think I'll stick around."

I wonder if he would've said that yesterday, but we're good now.

"Be careful, okay? Don't drive like maniacs," I say because it's something *to* say. We all know there's no chance of it happening.

"We'll help Phoenix and Mage, find out what's going on out there," Fable says, kissing my cheek. "We'll let you know."

"Check in on the way."

"Will do."

I hug Sabine, step back to stand against Jonas, watch them leave. Their choreography has changed, slight shifts in every movement to harmonize with the other. And I'm not envious now.

"You'll be fine here for a bit?" I ask Jonas. "Omega'll be back soon, he was just taking Haven breakfast." A flutter of nerves had rippled through me when Omega left, but it passed. If Haven and Ant tell him what they're doing, they tell him. He'll be as hopeful as I am, or not.

Jonas knows I'm not keeping secrets from him now by leaving, at least not my own. He kisses me. "Don't worry so much. Say hi to them for me."

Pixel and Isis live over in Quadrant Three, a small, nice apartment that holds no memories for either of them except the ones they've made together. As Isis and I sit in their living room, burning our tongues on mugs of peppermint tea, Isis waits. She can tell I haven't just dropped by for tea.

Now that I've told the story once, twice, it is almost easy, but telling her is about more than unburdening my soul. If anything, she's the person I should've told years ago, before Fable or Ant or Jonas. A Corp-trained med-tech who has spent all her time since the rebellion gathering every scrap of medical knowledge she could.

I wanted to do this myself. Find my cure. I should be at home in Los Angeles, relaxing after all the exams that would let me back into school in September, but that's not the way things are.

"Will you help?" My mug is empty, the metal still clinging to remembered warmth, my hands clinging to the metal.

"You've only ever had to ask."

I blink. She looks at me, deep brown eyes liquid, wise. "I always felt like there was something. Just a hunch, I guess. That and I have a lot of experience seeing the kind of damage the Corp did. But I saw both you and Omega . . . right after. Took care of you, and it wasn't really like anything I'd seen before, your reactions, the way you came out of it. Could've been because you were so young, I told myself that. Figured you would tell me when you were ready. Are Omega's flashbacks the same as yours?" she adds.

"We don't think so. Similar, but not exactly the same." I shrug. "But who knows? We don't describe most things the same way."

"Makes sense. Okay. Can both of you come to the hospital tomorrow? I want to run some tests." My apprehension must show on my face. "Completely safe, promise."

"Okay."

I hang around a little while longer, only because I've always liked it here. Always loved Isis, and Pixel, too, though he doesn't come out of the bedroom while I'm there. I think about what happened, losing his brother, how I'd feel if I lost one of mine that way. The last shards of my iciness toward Haven melt and slip through my veins, away from my heart.

It's a long walk back over to One, but the weather's nice and the wind off the river is almost, *almost* the same as the one that blows in my bedroom window from the beach. Head clearer than it's been in days, I let myself into the apartment, feel the intangible stillness of solitude. Music drifts from the radio in the kitchen and I hum along as I clean, scrubbing away the dusty remains of bigger problems.

We still have problems. I don't know what the hell is going on in Los Angeles, but Phoenix hasn't told me anything else, which means there *is* nothing else yet. Sabine and Fable will be there as soon as they can. Tomorrow before I visit Isis at the hospital, I'm going to ask Lynx and Spectrum if they know how someone would get large numbers of tracks into Los Angeles without detection. They can be transmitted, sure, but no one's dumb enough to try that.

One song fades into the next, something I know this time. I hum along, let the melody turn my limbs loose and liquid as I move around, cooking dinner. The unmistakable sensation of being watched tickles the back of my neck. I turn, smile at Jonas leaning against the archway.

Behind him, the door closes and Omega calls out a *hi*. Jonas and Omega apparently went shopping. I'm torn between laughter and dragging Jonas to my bedroom when Omega holds up a black shirt held together with red lacing.

"Might as well fit in." Jonas shrugs, tries to pretend it doesn't matter.

"I like it." I kiss him, properly, wishing I could just fall against him and ignore the burning smell coming from the stove. I don't give a damn if my brother's right there on the couch taking off his boots.

The song changes again. I don't know this one, but it's immediately catchy, a guitar hook tugging on my brain. Boiling water froths and blurs my vision.

The hook tugs harder.

Pulling.

Pulling.

White tiles and stainless steel shimmer. I'm in another room and *the music is playing*.

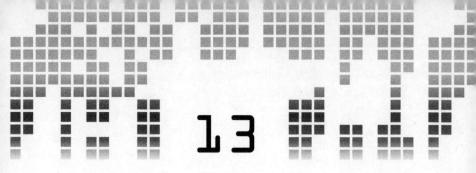

13

Cold, it's cold against my back, smooth as glass and I gasp at how cold it is. Air fills my lungs and that's so much better. The claws dig into my skin, white teeth bare in a smile-grimace. Now I'm too hot because I'm floating above the cold place, or maybe I've fallen right through it. Everything is weightless. Weightless and not right.

Wrong. So wrong. I have hands somewhere, and feet, legs, a whole body. Not just my mind, white at the edges and brilliant prisms of color in the middle of my brain, sparking and twisting with each note. High notes are blue, I think, and low are more like fire. The warm guitar is sweet on my tongue, like chocolate.

No. This is wrong. I try to feel my toes first, remember where they are, and then, slowly, the rest of me. My hands in fists that beat the claws away until I break free . . .

I gasp, choke, stumble across the room to the tiny black box.

"Al—?" Jonas's voice sounds faraway, faint. My fingers wrap around the radio, I imagine the drug seeping in through my skin.

Jaw clenched, I stare at Jonas, at his dilated pupils in the bright, sunny kitchen. The smash is loud, plastic and wires smashing, skittering across the floor. Omega runs in, looks from me to Jonas and back again.

"The radio," I say. My jaw hurts. My ears hurt. My whole head hurts. "It's coming in through the radio."

14

Haven's never been dumb. She can see it on our faces, read it in the way we burst into the room. "What is it? What's wrong? We haven't found—"

"No, not the cure." I pant. We hadn't been able to park the pod anywhere nearby. I ran the last five blocks, the guys right behind me. "Something else. Damn it! Something else!" I shout, facing her fully.

As I tell her, her skin drains as if there's a hole in her foot and the beautiful color is about to pool on the floor. I try to will the last remnants of the track and the way it skews every perception from my brain.

"No." She shakes her head. "No, Al."

"I was there," Omega says, stepping in before Haven can ask me if I'm sure. "So was Jonas, and it affected him, too." Omega's eyes are too wide, tiny tremors make Jonas shake beside me.

Well, he'd wanted to try it. He got his chance.

"Maybe it was a mistake?"

"Like, someone got the tracks confused with regular music?" It's Omega's turn to shake his head. "Tell her the rest, Al."

I pass Haven my tablet, the messages from Phoenix open. Watch her scroll through them twice.

"Something's happening. I can feel it," I say. Haven jacks my tablet into her system and a shower of text begins to fall around

Ant. His translucent hands curl into fists.

"We always knew people were going to keep tracking," Haven says. "We knew it when we decided not to destroy them all. But getting people hooked out there? And if people here don't know what they're listening to until it's too late?"

I think Ant would kick something if he could.

"The track on the radio didn't come from nowhere. Neither did whatever's happening in L.A. There has to be something, somewhere."

"Okay," Ant says. "Why? No matter what this is, why here, why there? Why now?"

"Someone thinks it's funny?" I shrug. Bitterness is sour on my tongue, and I don't really think that's the answer, but I don't have another one. A tiny part of my brain tries to tell me that this isn't my problem, my fight, and it definitely isn't anyone else's in this room.

Except it is. Los Angeles is mine; they're not taking that from me.

A bigger part of my brain knows what I'm asking—for them to stop looking for what Ell made me listen to.

The biggest part kicks and screams against the idea that it might not matter anymore. However briefly, I've tracked again.

"We can try," Haven says. Her eyes meet mine and I know what she's thinking—I was so pissed about what she did, and now I'm letting it go because I need him, I need both of them. And I know she's not mad about it.

"I'm sorry," I say, barely whispering, but she's reading my lips anyway. "I know I . . . I should have told you before, but forget that now. Do this?"

"I'll do it."

"Ant." I'm not exactly sure what to say. He wanted to die and I was the only one who agreed with him. It was bad enough that I got over it when I thought he could help just me. Me and Omega, anyway. He thought his time here, fighting, was over, and it should've been. "Maybe it's nothing."

"Never nothing in the Web, little sister," he says, smiling wryly. "Learned that a long time ago."

"Do you remember what song it was?" Haven asks.

"I didn't know it."

"Any of you?" Everyone shakes their head in unison.

"Okay. Look for equipment purchases." Keys click and a bank of computers comes to life. Lights blink, beeps of a dozen different pitches form a discordant melody. It takes a minute for my eyes to adjust, to make out even a few digits in the lines of code raining around Ant, but he's reading them before they burst against the floor.

"Wow," Jonas says. I nod. Haven's rapid typing blurs to white noise; Omega leans over her shoulder. Ant lets her know when to change files, or storage sectors, or other terms I don't really get. In death—if it can really be called that—he is as careful as ever to face her when he talks.

I don't want to leave, but it'd be miraculous if he found anything right away. Jonas and I go in search of food for all of us, bring it back, and eat cross-legged on the hard CRC floor, helpless, unwilling to pretend there's somewhere else we should be.

After hours of no answers, I stand and stretch, my feet hot and restless inside my boots. Omega's sitting against a wall, cracking his knuckles, trying not to fall asleep. Fingers brush the back of my leg; I touch Jonas's head in answer. I'm fine. His hair is softly spiked, silk and needles against my palm.

"Can one of you go out and buy a radio?" There's a gentleness in Haven's eyes aimed at Jonas and me, but her voice is all business. I hesitate.

"You don't need to listen," she says. "None of you do."

Right. She can't hear it, and Ant can't feel it.

It's late, but it's still summer, with the warmth and the breezes that come from the river, wisp-thin in the middle of the island. I grab the first radio I find on a shelf of electronics in a store a few blocks away, avert my eyes from the glass case of portable consoles that anyone can sell now.

And anyone can buy.

The guy behind the counter sees me through glowing yellow cat's eyes, asks if I want to test one. I wish I could see my own face, the look I give him, but his reaction is satisfying enough. He doesn't say another word, just waits for the scanner to beep after it reads my wrist chip.

I don't thank him.

As soon as I get back, Haven orders us out. "Go get some sleep."

"You, too," I tell her, pulling her from the computers long enough to give her a hug. A sort-of apology. My mind is in knots, but my shoulders relax completely for the first time since that night.

She squeezes me. "I'll be back in a while."

More like she'll sleep here again, but I'm not going to start another argument.

The apartment's dark, quiet. Plastic radio fragments glitter in the moonlight around the table. Omega offers to clean up and I don't fight him on it. I just smile gratefully and grab Jonas's hand, pulling him to the bedroom. Back down the hall, my brother makes some comment I ignore and laughs to himself.

There's a way Jonas touches me most nights, lingering, fingerprints smudging on my wrist or shoulder, and a way for nights like this, firmer, more practical. Under the covers, we lie back to chest, his arm over my collarbone. Sleep comes much faster than I would've imagined after this day, warm and soft.

128

■

Buzz. My tablet goes off again on the nightstand, loud and angry like a trapped wasp.

    Someone OD'd here last night._

Shit shit shit. I tab Mage back, the time clear in the corner of the screen. If he's awake now, he hasn't been to sleep yet. What happened?_

    I don't know. The police came back to
    talk to us. I told them there are other
    tracks that can help, but we don't have any
    of those here. They said they'd get in
    touch with Lock._

No. They've never needed them in L.A before. My beautiful city, clear-eyed and sunlit, a city that lets people breathe. Here, now, I feel like I can't, chest tight and aching. Jonas props himself on an elbow and puts his hand on my back.

    Mage, do me a favor. The body . . . Find
    out if it was near a radio._

■

I stand by my bedroom window, Jonas cross-legged on the bed, the weight of the past few days heavy as a thunderstorm around us.

Only with thunderstorms, the air clears after. I'm only just beginning to smell lightning; it's going to be a while.

My shins start to ache and I walk across the room to toss stuff into my bag. We have to leave, though we're not going far.

We don't talk much on the drive, but it's a comfortable silence, as comfortable as it can be when we're both thinking of what's happening out west. Jonas doesn't understand, and I understand too much. I stop him when he heads for the door of the CRC, remembering too late that he can't unlock it.

"I need one of those chips if we're going to stay here much longer," he mutters, looking at his wrist.

He might have a point, but the thought of anyone cutting into him turns my stomach. I shake my head and lean against the center's sign, still out front even thought this hasn't been a real CRC in years.

"You don't want to go inside?"

"I asked some friends to meet us." Seeing Ant is so much easier than explaining him, especially over tabs. "They'll be here soon." It occurs to me that Jonas should know this stuff already. Should've heard about my friends back home over lunch or dinner or by the light of a bonfire.

I've only ever told him what I really had to. Every day I spend here, I realize more just how far I tried to run, how much I tried to escape. And just how hard it is to run when you don't know what you're running from, or who the person is you're supposed to be when you arrive.

In the distance, a trans-pod comes into view, taller than most of the others on the road. The Web is awake, traffic thick as always. Squinting, I try to see inside, past cityscape reflections on the windshield, and will the pod closer with my mind. Neither work.

Finally. Lynx and Spectrum hop off the pod onto the curb, blond and purple heads turning to search for me.

"Al, why did we have to kick out paying customers and drag ourselves all the way up to civilization? *Here?* You have a pretty face—"

"But not that pretty," Lynx finishes. Jonas looks at them, then me, his eyebrows raised.

"Meet Lynx and Spectrum," I tell him, waving my hand at them. "Ignore almost everything they say. Guys, this is Jonas."

Cute, Lynx mouths as Jonas and Spectrum shake hands.

I know, I mouth back. "It's not consoles," I say out loud. "Guys, someone's transmitting tracks over radio waves, here, all the way out to L.A. Or *from* L.A. I don't know. Long story, but there's something you need to see." Before they find out on their own, which they will, and we need their help before that. I lead them inside.

At any other time, in any other situation, their reactions to Anthem's hologram would be priceless, comical. It gets even better when Anthem says hello. Haven has to slap their shoulders before they look away and see her for what I'm guessing is the first time in months. Both of them start talking at once, asking her a million questions about how it works, how long it took her, whether she'll be able to replicate the results with other chips.

She answers them all. People tell those two anything.

Six years.

Lips touch the top of my head; I tilt my neck to kiss Jonas back. "Okay?"

"Yeah." My ears prick to footsteps on the stairs. More than one person, and my skin tightens until I see it's just Omega with Pixel and Isis behind him. Omega must have told them already, judging by Pixel's paleness, the tightness around Isis's eyes. Omega stops dead when he sees the guys, lips stretching thin over his teeth.

And then he's relaxed again. "Hey, you two," he says.

"Omega, man, long time no see."

"Been busy. How goes it?"

"Business is booming." Lynx grins.

"Great." Omega's smile doesn't reach his eyes. "So. Anything new here?"

"We're waiting for some scans to finish," Haven says. All of us scattered around the room, around Anthem like he's something we orbit, exchange looks. What we're afraid to say is a silence so loud it echoes. None of us want absolute confirmation of the things we suspect. Staring at Omega, I jerk my head at the door and squeeze Jonas's fingers once before letting go.

"What?" my brother asks, meeting me outside. Like I'm that stupid.

"What's the deal with Lynx and Spectrum? They said they hadn't seen you, and you were pissed when you saw them. Don't act like you weren't, I know you better than anyone."

"Nothing."

"Really."

"Yep."

"You're lying."

His laughter nudges birds from a straggly tree near a corner of the building. "I think you're not one to talk about telling people things, Al."

"And that means?"

"That you told Jonas everything what, five seconds ago? You let him follow you across the fucking country, but talk to him? Nah. That's crazy."

"You don't know shit about it." My skin feels hot, too small.

He crosses his arms, hands stark against his black shirt. "I've spent more time with him than you have since you got here. I know you knew about the tracks in L.A. and didn't tell any of us right away. Haven I could get—me, even—but Jonas is on your side just because it's you. If you even have a side anymore. You went off on Haven that first night here, but the minute you thought you needed Ant, boom, you're okay with all of it."

Never in my life have I wanted to hit Omega more. Even when

we were kids we got along, us against the world, dependent on each other because we didn't have anyone else, not completely. Ant was too lost in the music, then the war, then too lost in Haven. I was always glad to have my twin.

I turn, walk a few steps before I do something I'll regret. Words sting in the back of my throat.

■

I pace in front of the CRC, calming my pulse. I wasn't suddenly *okay* with Haven's choice, it's just I was willing to use it. At first to save myself, and now to find out what's going on in a city most of the people inside the building behind me will never see. My place. The place I left them for. Would I be so worried if it was just here, the track on the radio?

Yes. *Yes.*

A pod blasts its horn, setting off a chain that stabs behind my eyes. The door opens, Pixel steps out, finds me leaning against the wall. I've never known him as well as I know Mage and Phoenix, but he's always been around, Uncle Pix, there to help out.

"Want to talk about it?"

"Later?" Truth is he looks worse than I feel, but I don't say it.

"Okay. Haven needs you inside. Where's Omega?"

"He's not inside?"

"No."

Fine. He can do what he wants.

I follow Pixel upstairs. Lynx and Spectrum are on some of Haven's spare machines. Ant looks up from his lines of code, Haven's fingers keep flying faster than I can think over a half dozen keyboards.

"Tell me you found something," I say, crossing the room to stand with Jonas.

Ant makes a gesture with the beams of light that form one of his hands; a monitor flashes. "Maybe," he says as Haven looks up.

I'm still awed that Ant can process my voice like that. *Hear* me. "Maybe?"

"I'll be right back," Haven says. "I need to check something downstairs." She rushes past me in a waft of panic she's trying to hide.

"What the fuck is going on?"

Jonas puts his arm around me. Pixel does the same to Isis. Ant shakes his head, a cascade of rippling lines. "Nothing good."

Because I haven't known *that* much for days. For longer than any of them have known there's a problem.

"Ant . . ."

He doesn't need to breathe. Breathe or sleep or cry ever again, but his hologram looks as if it could use all three. "We think they were waiting for me to die."

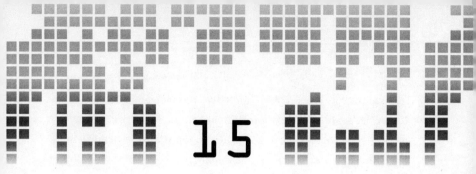

15

There's only one *they*. I know it, I just didn't want to believe it. Was trying *not* to believe it.

They.

"The Corp is gone," I say. Jonas flinches; my fingernails have left crescent marks in his arm. I loosen my grip but can't let go.

Hearing it makes it real.

Too real.

Ant stares at the floor. I don't know what he sees, if he *can* see, the same way he can hear. Now doesn't exactly feel like the right time to ask. I'm trying to breathe enough for both of us, I think. Sharp gasps, scratchy and dizzying. Over the ringing in my ears I hear Ant say something to Jonas, who helps me to Haven's chair.

Waiting for me to die.

So they could come back. It. The Corp. I want to ask how, but I'm not going to get any answers until Haven returns, and maybe not even then. I'm terrified—not at the idea, but by how easily I believe they could do it.

Mostly I remember uniforms and guns.

I remember fear.

And that Anthem made it all stop.

I raise my head. "You didn't fail," I say. "You protected us." My head starts to pound. *Protected us . . . mostly.*

Ant shrugs.

"I know," he says, voice rough, like the viewer's speaker is distorted by static. "But if we didn't end them, what the fuck was it all for?" The door opens, closes again. Jonas's hand around mine and the slight weight of his body against the arm of the chair feel like the only things I can believe in right now.

Haven nods, just once.

Ant starts to talk. It's so smooth, so practiced that I wonder for a second whether he's repeated the conversation in his head every day since it happened. Whether it just played over and over and over, the worst kind of track on repeat, every word President Z said to him.

She'd promised him the Corp was eternal. As Anthem stood there in her office, her death seconds away, she'd been sure of that. Sure that Anthem would die within a decade, that his name and his legacy would fade to silence.

He got eight years. Haven's not watching his lips.

"A contingency plan." Pixel sounds like the words are razor blades. My memories of Scope are vague outlines colored in by what I've learned since, but if there's anyone his death hurt more than Ant, it's Pixel. I look at Ant, think of Omega, and am struck again by how much better I understand Pixel's pain now.

"The Corp stopped the rebellion once," Haven says bitterly. "They were sure we'd never beat them. But it never hurts to have a backup, a fail-safe. They were half machine before we killed them; it wouldn't have occurred to them to do things any other way."

Killed. But she did exactly the same thing to them as she did with Ant. She did it *better* with Ant.

It's not *just* a contingency plan, though, and I say so as soon as I can trust myself to speak again. It's not just a plot to reclaim the Web, because why stop there? They aren't going to forget the other cities exist, and why should they, when they can be dragged—drugged—into the fold?

"We don't know everything yet," Haven says. I watch her with a new kind of . . . something. I'm not sure if it's respect or curiosity or a secret fluttering of fear. Because something in her knew to keep Anthem alive, however she could. She could have handled the grief, and she didn't do this just for herself. "So far we've found traces of weirdly encoded tracks, stuff Ant doesn't recognize, and a few references to him. Messages buried in the system code, but fragmented. Someone's tried to wipe it. I'm still trying to put everything together. And someone's bought a shitload of radio gear, but there's no record of *who* left in the files."

"Can they"—I point to the floor—"alter things like that?"

"Not like that."

None of us need to ask what that means. Someone's out there working for the Corp's return, and *out there* is a hell of a lot bigger than it was eight years ago.

I want to sleep for a week. I want to sleep for a week in my bed in Los Angeles, except that's not safe anymore either.

"So what now? Do we tell someone?"

"Not until we know who we can trust," Pixel answers Jonas. "And we have something to say more than *we think this is happening.* I don't want to believe it. No one else's gonna want to either."

Except whoever's behind it. Fuck, doesn't everyone remember? It wasn't that long ago. Not long enough for romanticized nostalgia for the Corp to sprout from nothing, like a fungus. Fresh nausea churns at the thought of how bad things could've gotten before someone realized what was going on. No one was expecting Ant to still be here, to find digital footprints not quite swept away. Outside this room and a handful of others, no one knows, and that might be the one bright star in a burned-out constellation.

Lynx and Spectrum close their computers in one motion,

stand, promise to do what they can. The shady shit that goes down in their bar isn't *bad*, mostly, but even a Web without the Corp must have laws, and some people will always want to be on the wrong side of them.

I can hardly judge.

"Thanks, guys," I say, which doesn't feel right at all; nothing does. Knots ache in my shoulders, my clothes scratch and twist against my skin. Pixel and Isis leave with Lynx and Spectrum, and I walk away into the stacks, rows and rows of empty lockers that once held memory chips.

Leaning against tiny glass doors that dig into my back, I send messages west, wanting the words I tap out to be wrong, knowing they're not. The Web recovered from the Corp surprisingly fast, the relief everyone felt lending new energy to tired minds. But always, always there's been a cloud, unacknowledged, looming on the horizon.

Now rain has begun to fall on the Web.

I press my hands to my eyes until I see spots. Heavy footsteps come closer and I look up, blinking, expecting to see Jonas. Omega smiles, but his eyes are sad, darker than usual.

"Sorry, Al," he says, putting his arm around me. I shrug underneath it.

"S'okay."

"They caught me up." He juts his chin back toward the viewer. "You really think this is happening?"

"Don't you?"

"It's just . . . yeah."

Yeah. That about covers it.

Eight years ago, Ant, Haven, all the others, they took the fight to the Corp. They were all *good* at something, each in their own way, but if the Corp's really coming back, we can't ask them to fight again. That's the whole point of their plan, if we're right. They were waiting for Ant to die, for the one who had beaten them to go so he couldn't do it a second time. And sure, he's here, in a sense, an unexpected one, but he can't hold a gun. He can't run to save us like he did back then. None of them are young.

Omega, Jonas, Lynx and Spectrum, me—we're the young ones now, and we have to stop it.

"You okay? Al?"

I swallow. "I'm fine. Thinking. Getting ahead of myself. C'mon."

Maybe we've discovered it early enough. Mage and Phoenix are already alerting people in L.A. about the radios, but we probably have some time before that information gets back to the mayor and everyone here. The authorities in L.A. have never trusted the Web, and I can't blame them for that. Citizens from here are welcomed there as refugees, not visiting dignitaries— they won't know who to trust here any more than we do. So we have time, a little, and maybe we found out early enough to stop anything really terrible from happening.

Right.

■

The Corp is eternal.

Maps stretch across Haven's monitors, dots for the three cities picked out in a bright color. I wish I could say we made these maps after breaking free of the confines of the island once the rebellion was over, or even that they're a few hundred years old, unearthed from the depths of a file somewhere. But I can't, they fall somewhere in the middle, because the Corp knew the whole time that Los Angeles and Seattle were out there, waiting.

For once, Anthem's alone, reading file after file faster than I can make out their names. I find Haven on the floor below and lean against a row of empty lockers, out of sight, as she wanders among the viewers that hold her parents and the other members of the old Board.

She's silent. The pink in her hair is faded in the bright lights, neglected during all the time she's spent here with Ant, hidden away from a world that's apparently always been bigger than we suspected.

I step out and wait for her to see me. She wipes her eyes, rearranges her face from rage into something approximating acceptance. I've never known how she could do that so easily. Maybe she just makes it look easy, and that, too, is a talent I lack.

"Let's go," she says, kicking the viewer that holds her mother. The image doesn't glitch.

"I'm going to meet Omega," I tell her. The night is one of those that's a little too warm, a little too beautiful, the rhythm of the city musical, tangible. There won't be many more before the trees in the park turn gold, then gray, then to stark skeletons against a dull sky. I've almost forgotten what the cherry blossoms in the park look like.

Cherry blossoms.

It's almost time.

I can give you everything you want.

Omega answers my tab right away and I head down the Web to the South Shore, through the hole we cut into the wire and into the warehouse. Voices drift up through the open trapdoor, falling away when they hear my boots on the ladder.

"Why are we here?" I ask, jumping down the last few rungs. Omega shrugs.

"Feels like the right place to be."

"For?"

"Inspiration? I don't know. Figuring all this out."

There's something about this room, the knowledge of what began here tucked into the shadows, quiet and watchful. The Corp was beaten once, maybe it can be beaten again.

"Ant thought about escaping with us," Omega says, forgetting I was there when Ant told this story, or just needing to talk. "He didn't because he thought there wasn't anywhere to go."

He wouldn't have made it to the west coast, but that's not the point. The point is that the Web itself looks different now, flayed, a layer of secrecy removed to reveal a hundred more. We were born here, raised here, taught by evil men and women that there was nothing *but* here, and now the truth is emerging of how little we know about our home.

Faced with that, this room is the only real thing, concrete and solid. A negative of the white room in the clean, glittering glass spider in the middle of the Web.

Headquarters. *Corp* headquarters. We'll be calling it that again soon enough.

No, we won't. My spine straightens and I squint across the space at my brother, think of Haven in the CRC, tearstained and furious at her parents' holograms. "What did we learn last time?" I ask, barely audible. It takes Omega a second to process my question, but he still looks blankly at me.

"What?"

"Same Corp, same tricks. It's never the person you expect, they were so good at hiding that." I jump up, legs greasy, not caring, and scale the ladder up into the perfect night. I don't find what I'm looking for right away. We have to walk a few blocks up north before the first one appears.

I always thought he was a slimy bastard. I point at the billboard, the mayor's face, his predator's smile. Ambitious, too slick.

"He's spent the whole time trying to get rid of the drugs, Al," Omega says.

"Except he's an addict, too."

"Wait, what?"

The problem with not telling people things is you forget what you haven't told them. "Fable found out."

"He's a creep, but you really think he's doing this?"

It's the same thing Fable asked me. Knees locked, I resist the urge to run back to the warehouse and hide in the basement. And I guess I don't know for sure, I don't know anything. I wonder if I want it to be him because that would be neat, easy, visible. Nothing—nobody—hidden beneath the surface.

If it's him, the Corp never left. There was a different mayor before him, but the Corp has been here, biding its time. Ant's victory would be completely hollow, for show.

If it isn't, the mayor's under the spell as much as anyone else who's tracking these days, and we need to drag him out of it. Tell him what's going on.

But it fits too well. His slithery, overkeen interest in Ant dying, his eyes lingering too long on me. The visceral reaction I've always had to him whenever I was forced to be in the same room. His liar's eyes and eagerness to lead this wreck of a city as soon as people would let him.

Omega and I race up the Web, dodging traffic, windows open to let the breeze in, river-sharp and buffeting my brain with noise that makes it so much easier to think. Straight lines of road. A direction, finally.

In the calmness of the CRC, Haven looks as if she wishes she was surprised, allowing herself a moment, just one, then tapping on her keyboard. Ant blinks, scanning the information she sends to him. Omega takes one of the computers at the end of the long table, matching Haven's speed, strike for strike. Jonas hovers, wanting to help but not knowing how any more than I do with that stuff. But I have something else: clarity zings around my head, refreshing, terrifying after weeks of fog.

Answers are easier to find now that we have some idea what we're looking for, but I get what Ant meant before about feeling helpless. I lean against Jonas, draw in some of his warmth, close my eyes.

"Here we go." A trail of evidence spells itself out in letters and numbers between the music database and a certain office overlooking the city from behind black glass.

"Is the radio equipment Lock's?" I ask. Haven frowns.

"Can't tell. But he knows," she says, twisting a strand of hair, "he knows what we did, giving Ant an extra chip so he could move around undetected. I told him years ago. If he did that, we wouldn't know who bought it. Anyway, he can do whatever he wants, he runs this place."

She left the scars off Anthem's projection, a perfect version of him, but if I look at his arms I can picture where the jagged white line was on his right wrist, all that was left of the untraceable chip they implanted in him during the final stages of the war.

Final. Maybe not so much.

"Where are you going?"

I'm already at the door; I turn back. "Don't you think this has been a little too easy? This whole plot, right there for us to find. They don't care—*he* doesn't care if we find out, why? Because he's already close enough to doing what he's trying to do?" I grip the door handle to stop myself shaking. A flashback creeps in from the edges of my mind. No. *Not now.* "What you guys did last time . . . obviously it didn't work. Enough. I'm going to see him."

16

The room turns red, then white.

It takes both Omega and Jonas to hold me back. "Calm down, Al," Omega says, pulling me from the door. "We don't know exactly what we're dealing with yet, or who else is involved. We don't know for sure that *he* is, only that it looks that way."

I can't fight him and my own brain at the same time and I bite my lip until the pain brings the room back into sharp focus. Okay. Fine, I'm fine. Think of the ocean, the ebb and flow. My breath evens.

"We should tell the others," I say. "I'll go get Lynx and Spectrum, get them to grab us some more untraceable tablets. Mine's not enough. Nor does mine seem to be entirely untraceable, but that doesn't matter right now. I'll be back soon." Haven and Omega both watch me warily.

"I'll come," Jonas says, and they relax.

"You can, too," I say to Omega, just to make the point. He shakes his head.

"Are you going to tell me what they did to piss you off?"

"Nope."

"But we can trust them?"

A reluctant nod.

"Awesome."

He rolls his eyes at my tone. Someday I'll unravel that puzzle, but whatever his problem with Lynx and Spectrum is, he seems willing to put it aside, more generous than I am. I hold grudges like hand grenades, and I'm not used to him not telling me things.

But I was the one who chose to leave, so maybe I deserve it.

Jonas heads toward the pod, but I shake my head. I need the walk, to leave my anger and adrenaline baking into hot tar behind us. I need the time. Feels like forever since I've been alone with him, even longer since we've been *really* alone. With Jonas's arm around my shoulders, wandering through the night, we could be anyone, or no one, which is a more attractive thought.

After the war, I wondered sometimes what it would be like not to be the great Anthem's younger sister, invisible and anonymous, just another figure in a tangle of heat and sound on a dance floor.

Around and around, my brain cycles through everything we actually do know so far: the radio waves, Lock, maybe. The Corp's return, I'm sure of it. Los Angeles, my home. Verse, chorus, repeat. I feel like I'm walking in circles around that same danger zone of ignorance I was in the day of the white room. Enough to know something's very, very wrong, too little to know how to stop it. Jonas catches me muttering under my breath and I tell him my thoughts, never wanting to stop.

The water bar is dark, locked, its sign a pool of shadow against the wall. Jonas knocks, the glass rattling in the door, but it's useless; I know where they are. *Idiots.* Indecision glues me to the spot, rainwater dripping down the gutter and pooling around the soles of my boots.

"Okay, come on," I say.

Jonas raises his eyebrows. I point to the opposite end of the alley. The club isn't far, just a few blocks down, tucked away in a maze of streets much narrower than anywhere in the Upper Web.

Near the club, I slow my steps, willing my tablet to flash, but

Lynx and Spectrum won't be checking theirs if they're inside, reality a distant and boring memory, dull and flat compared to the glittering drugs.

"This is what I think it is?" Jonas asks as I pull open the doors to the tiny entrance room and its cover-charge scanner blinking on the wall. Whoever runs this place and pretends to make sure nobody overdoses is gone, their empty chair kicked aside.

"Yep." I don't trust myself to say much more. "Wait here."

My hand shakes. The red light winks at me. Deep breaths. It doesn't matter as much anymore. The radio did everything I'd spent years avoiding, resisting. I won't be in there long. The lock clicks open and Jonas strides forward, swinging open the door before I can stop him or decide whether I want to. Music fills the space, my mind, a sudden hit like that second after a sneeze—blinding, beautiful, too short, then a ringing silence in the wake of the door's heavy slam. The white room threatens again. I stumble outside to wait, counting each second.

He's not in there long, but it's enough; his dazed expression when he comes back makes my chest hurt. Lynx and Spectrum are way gone, giggling, spaced, bodies still moving in time with each other and the melody stuck in their heads.

"You didn't have to—can you hear me?"

"What? Yeah. No problem. Here they are." Jonas's eyes light up and he kisses me with grinning lips. "Right here."

"Thanks," I say softly. I think I mean it, much as I wish he hadn't done that. "You two . . ." I snap my fingers in front of Lynx's and Spectrum's faces and they laugh louder, the sound bouncing down the street.

"Alpha! Hey, it's you!"

Oh, fuck it. I grab fistfuls of fishnet and drag them away, threads snapping in my grip. Lynx's wrist gets us into their water bar, the bright lights and hydration drag them into lucidity. *Complete* idiots.

"Feeling better?"

"Was feeling pretty good before," Spectrum says, pupils returning to normal and boring into mine. "You used to be cool with it, why the fuck drag us out?"

"I did that," Jonas says. For the twentieth time I check his eyes and try to look like I'm not. We'll talk about it later. Always *later*.

"Either way," Lynx takes a gulp of water, "what could possibly be so important?"

"The Corp's back." The sobering effect would be funny if I could remember how to laugh. "And it looks like Lock is behind it."

"No shit."

"Shit."

They both glance around their bar. A face to put to the Corp's return makes it more real, and when that return is public, the old punishments will be, too. Lynx and Spectrum have done enough to earn those a thousand times over.

"Okay," Spectrum says. "What do you need?"

Help. I don't know where to start; Anthem's the hero, not me. For now I'll settle for the tablets. Maybe some sleep. I feel it again, the suffocation the Web is so good at, the edges of the island contracting, smaller, smaller. Omega's right, we don't know who else is involved or all the steps the mayor has taken so far. The evil isn't in plain sight anymore so we have to be just as hidden.

Guess I get to be invisible after all.

■

Beyond the walls of the CRC, everything is too normal. Citizens going about their business, ignorant—which I have to remind myself is our fault. We're choosing not to warn them for now.

It's most obvious in the cluster of cameras, blooming again outside our building.

"Is it true he's dead?"

"Were you there when he died?"

"Are you proud of your brother's legacy?"

"Fuck off. Show some respect." I pull open the door and wrench myself away from grasping hands. Hard as it is to believe, those questions are a good thing.

It means they're not asking other ones. No one's discovered what Haven's done yet, and no one's guessed what's going on here.

Pixel's right. No one's going to want to believe it. The ones who do believe will panic.

The edges are too sharp; everything is too bright. There's nowhere I want to be, and nowhere I can be useful. Sitting around the CRC while Ant and Haven run more scans of the system will drive me insane, like I'm not halfway there already.

Jonas and I walk to the park, not talking, because it's somewhere to go. My fight with Omega replays in my head, but this time I'm not keeping quiet because I don't want to tell Jonas things. It's just a bad idea to talk about them on the street, in daylight, where people can hear us. Through the gates, along the path, I take him to my favorite spot, under my favorite tree. I wish I had my guitar, but it's at the apartment and this is good, too, sitting with my back against his chest while he matches up the streaks in my hair.

Calm. It's a weird calm. In L.A., we'd be waiting for lightning to set the ocean on fire.

"I don't understand all of this," he says. "If this Corp of yours is trying to come back, and we know who's behind it, why are we just sitting around?"

"We can't fight an enemy we can't completely see. The Corp is like that monster; you cut off one head and more grow back. You have to be strong enough to defeat it all at once." And we're not. "I never meant for you to get caught up in it," I say, because apparently saying exactly what I mean is a skill that left me somewhere along the broken highway. I feel him tense. "I'm glad you're here, it's not that, but there's a lot about this place that's hard to explain. I'd tell you if I could," I say, and his face clears, "but it's an atmosphere, a feeling. Hard to describe."

"Will you try?"

I close my eyes. "Okay. I think in some ways, we . . ." I'm not sure what the right word is. "We *inherit* fear. Like blue eyes or freckles or something. We've been kept powerless and scared for two hundred years here. Maybe it's not just tracking that makes us die so early. Maybe bodies start to crumble, break down under that kind of strain. Maybe terror is acidic enough to burn away our insides until there's nothing left. After a while, I think it became easier for people to just look down at their feet, keep walking, than look up into the eyes of the monster. You learn how to keep going that way. Your kids get it from you. And then, at some point, the view starts to look good. Comforting, because you know what to expect."

"You guys haven't had long enough to grow out of that."

"Eight years." I shake my head. "No, not long enough. It's why they were only waiting until Ant was gone."

"But he's not, not completely."

"Ant pretty much killed President Z with his bare hands. He can't do that again, and this is as close as they're going to get. Haven was smart when she put him in that particular building. No one can turn the power off without shutting down the other holograms, the Board. That would kill the Web completely."

Inhale. Exhale. *Buzz.* Relief and annoyance fight for control of my head as I take out my tablet. "It's Phoenix." He looks over my shoulder at the screen.

```
I'm coming out there._
Don't. Why? Did something else happen?_
```

"She can't drive here on her own," Jonas says. I wouldn't want to be the person who got on her bad side, but the idea of her sleeping alone in a pod by the side of the road squeezes my heart with panic.

```
Everything's fucked up here. Police all
over the place. Radio stations raided. I'm
too old for this shit, Al._
Bean and Fable should be back there
soon._
Yeah, great._
```

I hesitate, stung. What the fuck does she want me to say? That everything's awesome, we're all just hanging around, having a great time, maybe playing some tunes, she should come jam with us?

Under the grass and tree roots and soil it feels like the world is spinning ten times as fast as usual, too fast for me to catch any details, make any sense of what's going on. Like it's spinning too fast and can't hold itself together. Splitting, allowing darkness up through the cracks. There is *no way* Lock doesn't know what's going on.

My hands clench. I use fists to push myself to my feet. "I need to go."

"Where?"

I see the hurt in Jonas's eyes, the certainty I'm keeping

secrets from him again. "I'll tell you as soon as I'm back, I promise." He lets me kiss him and I don't want to stop, but I pull myself away. "Meet me at the apartment? I'll be back in an hour, we'll talk more."

"I'll wait here. Nice to be outside."

"Fine. Try to calm Phoenix down?"

"Uh, think I forgot my tablet at the apartment."

Mine lands on the grass by his feet.

I wait until I'm out of the park, out of sight, to run, defending my choice in my head, with nobody to convince but myself, and I'm failing pretty awesomely at that. Lock's more likely to tell me something if he knows I'm alone, which is exactly why Jonas shouldn't be there and exactly why he'd want to be there if he knew what I was doing.

The building looms ahead, in the center of a sea of light. Past it, out over the river, the sun is low, red.

When I see the elevators, the marble, feel the hum of the mainframe behind the curved wall, I remember.

That day. The white day.

"Alpha?"

I don't recognize my own name. A garbled collection of sounds. She has to call it again before I turn.

"Hey," I say. I can't remember her name, but we went to school together. She was the kind of person who was always going to grow up to wear a suit and never let her tablet out of her sight.

"Heard you went out west! Back already?"

My eyes flick to the lights above the doors of one of the elevators. Third floor, coming down. "Just to visit." I pretend to check my watch and notice too late that I'm not wearing one, so instead I just look like an idiot. "I have to go."

"Oh. Well, take care of yourself."

Sure. I don't give her a second glance, but her eyes stay on me as I dart inside and press a button. It rises too slowly. I curl my toes inside my boots.

The hallway's quiet, the door closed, and Pax's desk is empty. I knock. No answer. A scanner's blinking red eye watches me and I pass my wrist over it, not expecting the lock to let me in. I jump back when it does. At first sight, I understand why he took over this office despite what happened here. Huge windows offer a perfect view of the Web, and everything about the room whispers of wealth and otherness.

Up here, Lock doesn't have to be a man of the people, whatever he tries down on the streets.

"Hello?"

The carpet swallows my footsteps. I walk around a small seating area, smoked glass and leather and chrome. An enormous desk sits at the other end of the room, the chair behind it askew.

I wonder if it's possible to have secondary déjà vu, experience something that happened to someone else but you've heard so many times it feels like your own memory.

A lock of hair. That's what I see first. A lock of hair and then a head, then a still, cold, collection of shapes. A spine twisted at an uncomfortable angle, headphones over ears. A glowing console screen tucked into the desk, behind an open panel obviously meant to conceal it when not in use. Pale, waxy skin and unseeing eyes.

Oh, shit.

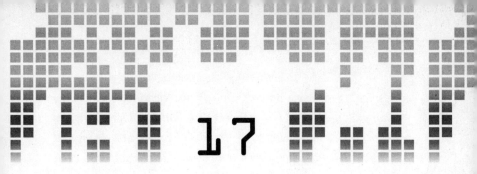

17

I get the fuck out of there as fast as I can. No. No way. No. Sixty seconds later I'm in the shadow of the building, hands on my knees, gulping fresh air, no idea how I got there. Lock's body in the office is crystal clear in my head, and everything around me is so sharp it looks as if it might break into a zillion pieces, but I don't remember a single step. Or if I took the elevator.

Or if anyone saw me on the way out.

Damn it.

I hadn't really wanted to believe Fable, even though I did. Seeing it for myself is something different. Maybe I would've noticed the signs before if I hadn't tried so hard not to look at him.

There are only two ways this could've happened: Lock chose to track, though someone would've known if he'd been walking the line between functional and overdose with that much balance for so long. Creep. Lying creep.

Or someone made him do it, knowing it would only take one song.

Just one. I imagine him slipping the headphones over his ears, the music starting, mellow or harsh, soft or loud. A swell of instruments that slowly crept into his brain, each note prying deeper, deeper.

Starbursts of color whirl around me and that's new, so beautiful after all the white. Red, blue, green. I try to grab them with my hands, feel them tingle and dissolve against my fingertips. Hands touch my shoulders and I push them away, hating them for trying to hold me down when I want to fly. I can't feel my toes anymore and it's amazing, drifting along each slide of the guitar, rising with each pure, clean note from the keyboard.

Oh yes.

And the voice, the voice telling me to move, dance, run. I laugh, hear it echo and become part of the music. Now the song is mine, really mine, and I let it take me higher, pull me under. Weightless. Floating, sinking, floating.

Sinking . . .

Cold stabs at my skin, sharp and mean. I don't like this. I don't want to be here anymore but I don't know where here is. I run. I see something horrible and I run and now everything around me is a blur and drums are beating in my head, each strike a new flare of pain.

Get me out. Help me.

Breathe. Breathe.

The Web reforms into defined edges, solid shapes. I really don't know where I am or, more accurately, how I got here. Across the street, the river drifts sluggishly past. My palms are scraped and bloody in the light from a nearby lamp. Outside the lamp's glow, the sky is dark. I dodge between two pods and bend over the guardrail to puke into the water. Tears sting my eyes, sweat beads all over me, chilled and feverish at the same time.

On shaky legs I walk to the nearest trans-pod stop, fumble in my bag for my tablet, but it's not there. Jonas has it.

Jonas.

I don't know what to panic about first. Calm wraps around me. Numb. Frozen. Take things one step at a time. Headlights come closer and I wait until the pod stops right in front of me before forcing my feet to move, climb on. All the other passengers stare at me. I hide behind my hair, watching through it and the windows. A neon clock on the side of a building stops my heart for a second and I try to count back, picture the time stamp on my tabs to Phoenix.

Three hours, give or take. I just lost three hours.

Jonas won't still be under that tree, but I check anyway, stumbling from the pod at the closest spot, up to the gates, into the park. I call his name; no answer.

The mayor is dead. I practice saying it over and over in my head, like that'll help it make more sense.

Dead, just like that.

My teeth chatter. The apartment is empty when I get there. It used to always be filled with people, laughter, but now we're all just orbiting around each other, or at the CRC which has become a second home. More of a home than this one. A dull black box sits on the coffee table—my tablet. So Jonas has been back, at least.

Maybe he's out looking for me. I scroll through the messages, find a new set from Phoenix promising that she and Mage are fine.

She's lying, but I can't worry about that right now, not when I have enough lies of my own curled in my chest, dark and sour.

The couch is tempting, my bed down the hall even more so, but I don't stop. I change into a shirt not soaked with sweat and leave again. When I open the door to Ant's floor at the Center, he and Haven are alone, her computers chugging away, their voices low as they talk, dropping quickly to silence as soon as they spot me.

I don't even need to say anything. Haven runs over to put her arms around me and leads me to the chair, all from the look on my face.

"What is it, Al?" Ant asks.

"Lock . . ." I stop. "He's . . ." I can do this. "He's dead. I found him. He'd been tracking."

"What?"

I watch their faces as it sinks in.

"Overdose?"

"I don't think so. We would've noticed something, right? If he was tracking that much?"

The room shimmers around me. We can't fight an enemy we can't see, and we were looking at the wrong one while the right one lurked on the edges of our vision. "So it wasn't him," I say. The words don't want to come out. I wanted it to be him. I wanted it—something, *anything*—to be that easy.

"Or he was part of it, until whoever he was working with didn't need him anymore," Haven offers.

"And they used a killing track to get rid of him either way?" I ask.

"It would make sense," Haven says. "It's a weapon they've used before."

"It's a weapon *we* used before," Ant reminds her. "I thought we destroyed the killing tracks. All of them, not just the ones we made."

But nothing's ever completely gone from the system. Traces of information lurk, hidden in fragments, digits, waiting to be pieced back together by anyone who wants to badly enough. I'm sure it wasn't a normal overdose, it couldn't have been. He's on TV all the damn time, healthy and charming in that oily way I didn't like to touch in case it wouldn't wash off.

"There's more." I keep my head up, but don't look at either of them while I describe the flashback. "I've never had one like that," I say, picking at a fingernail. "Losing that much time—"

"Al," Ant says. I wait for more, but it doesn't come.

"Where are Omega and Jonas?" I wipe my eyes. We have more important things to think about than what that evil woman did to me and the effects it still has. That it broke me so much more permanently than anyone expected. "I don't know if anyone saw me leaving the building, but someone saw me go in. They're going to find his body soon, this morning at the latest. People are going to remember who was the last to do something like that."

Haven has her hand on my shoulder. Ant is hovering, a projection of lights, in front of me. They won't be above suspicion when the discovery happens, and neither will I. Plus there's the small matter of what they'll find when they go looking for Anthem's chip. People will want to know what Ant knew, whether he was involved in any way. And then they'll want to know why his memory chip in his labeled locker down in Two is blank.

"Omega's on his way; he tabbed just before you got here." Haven's laugh is forced, unnatural. "Asking if I wanted dinner. Jonas is probably with him."

But when my brother gets here, he's alone, a bag in his hand that he passes to Haven as he looks at me. "What happened?"

I let her tell him, tune out the voices. I want Jonas, need to find him.

"No." Anthem's voice, firm, almost strident, jars me back.

"He's right," Omega says to Haven. "Hiding the body's too dangerous. Let them find it, and we'll deal with whatever happens next. Come on, Al."

He takes my elbow to pull me up, leads me downstairs and into the pod on the street. He drives fast, makeup stark in the streetlights. "You shouldn't be running around right now, let's get this all fixed first," he says, stopping outside our apartment building. Fixed. I want to laugh. Everything's irretrievably broken. "I'll find him. Go in and wait."

Sitting still isn't an option, however alluring the couch was an hour ago. There's one thing I can do, one tiny, inconsequential action I can take. I find what I need in the cabinet under the sink in Ant and Haven's hygiene cube. The marks around my neck are faded, green and yellow. I pace the living room for half an hour, climb into the shower when the alarm I've set goes off. Hot water needles my back and swirls around my feet, stained a bright, cerulean blue.

■

The Web explodes.

Not literally, but close enough. Panic is almost tangible, a simmering heat ready to blow, even from where I stand at the living room windows, looking down, watching. A cloud of it, heavy, blocking out the sun. Raindrops spatter on the windows and turn flashing pod lights to prisms.

On TV, a plastic newswoman repeats the same story again and again. The mayor is dead, found after a presumed tracking overdose. So that's still the official story.

Jonas puts a hot mug in my hand. "Thanks. Sorry," I say again, touching a fingertip to one of his bloodshot eyes. Omega found him eventually, looking for me.

"Shhh. You had a good excuse."

I wince. Yeah. Finding a body is the greatest reason to be late, ever. Jonas's eyes widen. "I know what you meant," I say, taking a sip of tea and leaning closer to the glass. My vision blurs to see nothing but the smudged reflection of blue around my face. "I'm not used to it yet."

"Me neither."

"I had to do something." Something to make me *not* the person who was in that office, and not only because maybe someone saw me. I want it to have happened to someone else. I want all of this to be happening to someone else.

"I know. I like it. Fuck, Al, what is going on? What are we going to do?"

The million-credit question. Tabs flying back and forth, Omega and Haven and Ant holed up at the CRC where I can't go because for now they think it's best I don't go outside. *They think it's best.* I take another sip to wash away the bitterness of the words. I'm the one who's been looking for a cure for a year, and yeah, maybe it was just for myself and Omega at first, but not now. I can help. I know more about this than anyone, and I know that setting everyone in the Web free is the only way we're going to get rid of the Corp. And if I *can* only heal myself and my brother, it's my only chance at fending off the urge to surrender. Track and track and track until nothing matters anymore and I stop caring.

"We have to tell people the Corp's coming back," I say. "Warn them about the tracks through the radio. About death tracks if they're using consoles."

"It's that easy?"

"Easy?" I shake my head. "No."

But we're out of time. We can't protect the Web, change the course like we hoped we could. Part of me—a bigger part than I'd like to admit—considers packing our stuff, throwing it into our pod, leaving and never looking back. Los Angeles isn't safe. Seattle might not be either, for all we know—Lynx and Spectrum are trying to find out—but I've been in the eye of this hurricane once before. Back then, I was too young to really understand.

I'd give everything I own, including my guitar, for that blind innocence again.

Any minute now, I expect Jonas to grasp the frayed thread of our conversation in the park, ask me to talk more. And I will, as soon as he asks.

He takes the empty mug from my hands and disappears into the kitchen.

■

Hours pass. My legs get tired from standing and I fold onto the carpet, the window smooth and cold against my shoulder. The voice on the TV changes, and then the story does. I close my eyes and listen to the sound of pure fear restrained as the reporter tries to calmly report rumors of the Corp's return. *Rumors*, she stresses, from a small faction of citizens who may or may not be a credible source.

We're a *faction*. That's funny. Not enough to laugh, but funny.

They'd believe it if it came from Ant, but we're not ready to reveal him yet. The longer we can keep him hidden from whoever's pulling the strings, the better. Lynx leaked the information to a few well-chosen contacts.

The door opens. My fingers dig into my thighs, but it's only Omega, black clothes soaked, hair dripping. Most of his overapplied makeup is gone and I realize how tired he is, the toll the past few weeks have taken on him, too.

He looks like hell. I don't say so because I don't want to hear the same about myself.

"Well, tracking's gone way up," he says. I stand and walk away, down the hall, come back with a towel for him.

"That was predictable," I say.

"Why?" Jonas asks. "Aren't they scared of what'll happen?"

I go back to the window. "If you'd been here before, and knew what was coming, you'd want to be high before it started, too. Why wait until they make you do it? Why be afraid if you can feel something else?"

"But you can't."

"I wouldn't anyway." I like to think it's the truth. I'm still clinging to the hope that my cure is possible, that somehow, among everything else, we'll find what I need. That my brain hasn't been damaged beyond repair by the music from the radio, and I can paint the white room over with a colorful cure. That maybe we can save the rest of the Web, too. Give them all the rest of the freedom Ant started.

Tiny figures run down the street. Beating the Corp to the punch is only half the reason they're racing to the nearest console. Most of them are probably trying not to believe it.

But it's a good excuse. Enough time has passed. Time wears ugliness away, leaving beautiful, polished diamonds behind. No one's thinking about the sickness, the death that will eventually come. They're thinking of how freeing it was, how much *fun*.

Oblivion is an appealing idea right now. The news report cycles back to the beginning of the story. I go into my room and close the door, shut the curtains so it's too dark to see. I slept like shit last night, jolting awake every five minutes.

Sleep should not be a guilty pleasure, and still I fight it. Voices in the living room tangle with half-conscious dreams. The voices swell, come closer. Bright light streams in and stings my eyelids. Omega's face is a mask of indecision.

I sit up, eye the uniforms behind him. Different than the ones the old guards used to wear, but there's still a quiet menace sewn into the seams, at odds with their apologetic expressions.

"It's okay," I say to my brother. "I'll go with them. Tell . . . everyone."

"You're sure?"

"Yeah."

"It's just that she was seen . . . ," one of them begins.

Appearance is everything. I might be Anthem's little sister, but preferential treatment only extends so far. I trip down the hallway in my unlaced boots, thankful that I'm not in handcuffs. Jonas is holding on to the back of the couch, knuckles white, eyes narrowed at the men behind me, and I shake my head, give him a smile I hope is reassuring.

The pod is comfortable, the guards' hands gentle on my arms, the entrance to *headquarters* underground, hidden from view. Hot fear gathers under my skin, but the room they lead me to isn't a cell. It's just a room, windowless, monochrome, not white. One of them locks the door, but he has the decency to shoot me a sympathetic frown from the closing gap in the second before I'm left alone.

Alone. The shell I pulled on in my room, already loose as my shoes, cracks, falls away. Innocence counts for nothing here if the Corp is back, and I'm guilty of wanting that asshole dead. Threatened it aloud, forgetting that in the Web, the walls have ears.

But I'm here now. I sit on a hard gray couch and breathe, in, out, until my heartbeat fades from my ears.

Counting the minutes makes me yawn, my jaw cracking loud in the sucking silence, and soon there are too many of them to bother. Night must've fallen by the time the door opens again, two different guards blocking the way between me and freedom.

"I didn't do anything," I say. "Yeah, okay, I was there, but I didn't kill him."

"I know," says the third guy, not in a uniform but in a black suit that fits like one, stepping into the room. "Don't worry, you're not in any trouble for that."

I'm in so much more. The room is too small. There's nowhere to get away from him, a guy I've never met but it's too much of a coincidence for it to be anyone else. He looks exactly like I imagined. Like I've heard him described—by Haven, and not where Ant could hear her. Shock traps my voice in my throat. I've seen him before, just once, a shadow between bright lights in the crowd at Mage and Phoenix's club the night word came about Ant. A glimpse, not enough to know what I was seeing.

Everything in me screams *no*—except for the parts screaming *yes*. Things that make sense are more frightening than things that don't, and this makes the kind of sense that turns my blood cold.

"I know you didn't kill him," he says again, adjusting a bright yellow tie as I look up into the eyes of the monster. "I did. It's so good to meet you, Alpha. Did you like the cherry blossoms?"

18

Wraith. That's his name and what he is. A ghost. Ant had a different nickname for him, when Wraith was alive, and after. When we thought he was dead.

"You're dead," I say. Stupid. It sounds like a threat and maybe it is. Sharp laughter fills the room and he waves his hand, dismissing the guards.

"I really don't think that's your biggest problem right now."

I back farther into the corner. He might have a point. "I don't understand . . . how?"

"Do you really think we weren't prepared for whatever might happen? It became convenient to allow your brother to believe he'd defeated us, and your so-called friends made it easy, deciding to tell everyone I'd died with Scope. Seriously, I should thank them for that."

"Stay away from them." And me, all of us.

He ignores this. "Anyway, the *how* isn't the important thing right now. What's important is what happens next."

"Which is?" The chances of me getting out of this are so low I'm not even scared anymore, I just want to know.

"Well," he says, smiling and smug, "now it's convenient to leave Anthem there in that clever hologram, where he has to watch all his plans crumble around him."

I want to puke. So we were right, and the Corp was waiting,

but it's even better this way. Haven is proof that they won't kill you if they can break you instead, stand over your broken body and laugh. Dead, Ant would've been out of the way, but at the CRC he's trapped, as helpless as he thinks he is.

"He's not the only one who can stop you," I say.

Another smile. "Can't wait. You'll get your chance, I'm not going to keep you here. Go back to your precious family and tell them everything. I should come with you, that'd be fun to watch. I know all about you, Alpha, I've been paying attention. Your brother's legacy is gone, the Web belongs to the Corp again, and the other cities will, too, especially your beloved Los Angeles. Fight me—us—if you want, but here's the thing: I don't think you want to. Don't you ever think about it? How good the drugs would feel, and what a relief it'd be for the Corp to make all your decisions?"

"No."

Pressed against the wall, I can feel the hum of the mainframe in my bones, stirring my blood, raising goose bumps on my skin. Wraith flicks a strand of yellow hair from his eyes, rounds the back of the sofa so there's nothing between us but shrinking feet and growing lies.

"Never?" He steps closer. "I think you want it, just as much as it scares you. I think you know how great the Corp was, and will be again."

"You're wrong."

He shrugs, an easy motion. "Okay. If you say so."

Questions. So many questions. I don't trust him to give me honest answers to any of them, but I try. "So, what? You just walked back in here"—I gesture to the building around me—"and announce you're in charge?" The news reports had said nothing about this in their clueless, mechanical recitations. "How do I know it's just you? How do I know you're not just some kind of puppet for someone else?"

He's so close now I can feel his breath, the heat coming off him. "I guess you don't know for sure, and you'll just have to take my word for it. I am the Corp now, and I'll bring it back to the glory it was before. One last question, Alpha. Would you like your cure?" My vision ripples. I see nothing but his eyes. Heart pounding, I duck around him and run, sure that he or one of his pets will try to stop me.

No one does. Repeat, repeat, like a song's chorus, I find myself outside the building, every gasp for air a knife in my lungs.

A flashback nudges at my brain, and this time I manage to push it away. Home or the CRC. Home. Omega and Jonas will be waiting for me, and they're the ones who can help, bodies that can move and run and fight.

At every corner I look back over my shoulder, almost wishing for sirens, lights, guns that would betray a tiny bit of Wraith's arrogance, his terrifying confidence that they can't be stopped this time. There are pods, sure, but none of them stop me or even slow down.

I'm invisible. Unimportant. Not worthy of attention from drugged eyes, and they're all drugged.

Fuck.

I hit the button for the elevator a dozen times. Finally the doors part, the trip up into the sky taking way too long. Jonas and Omega will know what to do, and we'll tell the others. Mage and Phoenix lied to him, to everyone. I think I know why. Somehow, I'm guessing Ant's going to be less understanding than I am.

"Hello?"

The apartment echoes, quieter than the room I was just in at the Corp—how easily that comes back—without the ever-present computer hum below all the other sounds. Nothing. Total silence. What the fuck. Maybe they're at the CRC.

Maybe they weren't expecting me back at all.

"Guys?" I call, louder. I head for my room, unearth my tablet from my bag beneath a pile of clothes where I left it this morning. No messages. I fire off one to Phoenix because some warning is better than none. I imagine her tablet flashing on the bar at the club, the little jerk of her shoulders because it always catches her slightly off guard. Then I remember they haven't opened the club in days. They're in our house on the beach, waiting, angry, afraid.

This is going to be messy. That's all I can think. Messy. My mind is fracturing, pulled in too many directions, cracked by too many questions. How? Who else? The *why* is pretty fucking obvious.

The Corp is eternal, eternal, eternal. They want their power back, and they want more of it than ever.

I sit down on my bed, catch my breath for a second. I should force myself back up, go to the CRC, and it's the last thing I want to do because this is the last thing, the last failure. Ant didn't defeat the Corp, didn't save us, he didn't even make sure the person who killed Scope was dead.

And I don't know how to tell him. Even in my head the words are fuzzy, garbled, vague impressions tinged with fear and confusion.

Okay. I inhale, stand, go back into the hall. The door to Omega's room is open, just a few inches, and I don't know what makes me push it the rest of the way. He would've heard me call.

Unless . . .

No.

Almost.

It's not him on the floor, ears covered. I wish it was, instead of the only person that's worse. The tiny console screen glows, a track title scrolling across it, the only light in the whole room. Enough light to see the thing I absolutely don't want to see.

Repeat, repeat.

This time, it's déjà vu of my own. I can't breathe, but he is, thank fuck. Stay with me. Please, Jonas, stay with me. I tab for a med-pod and throw the headphones against the wall so hard they crack. Hurry up. *Hurry up.*

Minutes drag, each one a day, a week. As soon as I hear the lock click I scream so they can follow my voice. The stretcher carves grooves in the carpet. The harsh lights of the med-pod make every vein glow indigo under his skin. I tell them to take him to Isis's hospital and don't say another word.

I love you. Don't leave me. Don't leave me now.

■

Isis says he'll be okay. I try to believe her and not the waxy sheen of his skin, the whimpers that are the only sounds he's made for hours. She's seen this hundreds of times.

The pillow is cool, his face an inch from mine. Crawling into the bed with him is a bad idea, I settle for leaning over, awkwardly bent in my uncomfortable chair.

I turn my tablet off. The Web really *could* be exploding for all I care, I just want to be left alone with him. Isis will tell the others for me, and will tell me if something bad happens. Something worse than everything that's already happened, if there's anything left. The thought that maybe all the bombs have dropped already is almost reassuring.

Ant dead, but not. The Corp returning. The mayor definitely dead, and I only got out of that by luck. Wraith and death tracks, addicts and dark clouds looming . . .

Jonas.

I'm still glad he came with us, and I don't know what that

171

says about me, how selfish I am. His fingers twitch against the stark white sheets. This is my fault.

Telling him everything, letting him in didn't stop him. Maybe if I'd told him earlier, warned him, let him really see. And it would've made him less pissed at me. He tried to hide it just as much as I tried not to see it. Sure, drive across the country with me and then sit back while I ignore you, run around dealing with my family and friends and this crazy fucking place I call home.

Because the Web is home, much as I miss Los Angeles and desperately want to go back. I can only hope there'll be a city to go back *to*, someday.

We *have* to beat the Corp.

Correction: *they* do. I'm done. Not that I did much to start with, but Jonas is pale, brow furrowed, grimacing beside me, and if this is the price I pay, it's not worth it. Call me a coward, whatever.

"He'll stay asleep for a few hours?" I ask Isis when she comes back to check on him, maybe me, too. Already thin lips turn down in sympathy.

"Another day, at least, I think," she says, checking his pulse. "He had no tolerance, Al, and tracks seem to work differently on people who don't have memory chips. I'm still running tests on that. Do what you need to do."

Chips. Wait.

"Who paid for it?"

She drops his arm. "The console?"

"Yeah. He doesn't have a chip, no credits."

"Good question."

One I'd really love the answer to. Those things aren't cheap, and he didn't bring anything with him he could sell or trade. Someone bought it for him, and that's another mystery I will get to the bottom of. There's no way to rewind time to before this happened, but I can fast forward it to a time when it will never happen again.

"I'll be back soon," I tell her.

Darkness—or what passes for it in the Web—blinds me after the hospital lights. Blinking, I wait until shapes begin to appear, define, grow into identifiable objects. Pods, lampposts, people in black and neon. I keep to the shadows, make my way down to Two as fast as I can. The water bar is packed, music—safe music— escaping through the cracks around the door. Loud enough that I can't hear myself think, but Lynx sees me as soon as I open the door, follows me back out into the alley.

"I heard," he says, hugging me tight. "Is he okay? Are you?"

"I need a pod. Something that isn't going to break down in five minutes."

One beat. Two. "You know what you're doing?"

"No idea. A gun, too."

Another pause. "Okay."

"And don't tell anyone I asked."

"Al . . ."

I touch his arm, leather cool on my fingers. "Please."

"Anything for you."

Like I deserve that, but I'll take it. He promises to bring both to the apartment as soon as he can, leave them in the parking lot behind the building. I head there now, pile my clothes and Jonas's on the bed. Not enough. Haven and I are about the same size, and Ant doesn't need any of his anymore. I come back from their room with an armful of stuff. Better.

Tomorrow slowly chases today to the horizon. I sleep—like shit, again—and wake before sunrise. True to his word, Lynx left a pod downstairs, its lock reprogrammed to open to my chip. Probably anyone's chip. A gun, black and menacing, is under the driver's seat. I pack the back with clothes, soap, medical supplies.

At the nearest depot, I fill every inch of remaining space with food that won't spoil.

I pull up outside the CRC. I should go in, say good-bye, explain. This could be the last time I'll ever see my brothers and Haven. My chest splits in two, tears fill my lashes and overflow. If I go in there now, this is the face they'll remember—the one that ran away.

When I moved to L.A., I said good-bye to everything. People, places, things I couldn't take with me, and here I am. Maybe the trick to running away for good is to pretend that one day I'll come back.

The pod stirs to life again. I don't look in the mirrors, and I turn out of sight as soon as I can, circling around to aim toward the hospital, fingers twitchy on the steering wheel. Isis would've tabbed me if Jonas had woken up, but the closer I get, the deeper the panic digs in, talons matched perfectly to my ribs.

Echoing hallways and a soundtrack of soft beeps coming through open doors. A generation of people who grew up with the Corp and were too old to quit tracking when they could are all dying now, replaced by ones my age—young, strong, healthy, and unsullied.

Okay, I'm not *unsullied*. But I didn't have a flashback when I found Jonas like I did with the mayor, which I take as a sign of . . . something. A scrap of hope I can cling to, a blanket to keep me warm.

Jonas's door is ajar. I square my shoulders, prepare to see him unconscious and weak, exactly the opposite of who he is in my head.

Rumpled sheets twist on the bed, but he's not in them. I spin, looking down the hallway, right, left. There's no sign of Isis or anyone and the near silence is unexpectedly unnerving. Too quiet. She said she was running tests to do with the memory chips, maybe they're doing that.

Behind me, the door to the hygiene cube clicks open, a rectangle of light set into a wall of deep shadows, framing him. Clean, dressed in black, hair spiked. Angular cheekbones jut through thin skin, sharper than usual. I shouldn't like it as much as I do.

"You're okay," I breathe, crossing the room so fast I don't realize I'm moving. Jonas flinches at my touch and I jump back, apologize. OD'ing is hell, or so I've heard. "We're leaving," I say. "I have a pod outside, everything we need. Let's get the fuck out of here."

He grits his teeth, tilts his head to look at me. A fresh wave of guilt washes over me, raises the hairs on my arms, but there'll be plenty of time to say I'm sorry when we're on the road. "Leave? Why?" Scars from yesterday's screams roughen his throat.

"We don't need to be here." That's a lie. "They don't need us." And another. I reach for his hand. "Please. I can't watch this happen again." I'm not sure if *this* is him or the Corp, but both are true.

"I like it here."

My pulse thuds at my temples. He's not himself, I shouldn't expect him to be. Eight years since I properly tracked—not counting the radio—and I still want to, still miss it, still need to resist the siren call. "Please," I say again. "Come on."

I'm watching him so closely. The soft laugh doesn't come from his lips. I know this laugh, too, exactly as well as I know my own. Omega steps out from behind the curtain drawn along one side of the empty bed.

"He can't go with you, Al."

Heat crackles over my skin. My scalp, palms, the soles of my feet. He's my brother; there's no reason to be afraid except the look in his eyes is giving me one, piercing, pinning me to the spot.

Where is Isis?

"What the hell?" I ask, voice steady. Good. "Omega, this isn't funny."

He laughs again. "No, dearest sister, this is not funny."

Footsteps sound out in the hall. Isis, thank fuck. "Come on, Jonas." I take his arm and he wrenches it from me as if my fingers shocked him. Omega comes another foot toward us.

"He can't go with you, Al, because he's coming to headquarters with me. Don't make me do anything I'd regret. I understand a little more about loyalty than you do." Sleek steel catches the light. A gun.

"Loyalty? To who?"

A smile. All teeth. "To the Corp, of course. Right, Jonas?"

"Right."

No. I back away, far as I can from both of them in the small room. I don't understand.

The door opens. And then I do understand.

"Alpha, so good to see you again," Wraith says. "Now you learn another little piece of the puzzle. It should have worked on you the way it worked on your brother. The way the new version is working on everyone else right now. Oh, well. You won't be able to hold out forever. Let's go, boys."

19

Pain shoots up my legs, twists my stomach, drives straight into my heart. Cool fingers wrap around my arms and I'm hauled to my feet, to the bed where the sheets smell like Jonas. A beam of light pierces my eyes and scatters a million stars across my brain.

Somehow I tell Isis we need to get to the CRC and suddenly we're there, the trip a blur. I always thought that phrase—the room spinning—was just something people said, but nothing will stay still.

They're probably at headquarters now. Jonas. Omega. *Him.* A ghost with yellow hair and eyes and fingernails.

I didn't have to see Ant's face when Isis told him about Wraith, I was too busy worrying about Jonas. Omega, though, is a heavier blow, one that seems to make Ant's lights dim in the CRC's reverent stillness. "He pointed a gun at me," I say, unable to catch my breath. Isis's arm wraps around my waist, ready to hold me up if my muscles fail me like everything else has.

"This is crazy." Haven puts her head in her hands. "Omega." But it's not a question, the truth a perfect note you know when you hear it, singing through the air.

The room spins a little faster. "He said it was supposed to be both of us. Me and Omega."

Ant's glowing lines glitch and reform, Haven's chrome

eyebrows knit in shock, confusion. The ability to brainwash all of us, that's what they'd finally figured out. And when there was even the slightest chance they'd lose, Ell took me and Omega and made us track.

Click, click, click. Wild, untethered thoughts finally slide into place. "It was supposed to work on both of us. The flashbacks," I blamed them getting worse on being back here, the cravings harder to fight in the face of immediate temptation.

"She, what, programmed you with some kind of countdown?"

"Waiting for you to die," I say, staring right at Ant.

"But I didn't, and Omega was *happy* about"—trails of light streak behind his hands as he gestures to himself—"this."

Because this way, Ant is a surprise security blanket Wraith is only too happy to have. Theoretically, Haven could shut down the entire mainframe by unplugging the viewers downstairs, disconnecting her mother and the Board from the system and plunging the Web into darkness and chaos.

In front of me is the moving, speaking, glowing reason why she never will.

"Say that's what happened," Haven begins, glancing between Isis and me. "Why didn't it work on Al? Why isn't she—"

"They're twins, not clones," Isis answers.

"Doing it to both of us just upped the odds that it'd work on one." My voice is more confident than I feel. *Like it's working on everyone else right now.*

The tracks people have been using pretty much since I got here, maybe earlier, are what I've been looking for this whole time, or at least a close version of it. I only ever had to look up the latest console station hit.

I could snap anytime, if it's like that. I don't know. Maybe Omega's mind slowly bent until it inevitably broke him in two. Or it *was* quick, a switch flicked. Either way, no one knew. I was the only one who could've, maybe, if we'd stayed as close as we once were and I was here to see it happen. And maybe I was too busy trying to stop it from happening to me to see anything else.

"I need air," I say. A lot more than that, but I'll settle for breathing, and I don't go far. The streets around the CRC are dark, breezy with expectation. I imagine I can feel it, whatever Ell put in my head, like a loose tooth.

Just ready to snap free.

Around me, the Web seethes with life, different than just a few days, a week ago. More faces—almost all the ones I see—show the signs. It's impossible to tell how many have gone back to the tracks of their own volition, or at least to beat the Corp to the punch, and how many are victims of the radio waves and whatever other secretive means Wraith has used.

My brother has used.

Jumbled, jarring, my thoughts cycle around. Repeat, repeat, repeat again. Haven left the coda symbol on Anthem's hand, but I have nothing. No symbols, no ideas. And even if I did, I don't know what I'd do with them.

The Corp never kills you if it can break you.

Jonas.

I kick the curb, the steel toes sending chunks of concrete spraying. Blaming someone else—Omega, Wraith, anyone— would be so easy. Nobody knows my twin like I do, or did, and I try to look back through the fog of grief and sadness and anger I've lived in since that last night on the beach, figure out when his plans changed.

The subtle questions about my flashbacks that I passed off as trying to unravel his own. His willingness to keep Jonas amused while I mourned Ant, fought with Haven, began to put

179

together the clues of the Corp's return.

I'm amazed he managed not to laugh where I could see.

Turning away from the lights, the Vortex, the Corp, I slip back through the doors of the CRC, up the stairs, into darkness much deeper than I'm expecting. A lamp on Haven's table of computers is the only illumination. Haven's watching for me, for my surprise at the empty viewer.

"You didn't—"

She has to squint at my lips, but she gets it. "No. He's still in there, just switched off."

If that means he doesn't have to think, feel anything, sign me up. "You can do that?"

In answer, she slides, cross-legged, to the floor and pats the space beside her. "It's been a long time since we talked, just us."

"And this is the time?" I ask, but I join her, our knees touching. We've had so many nights like this, my mother-sister-friend and I, my ally against growing up around so many guys. She was always the one I went to, needed, cried for.

"Where's Isis?" It's the simplest question.

"Went to tell Pixel everything."

Ah.

"He's not going to want to fight again." The revelations surrounding Scope's death alone will break him. Isis gave him as many minutes of ignorance as she could, which maybe is what love is. I don't know. For a while I thought I did with Jonas.

"None of us do."

There's a Sky-Club a few blocks from here; I bet there isn't a place in the city that plays unencoded music now. Surrender is minutes away, less than the length of a song onstage in Los Angeles. Haven's eyes narrow, darken to black, and her lips thin as she looks over my shoulder.

"You don't understand." A lump swells in my throat and her eyes snap back to me. "You don't understand," I repeat. "That's my brother. My fucking twin, Haven, working for everything I hate. Everything *you* fought against, and he took Jonas from me to help him."

"I don't understand?" Her tone is mild, but something steely and cold runs through it. "*I* don't? Remember what's downstairs?"

My face flushes with shame, because what's one more emotion in the mix. I'm not sure if I'm relieved that I can still feel or am disappointed that the numbness of earlier wasn't permanent.

"Right," she says, reading my expression like it's one of those ancient books she loves. "I know a little something about it."

"Sorry."

She touches my face, a single light fingertip enough to break the dam holding back my tears, hot and stinging. "Don't apologize, Al. I don't know what to do, either. Last time . . ." Swallowing, she looks over at the empty viewer, as if expecting to see Ant there. "He knew what to do, I just helped."

"You did more than that."

"Maybe, but we were young then. I was," she says, and I can't pretend I didn't have that exact thought before. "You can imagine how he feels now."

Defeated. Worse than defeated—like he never won in the first place. Her emotions have always been his, the reverse even more true. I open my mouth to argue, close it again.

"I'll tell you what I told him," she continues. "It's not Omega, Al. It's his body, his voice, but it's not him. I know a little something about that, too." Her fingernails tap once against the hard floor and a different kind of barricade collapses inside me, anger rushing forth.

"He should've fought harder," I hiss. "I did! Every day. I feel it there and I force it back and I left all of you to get away from it. Why didn't he?"

Haven speechless is a rare event, but even with rage boiling through me, there's no satisfaction in it. I want her to have the answers, say everything's going to be okay.

"I'm not you," I tell her. "Fuck knows I've always wanted to be, but I'm not. I can't fight my own family."

"Not even to save him, if you could?"

"If I can. Sure." My voice turns as steely as the gun under the bright hospital lights. The weight of the last weeks saturates the air, pressing down on my shoulders. Too much has happened already and I am not the person she seems to want me to be. I'm the one who runs away. "No." I don't think I've ever been so tired. "No. I give up. Let the Corp come back."

■

This is the Web of my childhood.

The neon seems brighter, blinding, and it absorbs the flashing lights of patrol pods as they speed up and down the Web. Guards call me *Citizen* and my steps quicken, eyes on the ground so they don't see, can't tell.

It's only a matter of time before all the old laws are enforced. Right now, Wraith and Omega and Jonas are too busy, enjoying themselves, laughing at us from their perch at the top of the spider, view stretching far beyond the Web now, all the way to the opposite coast.

Phoenix tabs me every hour, answering the messages I send except when I ask about Wraith. Pixel won't talk about it.

Haven hasn't switched Anthem back on. Her fingers poise above the keys, curl in on themselves, drop to her sides.

Love.

If the Web without the Corp was a slow, easy song, it thrums now like it used to, fast and brutal. Everyone knows their place—except maybe me, I don't know where I am at all. Time and space and the people who anchor me have spun loose. Around me, buildings seem taller again, viewed through my nine-year-old eyes.

Getting worse here._

Phoenix's tab blinks on my screen and I toss the whole thing away, letting it slide across the floor to hit a stack of lockers. Nothing I can do about it. Don't care.

I hear someone walking around out beyond the stacks, probably Haven, maybe Pixel or Isis. Whoever it is ignores me and I return the favor. I'm not afraid. Omega is leaving us alone and I can't figure out which hurts more: that we're not a threat, or that he doesn't care.

My tablet blinks again. Scowling, I crawl over to it, and my finger catches on a crack. Oops.

Resistance is growing, but it's not gonna work. They know too much about this place._

Because Jonas is helping, and the streets of Los Angeles run through him like veins. Weak spots and strong points and strategy, all there for Wraith and Omega to use, to learn how best to direct their growing armies.

And his parents thought I'd be the one to corrupt their precious son. I laugh, but it makes no sound in the quiet Center.

Wraith's had eight years to set this up—longer, maybe. The brainwashed drones on TV carry guns, and I don't mean the newscasters who read to us, smiles frozen, fingers twitching for their next fix.

Soldiers. Guards, their boots kicking up sand on my beach.

Stay safe._ Same thing I told Sabine an hour ago.

Do our best._

Phoenix and Mage are not tracking again yet, but who knows how long that'll last, by choice or duress. When they designed their club like a fortress of glass and steel and mirrors, I don't think they ever thought it would actually be one someday. The locked doors are cosmetic resistance. The guards will come for them.

Soon enough, they'll come for us all. Here, too, Haven's reprogrammed the scanner to only recognize a few chips, but I think that was only to give herself something to do.

"Alpha?"

My name echoes, bouncing off the lockers and floor, distorting the voice it takes me a second to place. "Over here," I call back, waiting for Spectrum to find me.

"Your brother's an asshole."

I cringe. He's not wrong, but it's pretty clear which one he's talking about, and there was a time when no one got to insult Omega but me. Now I guess anyone who can still think for themselves is entitled to hate him. I can just claim the title of the one who despises him most. Jonas's face flits in front of my eyes, replacing Spectrum's until I concentrate and it dissolves.

"Oh?" Nothing I can do. Don't care.

Maybe there's a track that'll make me give a fuck. All my clothes are packed into the pod down on the street. So easy to get ready, find Jonas, drag him to a club, dance with him. Belong.

"Tell him to lay off everyone in Two."

"I can't tell him anything," I snap. That alone takes all my energy. "What's he doing?" I don't really want to know.

"Three Exaurs already this week, for nothing, for stupid shit. If you ask me, your brother's trying to forget where he came from."

The Corp never kills you if it can break you.

"How long you figure the brainwashing lasts? You think it just takes one track and that's it, forever?" I ask Spectrum. He shrugs. My flashbacks have persisted for years. Wraith's had a while to perfect it even more.

Hiding. Plotting. Pulling strings.

"Where's Lynx?"

Spectrum's mouth twists. "At the bar in a truly pissy mood. Withdrawal doesn't look good on him. But . . ."

But it's not safe anymore, no way to know what they're listening to until it's too late. Even with their resources and black market consoles, I wouldn't trust it and neither are they.

"Sorry."

He sits beside me and takes my hand. "Not your fault, you know that, right?"

"Sure," I say, staring up at the rows and rows of empty lockers. I haven't been to visit my parents since this whole thing started and now I won't because I can't tell them what Omega is, the things he's doing.

"You couldn't have stopped this. You can't stop it." Irritation flares. I want to ask him if he remembers who my other brother is, remind him that I am the successor to the gang of revolutionaries who saved this island the first time.

Except they didn't save it, and even if they had, that was them, and I'm me.

"You need some fresh air," Spectrum decides. I give him a dirty look that he pointedly ignores as he stands and hauls me to my feet.

"I don't want to go outside."

"You're going to stay shut up in here forever? Let people bring you food and water until you decide even that isn't worth the trouble anymore? You used to be fun."

My eyes widen so far I think they'll fall out. "Excuse me?"

"This is what it is," he says, dragging me down the stairs and out into painful sunlight. "If you meant what you said to Haven, then the Corp is back. Might as well get on with your life, right?"

What the fuck life is he talking about?

He reads the question on my face, slips on a pair of sunglasses, smiles. "Tell me why you think what's happening is wrong."

I think he's actively trying to make me hit him. I grit my teeth and resist. "You don't? People shouldn't have choices?" Everything Ant fought for, washed away into the rivers.

"You're not making any. You're hiding. Omega's not going to hurt you, you're too valuable alive, so why?"

We get sucked into the spin of the Vortex, crowded with people whose dull skin fades to nothing against the bright paint encircling their eyes and lips. All walking in different directions, toward home or the Corp or a depot for food. I almost don't notice, and once I do, it's impossible not to fall into step with them.

All walking in unison. Unthinking. Robotic. Beside me, Spectrum matches my pace. Guards with guns stand outside their pods, watching, gazes sliding over us, nothing to see here. We cross to the other side, into the quieter streets of Three, closer to the water beyond.

"Why did you do that?"

Spectrum squeezes my fingers, features impassive, masked by his makeup. "Thought you could use a change of scenery."

"Thanks so much."

Across the road, a family struggles with heavy bags. Little

children, no taller than my hip, walk in such perfect time with their parents I could set music to the rhythm of their tiny boots on the sidewalk.

I look away.

Not my problem. Don't care.

20

My guitar is still in the packed pod, buried in its hard case under clothes and blankets.

We were so close to escaping. Now, I'm afraid to open the door, the case. Music scares me.

The Corp never kills you . . .

Turns out they didn't need to finish the process of brainwashing me to take away who I am. There hasn't been a real *me* in so long it might as well be forever.

The first of the big fall storms crashes down onto the Web in the middle of the night, lashing skyscrapers and ruins with rain stained blue, red, green, yellow in the seconds before it hits the ground. All day it hammers around the CRC and in these windowless rooms I can't see it. But I can hear it, a rush of white noise, scrubbing my mind clean of those tiny, marching feet.

I wish.

I break into a cold sweat for the thousandth time. That can't have been Omega's idea, or Jonas's. They would never. I picture Wraith, yellow-streaked and evil, behind a desk at the Corp, mind whirring with how he can outdo even the ones who set him up to take over.

We're trapped in a holding pattern. When we eventually give in, they won't even have to move us. Just take our chips out and plug them into viewers right here. For Haven, there is no other kind of surrender. I'm a different story. Console stations and Sky-Clubs blink on the map in my head, like the ones the Corp had here, L.A., Seattle.

Here there is weakness.

Isis takes her turn to bring us dinner, food I don't eat, though the scent wafts tantalizingly at me from across the table. Her eyes narrow, search my face. Again. Like she has every time she's seen me for days.

"How is he?" Haven asks.

Isis takes longer than she needs to finish her mouthful. "One day at a time."

Phoenix still won't talk to me about Wraith. Mage ignores my tabs completely. Fable keeps working on them for me, but can't get anything out of them, either.

In a way, it doesn't matter; I can guess what's going on. But I want to hear it from them, have something to give Haven and Isis and Pixel. Ant, too, if we ever switch him back on.

My shoulders jerk, Isis and Haven look at me.

"Nothing," I mutter. But their gazes don't leave me for more than a second or two while they eat and I feel my skin shrinking against my bones, tight and constricting and wrong.

Something has to break soon; hairline fractures crawl and spread across my mind. I want my brothers back, both of them. I want my ocean, and Phoenix and Mage, and Jonas, and Sabine telling bad jokes, and Fable, my oldest friend, with his unfailing loyalty and permanent smile.

A flashback presses in, a band wrapped too tightly around my skull. *The room is dark but all I can see is white, teeth, the music rising and falling in my ears. My muscles spasm and jump, wanting to dance even though I'm held down and I can't move. The Corp is eternal, eternal, eternal. . . . Yes, I will always fight for it, for this. Yes, I will make sure it lives on forever if it means I can have this all the time. Thrashing guitars and a rhythm like the only heart-beat that's ever mattered. Perfection, beauty, sound, light that flashes across my brain in a thousand colors, shades I didn't even know existed. Drums kick in and different hands grab hold of me, strong, wiry like the strings on Anthem's guitar that he won't let me touch. I sneaked into his room to look, don't tell him. And then the music is gone and he's there and I want to scream, but no sound comes out of my mouth. Give it back, give it back. I hate him. He took it away. I'll get it back, even if I have to wait until he's gone and can't stop me anymore. Even if I have to kill him myself.*

My screams ricochet around the CRC, filling the empty lockers that will hold fractions of terror forever now.

"She's back," Isis says. "Get her some water. Shit. Alpha? Al?"

"I'm okay."

"Was that a bad one? We need to make this stop."

Trust her to think like that, but it's too late now. Wraith has my cure, if he was telling the truth about that. A cure in exchange for my complicity.

He has my complicity, though. I'm doing nothing to stop him. So why not make him live up to his end of the deal?

"No worse than usual," I lie. *Even if I have to kill him myself.*

I drain the bottle Haven gives me. Somehow I ended up on the floor and my bones feel brittle, ready to splinter as I pull myself back up to my chair. They stop talking, leave me to catch my breath, or so I think. The silence, humid and tense from the storm, stretches out. Nobody knows what to say.

"I have to get back to him. You need to tell me if you start to feel anything . . . weird," Isis says eventually. Because what just happened isn't weird enough, no matter how used to it I am.

"Yeah. Sure. No problem. Are you crazy?" Angry tears always

sting more than sad ones. "You think it'll be that easy? You think Omega knew what was happening to him and just didn't tell anyone? Didn't tell *me*?"

Spots dance on my eyes and by the time I've blinked them away, she's gone.

"*Are* you okay?"

"Don't you start," I say, glaring at Haven. "I'm going for a walk."

"In this?" The rain isn't her problem, but she's not going to stop me and I can't explain my need to be out in it, to be flayed by the needles that soak me through by the time I get to the park. Maybe it's the only thing connecting me to my ocean, each drop sent to me from the beach, remembering that I would edge my toes up to it but never let it touch me.

There is no distance in the Web, no escape. You just have to stand still and let the noise, the light, the suffocating claustrophobia of it all slam into you, hope you're left standing at the end.

Lightning crashes, blinding white. I walk faster, deeper into the cacophony of rain bouncing off the leaves and grass and path in front of me. Steel flashes on my toes.

I dare you. But the lightning stays just far enough away for me to be safe. It's so loud I can't think. And this, this is what I wanted, to be surrounded by the rush and roar, finally something loud enough to drown out my thoughts. I wasn't sure until now that it was possible and when it comes it's the most beautiful kind of bliss, a kiss that steals your breath, a thrill of speed, the flood of adrenaline when a crowd calls your name.

The seed of an idea digs into the blankness and I try to pull it up by its long, curling roots, toss it away like I do the flashbacks.

But it takes hold. Rain bursts on my scalp, runs down the length of each strand. Noise, just noise. This is what OD meds are like, or so I've heard.

Louder. Turn it up.

The clouds crack down the middle, open for me into torrents that aren't individual drops anymore, just floods, walls of water enclosing me in a room of liquid glass, all my thoughts and grief locked outside.

I turn, break the spell. Fuck, I'm drenched. My feet squelch in my boots with each step back toward the CRC, cold and disgusting and I don't care right now. I have the streets pretty much to myself save for a few patrol pods whose occupants care more about the weather than a sole citizen running through it. I open the door on the second floor, expecting both Ant and Haven to see me, or at least for Anthem to hear me, but they don't.

"You can't ask me to do that!" Haven shouts. Haven never shouts. Long ago she learned to modulate her voice, to keep it at a normal volume all the time, and shouting is only satisfying when you can hear yourself. I step back out to the stairs, hold the door open an inch.

"I didn't ask you to do *this*. And I put on a brave face and I help and I love you like I always did, but when this is over I want to go, Haven. They wanted me to watch, I've watched. Take a good look at how Al's taking all of this—"

I step back. Shit. He's not wrong, I just thought I was hiding it better.

"I'm done, all right? I'm glad I could do . . . whatever I've done to help here. Still feels like nothing, but whatever, I'm finished, Haven. I don't even want to be in a normal CRC. Take my chip and throw it into the river, wipe every trace of me from the system. Let me go."

I move back, press my ear to the door.

". . . What I thought was right," she's saying.

"I know that, but I'm tired. I'm ready. Please."

"You make me sound like some pathetic girl who couldn't let you go."

Ant laughs. "*Pathetic* is the last word I'd use to describe you, the last word anyone would. I know why you did it. You proved you could, and maybe you guessed what was coming. But whatever happens, I'm done. I can't help anymore."

She's quiet for a long time. "I'm glad I met Scope, let him drag me to Pixel's club that night."

I lean against the wall. It feels like longer than ten years ago to me, I can only guess what it's like for them. So much has happened, a lifetime in a decade.

"I was obsessed with you."

"Was?" Haven teases. Anthem laughs, and I think I'm safe. But she can't unplug him now.

"Haven?" I walk in, touch her shoulder. She raises her eyebrows, arcs of silver. Water streams off me, pools around our feet, swirled with blue from my hair.

"We can't get into the tracking database, right?"

"Not anymore." Simmering fury mixes with grudging respect in her eyes. Omega's not stupid; he's taken precautions. She taught him everything he knows and he's almost as good as she is, but that's not the point. Different notes of betrayal, all combined to form an evil song. "Why? What are you thinking?"

I look at her, at Ant. "I'm not sure yet."

■

It takes a day to figure out what we need, another for Lynx and Spectrum to get it for us without arousing suspicion. Carefully out of sight, I tab Phoenix, Sabine, Fable.

`Can you get out?_`

My tablet beams a rainbow, different colors for each of them.

Yes._

Maybe._

Why?_

Meet us at Central_ is all I say. Sabine and Fable just got back; I'd feel bad if she didn't love to drive so much. It'll take them longer to get there, sometime between now and then I'll warn the others. Or not. It sounds harsh to think they have to just get over it, but I have no other solutions. I can't even begin to do this without any of them. I'm not even sure I can do it with them, but I have to try.

When we switch Ant back on—if it works—I'll have to ask him if this is how it felt, that moment in the basement, when he realized he had to fight back and that he had the tools to do it. Of course, it was a little different then.

He wasn't fighting his brother. His twin. I let myself have a second, just one, a heartbeat, a drumbeat, eyes closed. Okay.

It's not him in there.

Now I'm counting on the hope that it is. If it's him inside his head, trapped, maybe I can get him out again. Save us all.

We cram more food, more supplies into the already cramped pod, tucked behind the CRC, away from the gazes of any passing guards. Not that they're paying any attention to us. This is part of Omega's punishment for us; we're not worthy of attention. Beneath his notice.

"We ready?" Lynx asks, handing me a black box, dull black and heavier than it looks, wires streaming from one end. Hopefully Haven knows what it's for.

"I think so."

"Adventure." Spectrum grins, slightly, and I can't remember

the last time I saw any of us smile. "This'll be fun."

"The two of you deserve each other," I say. None of this is *fun*. But they're so perfectly in tune, I actually mean it.

"Seriously." His voice softens. "Do you know what you're doing?"

"Not even a little bit." But Spectrum was right. I can do something, or I can do nothing, and the faintest strains of a plan have been running through my mind since the storm, strengthening the more I think about it, like a fragment of music I dream and then compose around, note by note until it's coherent, melodic.

Haven is worried, Isis doubtful, Pixel indifferent. That's why I need the others. Phoenix with her fire, her fight, and Mage because he never lets frustration get in the way of what he's trying to do. Fable to keep time. Sabine with her bass and her brain that isn't like any of ours.

I look back down at the box and tuck it into the pod between crates of water. I don't have a fucking clue what I'm doing when we get out of here, and I have even less of one about what I'm going to do now.

"Tell Haven I'll be back in an hour." The sky is nearly dark. I won't be long and this is stupid, stupid, but I can't stop myself or make my feet move in any direction but toward the spider.

Headquarters.

Marble catches every footstep and cough; the receptionist's fingers click over keys. I'm watching for it now, can see that each motion is just a little off, too calculated, too stilted and stiff. I want to scream at them, wake them up, snap them from the haze they're drowning in thanks to the tracks, but it's going to take a lot more than my voice.

If it's possible at all.

I straighten, smile brightly at a guard whose dilated pupils contract slightly, his thumb brushing over the sleek edge of the gun on his belt. Into the elevator, up. Try not to think of what happened last time.

Try not to think of what might happen this time.

At least I guess right. Wraith has the mayor's old office. No doubt he'll take on some ridiculous title soon. For now, everyone is too high and dazed to care or know the difference. The door is closed, locked, and I have no interest in testing the scanner to see if it'll let me in. Along the corridor, the next one is open and I force myself not to turn, run away. I came this far. I have to do it.

"Alpha."

"Hi." I don't use his name. It's not really him in there. If he notices, he ignores it, gazes out the windows over the Web instead. My heart thumps harder in my chest. When we were younger and Ant gave us music lessons, Omega was always the one to give up first, frustrated, not good enough in his own eyes, not interested enough in Ant's.

Pride straightens his shoulders and it's a look I've never seen on him.

"You haven't started tracking again yet," Omega says.

"No."

"Do you plan to?"

I look away.

"Fine." He waves a hand. "You'll cave eventually. Isn't it great? Back the way things used to be, and the other cities are falling in line. The Corp is back, really back," he says like he can't quite believe it. I can't believe this is the brother I've known and loved all my life.

"I need to know how," I whisper. "I need to know why. From you." Guesses, conjecture, the evidence Ant finds aren't enough. I need my traitorous twin to tell me.

It's not really him in there. Echo, echo. I will the voice away.

197

It's too late for that to matter.

"You know most of it already. You were the one who started to put it together, remember? Gotta admit, that was a little surprising, we were expecting to have some more time. Especially once Haven did what she did. We thought you'd all be too busy with Anthem to worry about anything else. And I was right, just not right enough. And then you had to go and get those two freaks involved and we knew our time was running out."

"What did they ever do to you?"

Omega scowls. "They caught Wraith and me coming out of headquarters in the middle of the night. They didn't know who he was, but I was worried they'd ask around, find out. So I told them to forget they saw us, or I'd remember to tell Lock about all the illegal shit they get up to. Pretty sure they just thought we were stealing something, but I didn't want to take the chance."

Well, that explains why the sight of Lynx and Spectrum made him so mad, why he tried to hide it and wouldn't tell me what they'd done.

"I wasn't the one who put the radio on that day." There's no one point I can think of and say *there, there* is where it started, but if I had to, it would be then. Omega's lips twist into a grimace, a faint hint of the funny faces he used to pull to make me laugh.

"No, no you weren't. We have Jonas to thank for that, but he didn't know. Just an accident. Anyway, he's more than made up for it. Thanks for him. He's been a big help."

It takes all the strength I have not to lunge across the room, tear Omega's throat out with my bare hands, brother or not. "What did I ever do to you?" I hiss, the last trace of sadness burning away. Mourning who Omega used to be is a fucking waste of time. This is who he is, and even if I meant what I said to Haven about giving up, letting the Corp come back, I won't forgive

Omega for what he's done already.

Jonas is somewhere in this building, but he's lost to me. Stolen from me.

"Done to me?" My twin shakes his head. "Nothing, Alpha. But the Corp is eternal, and you didn't join me. What was I supposed to do?"

There's no answer to that.

"Leave us alone," I say, my voice fiercer than I intend or know I'm capable of. "The Corp's hurt us enough. *You've* hurt us enough, Omega." They're the same thing now.

He turns to face me fully and my brother—really him—flashes behind his eyes. "Get out," he says, flat, toneless, impossible to decipher as threat or warning, but the connection is momentarily so strong it knocks the breath from my chest. He can read my mind again. "You can't beat us. Go. If you leave now, we'll leave you alone."

21

I gape at Haven. "What do you mean, you're not coming?"

I knew she was worried about moving Ant, but she said she could, and I believed her. The CRC is quiet around us, everyone fading into shadows.

"Someone has to be here," she says, eyes flicking down to the floor and back up to me, my lips. "I don't trust Omega and Wraith with . . . them."

Fear bubbles. I can't do this without her. Without him. "And you're the best person for that? You're going to hear them coming?" Someone inhales sharply—Isis, I think. Haven jerks as if I've slapped her, and I have, close enough. The floor is too solid to open up and swallow me whole. "I'm sorry. I didn't mean that."

"Yeah, you did." She shrugs, blinking furiously. "And you should. Not like it's not true."

"So what if they do come?"

"They don't want us, Al," Pixel says, stepping forward. "An Exaur, an old addict, a med-tech. We're not stopping them, and they know it. Even if they didn't, the Corp is too arrogant to be worried."

"You're staying, too." It's not a question. I can see the decision in his eyes and wonder how much of it is because he doesn't want to face Mage and Phoenix. How much of Haven's decision is because of that.

"You have everything you need," Isis says. "You're the one who has to go somewhere safe. You have help and we're only an untraceable tab away. We'll see you when it's over."

I look between the three of them, my fingers curling, opening, curling, opening. I hate that I can see Haven's point. I hate that I've known since the beginning that this is the way it would be.

We're the young ones now.

But when I first thought that, I thought I had Omega on my side.

■

It's weird, watching Lynx and Spectrum's reactions. The last time I left the Web—which was also the first time I left the Web—I was too busy with my own. The realization of everything and everyone I was leaving behind, the sheer wonder at what was around us and up ahead. Long stretches of nothingness, of barren sky-lines, but it didn't feel empty. It felt ready to be filled.

Now I keep my eyes on Lynx, on Spectrum's hands on the steering wheel, their ties to the Web stretching out behind the pod. Thinner and thinner, preparing to snap. They grin at each other but their smiles have an edge of apprehension because they're not as glad to leave it all behind. They found perfectly shaped niches in the postrevolution Web, made a home for themselves. If I wasn't doing this, they'd manage, adapt.

I have no idea what that word *home* even means anymore. It's easier to watch them than think of what I've left on the island.

The drive to Central feels like it takes less time than the same stretch did on my way here with Fable and Sabine and Jonas. I can't believe that was only weeks ago, not years. I'm actually surprised that it's not ravaged by neglect and disuse, or polished to newness by the people who live here. It is exactly the same.

Just quieter.

Our wheels spray jagged pebbles as we stop in the empty lot. The silence from the wasteland in all directions creeps in, muffling our noise. "Wait here," Spectrum says, jumping out. Black metal gleams dully in his hand. Lynx and I trade looks as Spectrum walks slowly away, inspecting the cluster of buildings.

"Gone," Spectrum says when he comes back. "No one here. We should park behind there"—he points at the box farthest from the road—"just in case."

I'm hoping the Corp still think they've broken me, that I won't want to fight them, or dare to. That Omega meant what he said.

I close my eyes, remind myself that Omega and Jonas have been taken over, assimilated, usurped, their bodies turned to shells to march for the Corp. It's not *them* in their heads, not the people I love. Not my brother and my boyfriend.

"Hey." Spectrum touches my arm. "You okay?"

"Yeah."

We set up camp in a completely empty building, just walls and a floor, but there's power. Faster than I would've thought possible, Lynx has a bank of computers and the other equipment we need set up, assembled from components they and Haven collected.

It won't take long for us to be found if Omega changes his mind, but that's not why I keep checking the time on my tablet. I leave Spectrum crouched on the floor amidst a snarl of wires.

I'm not the Corp. I never will be, no matter what they tried to do to me. Imaginary sparks deep in my brain tickle at me. *We're here, we could blow up anytime, we're just waiting.*

No.

I look east. I can't see even the faintest outline, no matter how hard I squint, but that means nothing. I'm living proof that it's not possible to run far enough. There is no escape, so there can only be defeat. The loser remains to be seen.

When I go back in, Lynx is nearly done. Spectrum's moved furniture in, hard plastic chairs and one torn, ragged sofa. Food is stacked on a table, and the room has taken on a strangely homelike atmosphere. My guitar leans against one wall, a clean console next to it.

A screen flashes. "What's first?" Lynx asks.

Everyone looks at me. I wish I had my rainbow hair back. The blue is such a lie. I can't do what Anthem did.

And I can't do what Omega can do. One day, when this is all over, however it ends, I'll ask Haven what she would've done differently if she'd known what Omega would do. And I have to believe that Omega didn't know. That the slow encroaching on his mind was a surprise, or that he never knew it was happening. A quiet, silent surrender. I have to believe he hasn't been gathering information, learning Haven's tricks and secrets all this time.

I think of my flashbacks, their attempt to overtake me anything but silent. Why didn't he fight harder?

Maybe I've learned a few tricks of my own.

"Okay, move," I say, nudging Lynx out of the chair. He gives me a twisted smile but surrenders the spot, moving to stand beside me. From the corner of my eye I see Spectrum join him, their fingers linking automatically.

I remember Jonas's hand around mine. The strength, the kind that's always a comfort, never a threat.

Out here, the connection is weaker, glitching along lines strung like spider silk from the Web to the opposite coast. "Hey," Spectrum says as I kick one of the computers. "You know that doesn't actually help."

"Makes me feel better." I keep typing, navigating through layers of files like I've watched Ant and Haven do for days.

"You really think you can get in?"

There it is, the tracking database. Haven tried. Anthem tried. But Omega's not their twin.

"Yes."

Our birthday doesn't work. It's not the day our memory chips were implanted or our first day of school or the day either of our parents died.

It's not the white room.

"Damn it," I mutter. The screen flashes red and resets, taunting me. I know him. I know him better than anyone else.

"Maybe Wraith set it up," Lynx suggests. "We can try to get in another way."

I shake my head. Think. A hot, sick feeling curls around my heart as I try again. My breath catches and I hold it there, the password accepted, lines of code unfolding in front of me.

"What was that?"

Lynx shakes purple spikes at Spectrum. "The day Alpha left for L.A."

"Dude. That's cold."

Goose bumps break out over my skin. "Lynx, I need you to find whatever you can on the origins of the Web. How things got started. The first doctors, what they knew. Not just the crap we learned at school."

"Yo."

The Corp has habits like any other living, breathing creature, its own evils and secrets, pleasures and favorite ways of inflicting pain.

We're all too familiar with the latter, but I need to know everything.

The sky darkens. I check my tablet every five minutes for messages and time. Ears strained, I listen for approaching wheels from either direction, but we're too far back from what passes for a road to hear anything. I tap beats on my knees and pace.

The door opens to Sabine's outline illuminated by a fog light. I'm on my feet and across the room, hugging her so hard she can't breathe and has to gasp a hello. Another pair of arms wrap around my back. Fable. Tears soak into Sabine's shoulder.

I know what's coming as soon as we break apart. I can't say hello to Mage and Phoenix, not properly.

"Tell me why," I say to Phoenix. I need to hear it if I ever want to look at Ant or Pixel or any of them again, and I need to believe that I will, that those hurried good-byes in the CRC weren't our last. They need to know the first thing I did was ask.

"Because we couldn't find Wraith, and everyone had to move on," Phoenix answers. I've never heard her voice so quiet, weakened. Etched deep around her eyes are the marks this secret has cost them all these years. "They never would have let it go, and we were all sick, tired, hurt. You and Omega were little. Ant was half dead, and when he recovered he had to look after you, not go running after some guy who could've just gone somewhere else to die, for all we knew."

"And if he was alive, that fuckhead had credits, all the access he needed, probably hiding places already set up. Look at what's happening now and tell me you don't think he was prepared for all that to go down, just in case."

"Was that why you left?" I ask.

Phoenix nods. In the brightness flooding from the fog light, her hair is as alive as my bonfires. "It got harder to look at everyone, keeping the secret, you know?"

I know a little something about that.

"We're sorry, kiddo," Mage says. "Really damn sorry. If we'd known . . ."

Nobody did, nobody could've predicted this. "Okay." I sigh. "Okay. Let's get to work."

■

They brought everything I asked—I'm surprised there was room in the pod for the two of them, let alone Fable and Sabine. Fuck, am I glad to see my friends. Mage and Phoenix are speaking in low voices somewhere out beyond the spread of light. I slam the door of the pod, hidden with ours behind the main building, and lean against it.

So much history. History and time and secrets. More than can be crammed into eight years, and somehow not enough to tell the full story. We need more, the whole thing falling in lines of code down a dozen monitors.

"What are we doing?" Sabine gazes around the landscape blip that is Central. "Is it safe here?"

"Not even kind of." But I have no other ideas. "Hopefully we won't be here long. What's it like . . . back there?"

She grimaces. "Those . . . what do you call them? Console stations, everywhere. They were taking over the clubs when we got out, pretty sure ours was next. I've never seen anything like it."

No. She's only ever known peace and warmth in Los Angeles, and now uniformed guards walk her ocean-scented streets with guns and headphones on their ears.

I don't really want to stop working, but we won't help anybody if we're half dead from exhaustion. The food Sabine and I make is decent and I nearly fall asleep in my plate. The sheets are scratchy, blankets too thin, and I've never been so comfortable or glad to close my eyes.

Surrender is so easy, tempting.

The sun rises and so do the others. They stumble from beds to splash water on their faces before we all meet in our weird little command center. I turn a mug of peppermint tea in my hands— Phoenix is already forgiven, as far as I'm concerned—and try not to shrink under the weight of all the eyes watching me.

"Okay." I turn the mug again. The story has become easier to tell, sure, but strangely I think it might be easier this time if there wasn't one person in the room who already knows it. I can't skim or cheat the details, or Fable will call me out again like he did the day I told Jonas.

Jonas.

Focus. Pay attention.

Telling the story isn't a destination for once. Now it's the road that got us here. "Ell came and got me and Omega that day, the last day of the rebellion. She took us to the Corp and made us track. You all know that; you helped rescue us. Some of it was Ant's music that she'd had specially encoded to . . . I can't explain it exactly. To stick in our heads and strengthen over time, making us want to bring the Corp back when the moment was right. What she made me and Fable listen to that day was a version of what Wraith and Omega are using on everyone now," I say.

"Pretty much the last thing Wraith said to me was that it was supposed to work on me like it's working on everybody now. The thing is . . ." Deep breaths. "The thing is, I don't think he knows how close it came." Is still coming. A ticking clock in my head.

"I know he knows about my flashbacks and that I'm looking for a cure for them, because Omega told him. But Omega and I have never been good at really explaining them to each other. It's the one thing we can't really find the words for."

"I hear that," Spectrum says, glancing at Lynx.

"Trips aren't the easiest thing to explain." Mage nods. "Even to someone who gets you."

"Right," I say, as if I have as much experience with it as them. That Omega and I aren't the only ones who struggle—albeit differently—has always been a small, selfish comfort, though, and especially now I'll take the most microscopic ones I can get. "So Wraith hinted that there's a cure hidden in the system, or at least that one could be made, which is what I've always figured." Hoped. Counted on. "I wouldn't listen to anything he gave me, but I've started looking anyway. See what's there."

"And we do what when we find it, or make it?" Sabine asks.

"We'll have to make it. If it works on me, it'll be close enough to work on Omega. Reverse what's happened to him." Fingers crossed. I scan their faces, waiting, delaying.

"And Jonas?" Fable asks. "Or everyone in the cities out west? They don't have chips, it's different for them."

Waiting for that. I look at Sabine, see every heavy syllable of what I haven't said sink into her head, chipless and unsullied. Fable jumps up, eyes pleading anyone to have his back. "No, Al."

"Yes, Al," Sabine says. "What, Fable? I'm here so I *won't* help the only way I can? I've known Jonas longer than any of you; he's mine as much as yours. If I have to listen to this drug shit to do my part, I will. I'm a big girl. Let's do it."

"Thank you," I say, quietly because my emotions are thudding too loud. I was prepared for her to refuse, a little less prepared for her to agree so quickly because it means I have to go through with it, too.

"What about everyone else?" Phoenix asks quietly. "We're not just going to save Omega and Jonas, are we?"

It's a tempting idea. Save them and run, leave the Web to whatever evil Wraith has planned. I might, if there was somewhere I could run to, but he's stolen my sun from me. My ocean.

"These two can help with that," I say, gesturing at Lynx and Spectrum. I know they will. "I've already gotten into the tracking database; everything in there is what Wraith's using on people." Just him. He's the one pulling the strings, twanging them until they screech with the harsh feedback of control. I totally believe Wraith would lie to me, but I'm sure he told me the truth about this. "We'll make an antidote to that, too."

The room is too small now, crowded with people and words. I step outside, gulp fresh air that's warmer now, though not enough to stop my teeth from chattering against the wind. Fable's boots crunch on the gravel. I don't need to look up to know it's him, and he doesn't need to speak for me to hear what he wants to say.

Yes, I know what I'm doing. Or, I know what I have to do. The thing I've always resisted. The chance that we'll get it right the first time is nonexistent, and tracks can fuck up your brain at the best of times. I touch my throat, the healed places where the bruises were.

These definitely aren't the best of times. But I'm ready.

22

There's an old television in the kitchen, tucked away among battered utensils and bags of rice. I can't imagine the boredom here, endless days and nights waiting for someone to come by for an hour, a day at most before continuing on their way.

Maybe they liked it. Maybe the infinite quiet held its own appeal after the relentless noise of the Web, required sound, enforced music.

But everyone has limits, and being completely cut off from the rest of the world is dangerous if nothing else.

I flick channels. Static-fuzzed images of Los Angeles make every muscle in my body weigh twice as much, pulling me into the hard tile floor. There's the street the club's on. I don't call Mage and Phoenix to look. And that's the road we drive down to the beach, now barricaded and guarded, as if any last holdouts are going to swim to freedom.

There's nowhere to go.

I flick again, see more landmarks I know too well, the jagged edges that they cut into the sky as familiar as the lines in my palms. Memories collide in my head with the images in front of me; it's just like it was before. Patrol pods, uniforms, guns. The camera pans across the Vortex, catching a thousand pairs of dead, drugged eyes.

But there's one difference. The sleek, overgroomed newscaster isn't trying to convince us the Corp is our friend, like they did when I was little. No false cheerfulness; he was probably helped along by a hit or two before the cameras rolled.

Friends don't matter anymore. What matters is what there is.

A knock at the door makes me jump; metal bowls clatter to the floor. I relax a little as the ringing fades, but not completely.

"Hey, Bean. Everything okay out there?"

"They're setting up."

Good.

"Want to talk about it?" Sabine asks.

The usual answer to this question is *no*. Sabine sits on the floor near my feet, thin arms and legs folding up, comfortable as she always is.

"I deserved this," I say.

The slap stings my knee. "Don't you dare."

"I ignored him. Hid things from him."

"You had other shit to be worrying about. Jonas chose to go to the Web; we all did, and your brother got him into all this, not you."

"Oh, that's so much better." I can't describe it to anyone, how responsible I am for everything. I should've seen it coming. I should have known something wasn't right with Omega. And I wasn't looking because I didn't want to know, or stay in the Web longer than I had to, or think about anything except myself and my ocean and going back to where I could dig my toes—and my head—into the sand.

She puts her hand on the spot she hit, gently this time, leaves it there. On the screen, someone new is talking about a fresh collection of tracks, just released, stronger than ever. They show a picture of Wraith, the Web's new leader. Sabine gasps. I look away, anywhere, everywhere else, but it doesn't help. The sight of him bothers me less than it should. I know who he is, what he's done and what he's capable of. He won't let anything stop him. Yellow nails glint on his folded hands.

Omega stands behind his left shoulder, Jonas his right. Sharply cut suits line their bones. Jonas's eyes and lips are painted deep red and he's so beautiful I can't breathe, can't think.

"Was it just to hurt you?" Sabine asks softly.

I thought so at first, and fuck did it work. "No," I say, staring at the wall above the TV. "I mean, that was part of it. Omega knew I wasn't going to help, even if I'd just given in and let everything happen . . . as it's happening back there, I guess. And if I wasn't going to help, he needed someone who could tell him things he didn't know. Hurting me was just a bonus."

"What the hell could Jonas tell him?"

My eyes flick back to the screen. "About L.A. Omega's never been. Wraith has, but I don't know how long he was there."

Cherry blossoms sit in a vase in the dressing room. Worse than that. I know he *was* there. Everything about that night is crystal-line, sharply rendered. The tab from Haven, telling me Ant was dying, before that the hours on the beach, before that, the club, and the flashback I had onstage. I've never been able to pin down exactly what triggered them other than exhaustion, but something always does. That night the something was a description come to life. A shade of yellow I'd promised Haven I'd never wear because it made Anthem want to put holes in the nearest wall.

Jonas lived out west all his life, knows the city as well as any-one. He knows how to help them take it from me.

And I'm much less sure I know how to take it back.

We head out, crowd into the building that now looks like the strangest cross between a club, a recording studio, and someone's living room. Instruments, amps, and microphones line the walls. Monitors fill with text. Lynx and Mage type, their fingers a blur.

We're never going to be ready, which I guess means we can start anytime.

■

The Web started with a war. Actually, it started a little after that, a weed growing from a crack in concrete, searching for the sun.

It didn't find any light. But somehow, it flourished in the darkness and despair that covered the island.

People want leaders. I think of how quickly Wraith and Omega took over after assassinating the mayor. It was almost easy. There's a security to having someone make decisions, even if those decisions are cruel, harsh, unforgiving.

After the first war, over a hundred years ago, people wanted leaders then, too. The leaders themselves fought, survival of the fittest, and from there, the Corp was born, a group of power-hungry men and women with a city on their hands to feed and sub-due. It only takes a handful if they are determined, devoted, strong, evil. Whether those come from within, like Wraith, or drugs, like Omega and Jonas, doesn't matter in effect. History repeats itself because the past is familiar, and familiar is comforting.

Is that what Omega wanted? Comfort? For the constant push-pull of the flashbacks to just be still for one minute? Did he have any kind of choice at all?

I have too many questions, and not enough answers. Yet.

We learned about the first war in school. How it was taught changed after Anthem's rebellion, from reverence to warning, but we all know the story. It's the details we weren't given that I need now.

A picture appears on one of the screens. None of us know the man in it. He died long before any of us were born. His white coat hangs limp, creased from thin shoulders, wispy eyebrows are raised, surprised by the camera, above faded eyes and a weak chin.

It would be easy to hate him. Easy, but pointless.

He's where it all started. The first doctor to come up with a track to help his patients. And I do believe he was actually trying to help them, that he didn't know what others would do with the drug he created.

"There's whole studies in here," Phoenix says, awed and afraid in equal measure, like she's looking at instructions for building a bomb—which she is, kind of. "He ran out of medications. No one could make more back then. Half the equipment was destroyed and pretty much everyone who knew how was dead. Making chemical drugs is hard, but the patients responded to . . . ," she trails off.

To music. And so he did what he could to ease the people's suffering from injuries and disease that come when a place tears itself apart from the inside and leaves nothing but a few concrete bones jutting from scorched skin. From there, it all unfolded easily. Experiments, test subjects, instruments and computers melding in perfect harmony.

When Ant beat the Corp the first time, he had the weapon he needed because the Corp had already developed it. Mage stole it, right in front of a Corp tech's face. We have almost the same thing, but with one major difference: Ant was never going to use it on himself, on anyone he loved. He could trust that the code he stole would work, because he could trust the Corp to kill.

I can't trust anything in that system to save me, Omega, Jonas.

My head hurts. A flashback from an hour ago is still gripping my neck. There's nowhere to be alone here, to escape the eyes of people who love me and trust me and are waiting for me to turn on them. I can't pretend I'm not half waiting for the same thing.

I think they think they're hiding it well. Fable has stopped asking me how I am every five minutes.

Not well enough. Eyes follow me everywhere, tangible as fingers on my skin.

I turn away from the computers, cross the room, loop my guitar strap over my aching head. Sabine picks up her bass, Fable his drumsticks. Spectrum stands in the place Jonas would normally be; Lynx's eyes spark with quiet confidence over a table full of electronics.

Every Friday night in Los Angeles, I counted on the music to take me somewhere else and keep me myself all at the same time. Hands poised, I remember Ant telling me once of the first gig they played at Pixel's club, the true start of the rebellion, that his guitar had seemed to speak to him.

Mine isn't talking to me, I'm talking to it.

Save me. Save all of us.

■

Music. I haven't played properly in weeks, beyond a few strums of my guitar for Ant, or for myself in the park.

It's all wrong, the rhythm off. I've jammed a little with Spectrum before, when we were younger and taking over whatever water bar would have us, but he's not who I expect to see when I glance up from my hands.

I wonder what Jonas is doing right now.

No, I don't. I can't think about that.

After so many nights at the club I should be used to an audience, long past the point where every movement in the room is a distraction that slips my fingers off the strings.

Phoenix's foot taps, the wrong note squeals from my guitar.

The soles of Jonas's boots probably know the Web by now, the streets as much his as they were ever mine.

Always belonging exactly wherever he happened to be.

The string snaps.

"Take a break, Al," Lynx suggests.

"I'm fine. Can everyone just go eat or something?"

Soon, I'm alone, my playing smoother, better than it's been for an hour in a preemptive effort to drown out my thoughts. Fluid, pure notes fill the air around me, a song I wrote back in L.A. and haven't played for anyone yet. It's like old times, almost, Ant teaching me everything he knew and then letting me go off to figure out the rest on my own.

I'm going to end up with more than calluses on my fingers this time.

We practice for days, the room growing musty and hot with our collective breath and frustration, impatience, and mounting fear. Time is running out. On TV wider and wider shots are needed to show the uniformed guards in the Web, Los Angeles, Seattle. Mage taps into tracking records, kept again now, the numbers climbing up, up, up in white on a pitch-black screen.

Verse, chorus, repeat.

I barely sleep, have to force food down past the permanent lump in my throat that I blame on all the singing after such a long break. Excuses. Sabine lends me clothes that don't fall over my wrists and fuck up my fingers on the strings.

Through it all, they watch me. I can guess what they're thinking, whether I'm subconsciously resisting, making myself screw up over and over, but I'm not.

It's just that nothing sounds right without Jonas now.

"Fine," I say at the end of the next afternoon, putting down my guitar. Sweat coats my face, my fingertips burn. "We've got it." I don't stay to see their reactions and leave, crossing to the building that holds beds and showers. In a cracked mirror, I trace the thin lines of blue my hair has stained across my forehead like new veins filled with fresh blood.

More to spill if this goes badly. Omega said he wouldn't chase us and so far he's held to his word, but if we go back and attack, all bets will be off. Especially if he discovers our weapon of choice before we have a chance to use it. The element of surprise was on their side with the radios, the console tracks changing without warning. It has to be ours now. Take what you know and use it against them. It's the only way.

The shower is hot, the noise an echo of the rainfall in the park. I stand in the spray for an hour, past clean and into avoidance, until I'm dizzy from the steam and stumble out to dry myself on a towel as soft and absorbent as sandpaper.

When I get back, new equipment has joined old, nestled up against keyboards and the drum kit. Lynx issues directions, though Mage and Phoenix know what to do. They've spent more time in a recording studio than anyone here except maybe me.

My hair drips onto the guitar, *plink, plink, plink*. Another time, another place, I'd think what a cool sound it was. Now I just shake it from my eyes, let Sabine pull it from my forehead and tie it in a knot at my neck.

"Thanks," I say. She kisses my cheek, goes back to take her own place, her eyes on Fable.

One, two, one two three four . . .

The *click* is almost audible, another layer of sound to match the instruments. Energy gathers in my feet and climbs, melting away all the tension, everything but the music. Finally I can move easily in my own skin, breathe, lose and find myself again in every rise and fall of the melody. Nothing matters but this. We are nowhere, everywhere, with no obligations but to hit the next chord. Fable's arm crashes down on the drums behind me.

Magic. Alchemy.

"Again," I say before my strings have stopped humming from the final notes of the coda. "We're going to get this right."

"Perfectionist," Lynx says. I flip him the finger. There is nothing outside this room.

"You heard her," he says to the others.

Verse, chorus, coda, repeat.

I know when we have it. The sixth time, five minutes pass in a blur of sound and instinct. I don't realize the song is over until we're all staring at each other, breathless and shocked. The ghost of Anthem hovers over us, a presence in the room because he taught me everything I know. If I can do this, it's only because of him. "Good job," he used to say. I know he'd say it now. Pride swells inside me, tempered by the knowledge of what comes next. I'm not thinking about it. For a few minutes or hours, this is out of my hands, the recording a mass of wavy lines on one of the monitors. Lynx and Mage sit down and get to work, Phoenix leaning over their shoulders.

I can't help with this part, and I need to rest, summon my strength. Sabine falls onto the couch, pulls me with her. We could be back in the club in L.A., adrenaline buzzing after a gig, nothing on our minds except what we want to eat before we hit the beach.

I can't believe things were that simple, for just the blink of an eye, a single beat. There and then gone, my neatly woven life unraveled into chaos by one simple tab.

It's time, come home. And now I'm not home, or by my ocean, but stranded in the middle of a wasteland, praying that my plan works better than Ant's once did. The thought doesn't sit right.

Ant didn't have any arrogance to teach me.

Okay, not much.

I drift off, too exhausted to battle my eyelids, and when I open them again, I'm alone on the couch, the first hints of dawn streaking the sky Haven pink.

"We think we've got it, kiddo," Mage says softly.

"Think?" My mouth is dry. I'm just killing time with the question. Sabine opens the door, Fable right behind her, the two of them laughing about something, a tray balanced in her hands.

"Sure as we can be, without—" Mage begins. Yeah.

"Eat first."

"Thanks, Bean." Not sure what the food'll do, but I'm glad to steal whatever few minutes I can.

"Promise me you're sure about this," Fable says, low enough that the others can pretend they didn't hear it. If it's anyone's job to check that I'm sure I want to take the next step, the risk, it's him.

I stop, fork halfway to my mouth, look up at him. I'm not, and I am. I know the same things that will make the track work, dig its hooks into my brain, are the same things that could shred it. But there's no one else, not for this part, and I've always known I'd reach this crossroad. The reasons haven't even changed. Save me, save Omega, save us all. My brain isn't identical to Omega's, but we think the same, sober, anyway. See things the same. Grew up the same until the road forked and I took it across the country.

"I'm sure," I tell him. He nods once, looks away. Lynx unplugs the portable console from his computer and brings it to me. A small black box, menacing as a weapon. I pass my half-eaten food back to Sabine, lie down on the couch. In some ways, the idea that I'm not just doing this for myself anymore makes it easier. My fractured parts can hide in a bigger, more important whole.

"I'm ready."

23

Red. The room is red now, with blood and anger. Pain like fire shoots through my veins and above the music I hear myself screaming. Hands try to take the music away. No, no. I need it and I'll kill anyone who tries to take it from me. Who are all these people? I don't know them and they look frightened. Good. They should be.

Now the hands try to hold me down, but I'm stronger than they are. I'm stronger than anyone. The rhythm shakes my bones. The pulse that keeps me alive, more alive than ever. Glass smashes, loud, and it should be discordant but it's not. The shards fall among the keyboard's notes, sharp and painfully beautiful.

Fresh air hits my lungs. I cling to the box in my hand, the thing that keeps the music running with me as my feet thud over the ground. There's somewhere I need to go. An island of steel and color. Home. I don't know why I'm not there now, but guitar strings whine in my ears like the power lines stretched across the sky, leading me back. I have to get back. I know things, I feel things no one else does, and the Corp needs me to help make them great and powerful again. Fix the tiny blip caused by someone . . . someone . . .

Blue streaks across my mind. My chest hurts. Footsteps hammer loud enough behind me to hear over the music that's still playing, that I'll never give up. Running is like dancing, marionette bones strung with melody and euphoria. But that voice isn't part of it, saying a word again and again that I feel like I should know.

Alpha! Alpha!

I don't look for the voice. I am Citizen W2750 and the Web is singing, calling to me, Citizen W2751's voice loudest of all. Omega.

Alpha!

Rocks tear at my boots. Jagged metal catches my clothes, gnarled fingers of iron reaching up from the earth, all that's left of what was here before and the people who built it. They were lazy and stupid and didn't have the Corp to care for them, about them, show them how things should be done.

Never again. Because the Corp is eternal.

Alpha!

I can't breathe. Arms wrap around my chest, crushing the life from me. Red stains my vision again. Get away from me. You can't stop me. I punch and kick and scratch with pointed fingernails and the screams, they're like music, too. But he doesn't let go, he has to let me go.

Let. Me. Go.

I grit my teeth and push, watch the boy stumble. It happens so slowly, a different rhythm than the music, like my eyes and ears aren't running at the same speed. Slowly, he staggers back. His boot catches on a shapeless chunk of cement; he falls against an old fence just waiting to catch him. It happens so slowly, the rusted spike piercing him first between his shoulders as he sinks onto it, the point slicing through him, bursting from the hollow below his throat.

Warmth spatters across my face.

Red.

24

We bury Fable in the dry, destroyed earth a hundred yards behind Central, or more accurately, they do. The kind of funeral I told Jonas we didn't give our dead. My restraints stretch far enough to let me see out the window, but my tears turn them all to shapeless blurs. Breath freezes in my lungs until I gasp, cough, scream.

Nobody looks in my direction.

Every one of them has assured me it was an accident, which is a generous way of looking at it. We made the track on purpose. No one forced me to listen to it.

I'll take their version if it means they forgive me, but forgiving myself will take longer. I've known Fable for seventeen years, it'll take at least that long again to feel as if I've washed his blood from my hands.

If ever.

If I survive this anyway.

We can't do for him what Haven did for Ant—we don't have the equipment, or knowledge, and he died too quickly—but I made sure Mage took his memory chip. Symbolism. The way we do things. He doesn't have any family left in the Web to watch it. He had me, Phoenix and Mage, Sabine.

Sabine. I only watch her when her back is turned. She was the first to say it was an accident, voice robotic, lips barely moving. She's the first to turn her back on the shallow grave, steps slow, measured, deliberate toward the cluster of buildings, toward me.

The others follow, most heading for the one cube in which we've practically lived for days now. If I'd . . . *killed* . . . anyone else, it'd have been Fable who would have come to check on me, Fable who wouldn't be afraid. Instead, it's Phoenix who veers from the group, disappearing from my sight, the lock on my door snapping open a minute later.

"How're you feeling?"

I don't begrudge the question anymore. "Okay," I say. Not *better*, because my oldest friend is out there, cold and already beginning to rot, but the regret, the unbearable sadness that threatens to suffocate me is promising. I am myself, I think. If the track still had complete hold of me, I wouldn't be sorry.

"Good. Al, it was—"

"An accident."

She nods, comes closer. "They're making adjustments. I tabbed Isis. I need to examine you, and you need to tell me if you don't want to try again."

I *don't* want to try again. "I have to. Isis spoke to you?"

"When I said it was about you, yeah. Not about anything else."

With exaggerated slowness, I move so she can do what Isis has told her, keeping my hands at my sides, statue-still. It's all for show, whether my pulse is normal or not isn't going to tell her what's in my brain, but I'll do whatever makes them feel better, whatever convinces them I'm safe.

Omega and I barely look alike, especially now that we're literally opposites, orange and blue, but we have the same expressions, sometimes. The same laugh, identical frowns. I remember that awful, searing fear I felt in the hospital room with Jonas and Omega and Wraith and know exactly how Fable saw me in those last few seconds.

Phoenix jumps away just in time as I bend over. Fingers comb through my hair and hold it off my neck until I'm done retching, eyes watering, goose bumps raised on my arms. I straighten and she leaves, returning with a mop.

"Let me," I say.

"Are you sure?"

"Yes."

She tries to hide the nervousness in her eyes as she unties the rope around my wrists. But I'm okay. Calm.

Numb.

Adjustments take hours, the room grows dark and quiet around me. I don't bother to turn on a light, don't need one to sit on the floor with my swollen eyes closed, thinking, remembering. Fable's mother was friends with mine; if anything, I knew his mom better than I ever did my own. She used to look after me and Omega every day while Ant was still at work—or in the basement down on the South Shore, but I didn't know that then. Fable was the one who first told us about the music. To this day I can picture Ant's face when we asked him what drugs were.

Years later, I hadn't even finished telling Fable what my plans were when he went to pack his bags, like it wasn't even a question that he'd come. We climbed into the back of the pod together, and when I couldn't stare out the windows anymore, I fell asleep on his shoulder.

He loved Los Angeles maybe even more than I did.

Pain jolts through my knuckles; the window shakes in its frame from the blow. I wish Haven could save him like she saved Ant just so I could tell him how sorry I am.

It's late when Mage and Spectrum come to get me, each taking one of my arms, and I don't fight them. Leave the restraints on, I don't care. In the other building, Lynx waves from his computers, Phoenix from the couch. Both shoot me soft, sad looks.

Sabine turns away.

"Ready?" Spectrum asks, touching my cheek. I inhale.

"Let's do it." I don't watch as he puts the headphones over my ears, swaddling me in a few seconds of total silence that make the first notes, when they come, unbearably loud.

Guitars, a keyboard, drums thumping. These people are wrong, they want to stop me and they can't. Nothing can stop us. The Corp has risen again, better than before. Cities everywhere know our glory now. The peace we bring with music and rhythm.

Eternal, eternal, eternal.

That one, there, with his skylit eyes and bodiless mind, he's the worst. He's the one who tried to stop us before.

I laugh, the sound curling like smoke into a snarl.

Tried.

They are all failures. We are the Corp.

"Let me go," *I order. How dare they ignore me? My bound hands lash out, just missing the nearest face.* "Let me go," *I say again. The Corp needs me; the Web needs me; my brother and the man I love are doing all the work without me and they need my help to raise us to greater heights than ever before. Legs kicking, back arching, I connect with one of these traitors. Coppery blood stains the air. Good. Good. Bleed out for the Corp. This is your sacrifice.*

Crash. A chair flies from the toe of my boot, through the hologram, against the wall. The image breaks, a tiny joy pulses at this brief destruction. But then he's whole again, unharmed.

The music changes, away from the harshly beautiful sound of my rage. This is water, air, lightness. A long note drawn from a violin string. Fractured faces pass in front of my eyes. Haven. Pixel. Mage. Warmth ripples through me, collides with my icy resolve. I am steam and mist, a million crystal drops, my thoughts dissolving into nothing, blissful nothing . . .

Black. Distant melodies I can't make out. I try to lift my arms and can't, too heavy. It's all too much, too dark and it's nice here. I don't have to think anything. I can just keep my eyes closed and fade away. . . .

A hand slaps my cheek, not hard, but the sting makes me blink. And again. Phoenix, deep eyes staring down at me, tied and twisted on the floor. "You with us?" she asks.

Am I?

"I think so." Ow. She hands me a bottle of water to wash down the razor blades in my throat, down to slice my stomach into ribbons of pain at the expressions turned my way. Everyone's looking at me and I want to crawl under the table, but I can't move. They're waiting. Like most of them don't know how hard it is to put tracking into words, a Technicolor sensation painted with monochrome syllables. "Better? Maybe?" I say. I didn't kill anyone this time, and it's a fucking weird day when that's the standard to judge by.

But weird days are the norm now. The last one that wasn't, I had sand between my toes and the purest music in my ears, mingled with Sabine's laughter and Jonas's gentle voice. Exactly none of those things are anywhere to be found anymore.

"You seemed to recover faster," Spectrum prompts.

I nod. "But at the end . . ." The blackness. That can't be good.

"Okay." Lynx and Mage go back to work; I promise I can handle another track or two today.

I want the music. My thumb runs over the edge of the headphones. Under the rope around my wrists, my chafed skin fits better than it ever has over my bones.

Let me do it again.

■

It gets easier every time. Alone in my room-slash-cell, I have hours to think about that. The sun arcs across the sky and with its descent, the itch grows, my skin shrinking again until I put the headphones on. Again and again. Again, please, again.

We're getting closer. Over and over the Corp's tracks blast into my ears, only to be wiped away by one of our own, leaving my mind just a little clearer and my craving to do it one more time just a little stronger.

I look like all the people I used to move away from on the streets of the Web. I look like Anthem used to. On TV, explosions tear through buildings and bullets tear through hearts.

We have to stop this. *I* have to stop this.

Mage and Spectrum come get me again. Honestly, I probably don't need the restraints anymore, but now I feel like they're holding me together. In the other room everyone is busy, all with their own job, just like I have mine. Lucky me. But now it's not only my turn.

They give us as much privacy as they can, backs to Sabine and me, busying themselves.

"I'm sorry," I tell her again. She nods, stiff, accepting because there's no other choice. "You're sure about this?" Her eyes widen and I curse myself. Fuck. I could've at least used different words, not echoed Fable's almost to the syllable when he asked me.

"Has to be done."

It does. If the brainwashing tracks are affecting people without memory chips differently, like Isis said when Jonas overdosed, we can't save everyone in Los Angeles and Seattle without making sure it works.

We can't save Jonas.

She goes first. I grit my teeth and focus on her, not the creeping envy at the headphones over her ears. My turn soon enough.

Not soon enough. But I wait, and watch, a strange mirror of myself, seeing what the others have seen since we started this. The anger that seeps like fever from her pores, flailing limbs, bared teeth, screaming. And then the next track, wiping it all away, repainting her features one brushstroke at a time. Phoenix pulls the headphones away to ask her a million questions that she answers in a dull, slow voice, words uncertain on her tongue; Lynx makes adjustments before Sabine's even stopped talking.

I know what to expect and still somehow it's a surprise, the rush of fury with the first track, the raging storm blown from my mind with the second, painfully blue skies left in its wake. *You were a rainbow.* My pulse matches the rhythms and my feet try to move—not kicking, dancing. Oh, to be at one of the Sky-Clubs now, floor spinning, the Web a pattern of sparkling gossamer strands beyond the windows.

Mage helps me up and, without asking me or anyone, pulls the rope from my wrists. "She's fine," he says.

No one argues. He does the same for Sabine, freeing her to cross the room and slip outside, Phoenix right behind her, keeping an eye on her just in case. I think Sabine's okay—dazed, but okay.

First hit's free. The distance between us stretches to an uncrossable chasm that cleaves my chest in two. Other than Omega, Sabine's the only person I know of whose first tracking experience was like mine—held down, an experiment, dangerous, for the greater good. I want to tell her it'll be okay, but it probably won't. We can reverse the brainwashing in ourselves, maybe in everyone else, but the cravings will haunt her forever, the way they've always followed me, one step behind and ready to pounce whenever they sense any weakness.

"Give us a sec, guys?" Lynx asks.

It stings, how willing they all are to get away from me. Love at war with fear of what I might do next; though Mage is right, I'm fine now. We've done it, I think. Close, anyway.

Fine. Fable's expression in the seconds before he fell is seared permanently across my brain. I'm never going to be fine again.

But what matters is what there is. Much as I don't want to admit the Corp is right about anything, they might be right about this. We can erase, not rewind.

"You have to promise me you'll stop."

"This is coming from *you*?"

Lynx's hands toy with his purple spikes. "Yes, dearest, it's coming from me. This was never you. This is the opposite of what you wanted to be."

I sit on the couch, don't say anything else. Lying to him will get me nowhere and I don't want to. Enough.

"I get it," he whispers. I have to strain to hear him. "I get how easy it is. That you've seen things you'd rather forget, and if something can help you . . ."

Yes, yes, that's it, exactly. I tell myself that each tracking session is to help refine, hone what we've done, make sure that when we unleash it there's the smallest chance it'll work.

"Did you ever want to stop?" I've never asked him this before.

"Yes."

I wait.

"Sometimes I've wondered what life would be like . . . would *have* been like . . . if Spectrum and I were good little boys. Clean, playing by all the rules." He shrugs. "But that's not us, Al. We liked our life, at least before your brother lost his shit. We were never fighters."

"You are now."

A faint smile. "For you. I don't think you realize how cool you are, Al. People want to be around you."

That's wrong for so many reasons. One, I'm not. Two, I haven't been *me* for eight years. "That's just because of Ant," I say instead. Lynx laughs.

"No, honey, it's not. Not the way you think. Nobody who matters

230

cares who your older brother is. Was. But you're a lot like him, and there's a reason people helped him back then. Be who you are, Al. You have to stop. Make sure what happened to Fable"—Wow, that's a nice way of putting it—"at least happened for a reason."

But my skin fits better. So much closer to covering the person it was meant to—the one who would stand beside Omega to raise the Corp up, again and for good. And every time the headphones cover my ears, I'm guaranteed a few minutes of *other*, of a sense of presence so overwhelming it drowns out past and future.

Across the room, my tablet flashes. I ignore it. Probably one of the others asking whether they can come back. And since they had to chase me, I get how much more exposed the outpost feels, nothing beyond for miles. There's something comforting about being huddled together as a group.

Even if that group includes me.

"I'll stop," I tell Lynx. Or else there's been no point to all of this. I could've given in weeks ago, stayed in the Web or gone back to Los Angeles. Drifted off into a sea of tracks and never cared about anything again. Ruled with Omega and Wraith. And Jonas.

"Good girl. Now I guess it's our turn."

"Won't be like that club you love."

"That much I've guessed. I'll get everyone."

I deserve the looks, the worry, the anger, but it makes the room small and airless and it's already hard enough to breathe when Fable isn't.

"Give them time."

They can have as much as they need; I just worry we won't have enough. I'd be an idiot if I believed that anything would work before I actually saw it work. Based on recent history, that much isn't a guarantee, either.

And here we are.

I stand in the corner, watch Lynx and Spectrum on the couch. I don't know if they cope with it better because they never stopped tracking, or if the constant refinements we've done mean the track is doing less damage.

My tablet goes off again. I finally move to grab it, tear my eyes away from Mage and Phoenix asking Lynx and Spectrum a hundred questions, taking them away for food and cold water to splash on their faces.

I was right about the earlier ones, all Mage asking if we were ready, but the one that came in a minute ago is Isis. I don't even have time to read the whole thing before another comes in, another, another.

```
They got her._
We were sleeping. She was awake._
```

But Haven didn't hear them coming. I can't . . . I can't . . .

```
ALPHA?_
Hiding. TAB ME BACK._
They know where you are and what you're
doing._
```

My hands shake and the letters blur. No, this can't happen.

But it is happening. Voices reach in from outside, shouting. They must be loud or I wouldn't hear them. Something breaks. The screech of crumpling metal.

"Al?" Sabine's panic matches my own and I freeze, no idea what to do, where to go. An instant of perfect, fragile silence shatters, no match for the force of the gunshots.

25

Cold steel sucks the warmth and feeling from my hand, the gun Lynx got me heavy, loaded, apprehensive. Sabine is on her feet but frozen, breath held.

"What—?" She doesn't understand. She grew up with peace, kindness.

"Stay here," I say.

"Fuck that."

"Please." *How much sorrier will you be if you don't make it back in time to say you're sorry?*

I've said it, but I need more time for her to believe it. Another shot rings through the night.

The door is shrouded in shadow. I slip outside, into a pocket of pitch black. Floodlights over the main building shine on a patrol pod, dented from a journey harsher than any on Web streets, one tire half deflated. No one behind the windshield.

I can't call for the others, but I can't see them, either. My hand tightens, the gun's rough grip biting into my thumb. I squeeze harder, make it real. A solid object in a shifting landscape.

Fifty feet away, out of the corner of my eye, a patch of darkness moves. Gravel crunches under thick-soled, Corp-issued boots.

I can't believe he sent fucking *guards* after us. Whichever *he* it was.

Yes, actually, I can.

The air cracks, a bullet pings off metal and ricochets away. My heart hammers so loud I'm amazed the guards can't use it as a homing beacon. A rush of footsteps comes, my too-slow scream smothered by a large hand.

"It's me," Mage whispers, touching a gun barrel lightly to my bicep to tell me he has it.

"Where are they?"

"Phoenix is by the showers. Lynx and Spectrum are in the kitchen."

I relax a tiny bit. They're all still alive, or were seconds ago.

"How many?"

"Counted three."

Numbers mean nothing, but we know this place better than they do.

"You know how to use that thing?" Mage asks, eyes flicking to my gun.

More gravel crunches, closer.

"Not really."

"Stay here and don't shoot yourself."

"Excellent plan. Hadn't thought of that."

He moves away, my side instantly chilled. A spine-wrenching shiver runs down my back at the thought of what I would've done if I'd been thinking clearly enough to grab this thing that night after I tracked for the first time.

Another gunshot, a sickening *thud*. I never realized they sound so different when they hit flesh. Blood roars in my ears and I will it down, need to hear. But now I can hear cries of pain, keening and muffled, no clue who it is.

I step out from the shadows, slowly, my back to the wall, and round the corner of the building. Brighter light makes me blink, squint to see the body on the ground, a dark stain oozing out from under the uniform. Thank fuck.

The other ones are still here somewhere.

Deafening noise rings out, a staccato beat that rings, echoes, bounces off every surface long after the clips have emptied. "Mage!" I hiss. No answer. "Phoenix!"

"Oh yeah?" Mage. At least he's still alive. "Try again, asshole." Two figures move out into the light, swinging, punching. The guard's fist connects with Mage's jaw, but it's the last one he gets. Mage's hands fly, blood spraying in a thousand droplets, set alight by the glow above.

He falls, body flinching as Mage switches from fists to feet, steel toecaps crashing into delicate bone, hands thrown up to shield his face.

And then they just . . . fall away.

"Stop!" I yell without thinking. "He's dead! Enough!"

Mage hovers, midkick, and lets his foot drop back to the ground. He raises his eyes to me, blank and unseeing, and his teeth are stained red.

"Drop the gun." The voice is as hard and cold as the weapon. I spin, my heart falling into my boots. I don't know him, this guard, but I know Phoenix, her fiery hair spilling over the arm clamped around her neck. "Drop it."

I can't move or breathe or think. Small, mean eyes stare at me, challenging, waiting. Ever so slightly, Phoenix shakes her head.

"Not going to give you another warning," he says, jerking his forearm tighter. Phoenix gasps and the gun begins to slip from my hand, my palms too clammy to hold on to anything when the world is spinning so wildly out of control.

"Phoenix," Mage says. Her name, but so much more to him.

"Shut. Up." The guard spits, a disgusting, slimy blob that only just misses Phoenix's shoulder. "We're gonna get all of you and line you up, nice and pretty. You'll be picked clean by the flies before anyone finds you. Just dust." He laughs, a wild mania tilting his eyes off kilter a few inches above the top of Phoenix's head.

People don't look like this. This . . . inhuman.

"So just drop the gun," he continues. "Or this one'll be the first to go."

Mage makes a sound halfway between pain and pleading.

"Okay!" I say. "Okay." He's taller than Phoenix. That's my final thought, the last one I let myself have before I swing the gun up and pull the trigger. Agony shoots through my arm, up my neck, rattles my brain inside my skull.

I can't look. Something heavy hits the ground.

So do I.

Nononono.

Soft fingers reach under my arms, hoist me to my feet. Warmth surrounds me but my whole body is shaking. "It's okay."

I know that voice, or at least the version of that voice that hasn't had all the air squeezed from it. Phoenix holds me, Mage joins her.

"Nice shot," is all Mage can say. I can't explain where the laughter comes from but it fills my every cell, hysterical and loud. It's still coming when they help me inside, explain to Ant what happened, get the others and bring them back. My stomach hurts by the time it stops under the weight of everyone staring. Almost. Sabine is back against the wall, trying not to look.

"Better?" Sabine asks, watching me a little more closely than the others.

"Yes. No. Yeah. I'm okay." I think it's the truth, I want it to be. "Thanks for staying inside."

"Are you kidding?" Spectrum asks. "We had to sneak around and hold her back when that asshole had Phoenix."

Sabine grins. We're all shocked, giddy, fueled by adrenaline.

Phoenix pulls out a box of medical supplies and gives Mage such a look he sits still while she wraps his knuckles with gauze. Bottles of little white pills nestle among syringes and vials.

"Need anything for this?" Phoenix asks, touching Mage's jaw, crusted from his lip down with a line of drying blood.

"Nope."

"You can still talk, can't be that bad. Shame," Phoenix says. She kisses the top of his head and looks over at me. There are no *thank-yous* or *your welcomes*; those imply a favor, a kindness instead of an instinct.

Somehow, we're okay, but we can't stay here anymore. Soon enough Wraith or Omega—or Jonas—will learn their mission failed and they'll send more after us. We only packed so many bullets.

I dig out a secret stash of chocolate. Haven always used to have it when we were kids, bringing treats when she thought we needed it most. The sugar shouldn't be as calming as it is, a warming sweetness that gradually returns our pulses to something approaching normal. I eat in silence, thinking. Almost everyone I've ever cared about is in this room. The rest have been poisoned, broken, turned into something other than themselves, but we can change that.

"We have to go back," I say. Everyone turns to me, midchew. "We're done, or as close as we're going to get."

"We can broadcast it from here, Al," Mage says. "And start sending it to consoles, DJ-comps. We're in the system."

He's right. Technically, I mean, he's right. But still, I shake my head.

"No." If that bullet had missed . . . My hands tremble again and I glance at Phoenix. She's okay, breathing, pale but alive. "They've got Haven, guys. What the fuck they're going to do with her, I don't know." I don't want to know what Wraith could come up with that would be worse than what Haven's parents did to her. I believe that he could find something. "We have to help her, and . . . and I want to see Wraith's eyes," I say. If the track doesn't work, I want to end them myself—for Fable, for that guard, for me. "I'm going. Come with me or not, but I'm going back, and they've just given us what we need to do it."

■

We approach the bridge at midnight, when the clubs are full and streets empty save for guards in uniforms that turn me into a kid again, ducking past patrols on my way to school with Omega.

A pod stops at the other end, Web-side, waiting, its headlights burning with challenge. Sabine urges ours faster and the corner of a speaker slams into my shoulder blade, slicing, pain stretching down my back. Mage reaches out to catch me before I slide forward, Phoenix grabbing my other arm.

Lynx and Spectrum pull their hands—not empty—from their pockets. I'm done with guns. Dull clicks are the only sound amidst our held breath. Closer, closer.

Stop.

Doors slam and the guards approach, one on either side. Bullets whistle through the air and they fall, mouths still open with the questions they'll never ask. Their blank, staring eyes bear the telltale signs of too much tracking. I look away—they didn't ask for this any more than we did. Some things just have to happen. There are no struggles as Mage and Lynx strip them of their uniforms, or screams or cries of pain as Lynx slices open their wrists to take their chips, the tips of his hair catching light from the Web, turning it purple. Twin splashes match the clicks and the gunshots, the bodies sinking into the river.

Spectrum climbs into the driver's seat of their pod.

Clearly, neither going back to the apartment is safe, nor is the CRC. If I know Omega—which I doubt now, but anyway—he'll have the basement staked out, too, just in case. The pods speed south, down to Two, and we park in a cluster of them around the corner from Pixel's old club, its door mercifully unlocking at the request of my chip.

"You're safe," Isis says as soon as we're inside, rushing to us before I have a chance to see anything. I hug her back, relieved as she is.

"Mostly," I whisper.

She steps away. Lynx and Spectrum are behind me, Mage and Phoenix and Sabine behind them. None of us are speaking, but I hear quiet voices. Look up to the balcony.

"Higher ground," Isis says, turning, leading the way.

"Do they know you're here?"

"Probably, but—"

"You. Asshole."

Pixel is a blur, a rush of air and color past me as soon as we all reach the top of the stairs. He's fast for his age and his health, stronger, too. Mage has just enough time to step to the side, staggering against the railing instead of tumbling to the floor below when Pixel's fist connects with his jaw. The crack of bone rings out and Pixel steps back, panting, eyeing Phoenix. Debating.

"Not a chance, man," Lynx says. He and Spectrum each take hold of a shoulder, pulling Pixel away.

"You deserved that," says a voice. Haven really, really made him too real. For the first time I look around the balcony, see Anthem, a glittering rainfall of glowing lines on a viewer in a corner, a long cable snaking away into the shadows.

"Not arguing with you." Mage holds his face, blood dripping

from his lip, too distracted by the punch to be awed by Ant, and I've done a good job of describing it to him and Phoenix anyway. "Not saying I didn't earn ten of these. But listen, okay?" He winces, Phoenix takes over, says basically what she told me out at Central.

"You think I would've forgotten about my brother?" Pixel asks in a voice that's worse, so much deadlier, than shouting. "He was all I had left."

"And killing Wraith wouldn't have brought him back," Mage says. "When we found Scope, we decided—"

"That wasn't your decision to make," Ant says.

Phoenix shrugs, the barest hint of her usual self. "Maybe not, but we all made those kinds of choices back then. You more than anyone." Ant doesn't answer.

"Guys, they're sorry," I say. Sometimes that just has to be enough. "We have bigger things to deal with right now."

Even with Ant as a hologram, it's weird to see him without Haven around. Maybe especially this way; the only times I have were when I asked her to leave. Pixel and Ant exchange looks, nod at each other. Lynx lets go of Pixel first, followed by Spectrum. We all hold our breath as Pixel heads for Mage, veers around him, and runs down the stairs, boots clanging. A minute later soft, safe music filters through the speakers. Harmonizing neon strobes flip on, slow and mesmerizing to watch.

"Echoes too much in here," Pixel mutters, rejoining us, and I get what he means, the way a certain kind of silence can drive you crazy. I want headphones over my ears, music, the drug.

"Do we know how she is?" I ask. Isis pauses her inspection of Mage's jaw to shake her head.

"No. They came, said"—Ant ripples, like he can't get comfortable, too human—"said if she didn't go with them, they'd delete me from the system, then come for you. Said that if she went peacefully, I could stay where I was and they'd leave Pixel and Isis alone. I would've been okay with the first, if it'd stopped them."

"They came for us anyway," Spectrum says. "Al, dude, your brother really is an asshole. Not you," he clarifies to Ant.

Ant smiles faintly.

"It's not him in there," I say. I *have* to believe that. "And Omega won't hurt Haven."

"Those things can't both be true," Ant says, choked.

I close my eyes, remember the flash of Omega—really him—telling me to get out, run. Some part of him is fighting it, and he needs me because he's mostly failing. "Yes, they can. Trust me." The neon lights begin to blur. A thick, sweet taste at the back of my throat is the same rainbow of colors. "Lynx, tell them—"

I almost trip down the stairs, across the dance floor, down the hallway, just about make it into a hygiene cube. A little over twenty-four hours since I last tracked. It's warm in here but I shiver, beads of sweat tickling down my spine.

The room is multicolored and sickening, curls of want looping around my brain.

There used to be a console here, in Pixel's old office. I grip the sink harder, shake my head. A waterfall of faded blue in the cracked mirror. Never again. I promised. I fold onto the floor, the ridiculousness of it all burning as much as the searing pain that shoots to my fingertips, my toes. It's too late to give in. Fable would kill me. Tears drip onto my shirt. This fucking place, this insane, evil island that does such awful things to everyone who sets foot on it by choice or birth.

Giving in is all I want to do. Over twenty-four hours since my last track, a little more than that since the white room last took over.

I stop breathing. It can't be that long. It's never been that long.

Someone knocks on the door; I flinch. Isis. I tell her to leave me alone and after a minute she does, footsteps clicking away to nothing.

The track seems to have worked on me. Hopefully it'll work on Omega. Before the cure, I wasn't myself, but without a desperate desire to find it, I don't know who I am. Easy for Lynx to tell me to be myself; he knows who he is.

You're on a beach. A campfire. A guitar. Jonas. I twist a strand of hair between my fingers, the same blue my ocean turns at night.

Aching, I push myself up, slip out into the hall. The others are all still on the balcony, talking too quietly for me to identify more than individual voices. I check the back room before I join them. Old shelves stand empty near the entrance to the tunnels, covered with thick dust. Evidence of years of silent emptiness, this whole place a mausoleum of memories. Someone, Pixel I guess, has sealed the trapdoor with a heavy chain and old-fashioned lock. It won't stop people from getting in here if they want to. Minutes. That's how we have to count time.

I walk back out, across the dance floor and up the stairs, voices silenced when they hear me coming. "I'm fine," I say to preempt Isis because I know she's about to ask, her mouth already open.

"Lynx was just filling us in on the plan," Ant says, knowing better than to ask.

"Plan's changed," I say, pointing at Lynx, Spectrum, and Sabine. "I need you three. The rest of you are staying out of it."

"Kiddo—"

"I'm not a kid anymore," I tell Mage, gritting my teeth, and face Anthem. "And don't you even try. You fought to protect me; now it's my turn."

When you can't trust anyone, you have to make choices or go it alone. I trust every one of the people in this club with my life, even if the reverse isn't as true as it used to be. Despite what happened with Phoenix, the guard, the gun, they will always remember what happened the time before that. So will I.

"Al . . ." Ant doesn't finish, doesn't need to.

"I will get Haven back. I promise you, I will get her back."

I'm not losing anyone else. And the less people I ask for help, the less I have to tell what I'm going to do until it's too late for them to stop me.

Some secrets are good. Some are just the only way.

26

"Al. *Alpha.*"

"What?" I blink at Mage. "Sorry. Yeah?"

Sabine's watching me, eyebrows raised expectantly. Nerves flutter through my stomach.

"Can we talk?" she asks.

I lead her downstairs, across the dance floor filled with the ghosts of a thousand citizens, ecstatic and unthinking and aglow. What was once Pixel's office is now stripped bare, walls crumbling. There's nowhere to sit, or hide from her unrelenting gaze. The console is long gone, ripped from the wall. Damn it. Good.

"Do you want me to apologize again?" A tiny fraction of my anger over Fable's death turns outward, points at her. "He was my oldest friend, Bean—"

"Don't call me that."

I fling up my hands. "Fine. I just don't know how much sorrier I can be."

"You hide it well."

"Forgive me if I'm not running around crying in front of everyone. I had plenty of time to do that while I was locked up to keep you all safe."

"Lucky you. And you didn't keep *all* of us safe. How can you even live with yourself?"

My head pounds and my fingers tremble. I shove them into

my pockets so she doesn't notice or guess what's causing it. "I don't know what you want me to say. I saved Phoenix, didn't I?"

"Maybe you just missed," she mutters.

"Fuck you."

I regret it as soon as I've said it. Emotions morph her face, pretty features shifting, not settling on any one feeling. She slides down the wall and puts her head on her knees. I have no idea whether she and Fable would've worked, but she deserved the chance to find out. Her shoulders shake, violently, then erratic tremors. When I touch her hair, she flinches but doesn't pull away.

Forgiveness can come later, when there's time. If there's time. Maybe. I sit beside her, words trapped in my throat because there's nothing I can say to her or to myself. The DJ-comp changes songs; the new one crawls into the room through the crack under the door. Omega's face flits across my mind. I quickly think of something else. Anything else. Food. We're going to need to get some, somehow.

"Just one thing," Sabine says, raising her head, makeup streaked down her cheeks in dark lines.

"Yeah?"

"*If* this works "—she stresses the *if*—"then everyone here, everywhere, they're gonna be normal again, you know, after a while."

I haven't told her yet. "I hope so. What's your point?"

Sabine gives me a long look. "You might be lucky enough to get Jonas back. You'd better make sure you really want him."

I've had good teachers in the art of forgiveness; Jonas isn't the one who has to worry. I let him come here, let this happen, refused to see the signs, didn't do enough to stop it.

I'm doing what I can now.

My skin crawls, constricts, wringing the oxygen from my

lungs and making my toes go numb. I stand, stomp the feeling back into them and leave Sabine alone. She'll come out when she's ready, and if anyone pushes her, it's not going to be me.

Spectrum's on a couch on the balcony, flipping a small black chip over in his fingers. Disappear, reappear. A magic trick.

"This is it?" Pixel asks.

"Yep. One of them."

"They work?"

"They work." We think. And we still need one more, but nobody knows that yet.

"You guys should go," I say to Pixel and Isis. "Safer if anyone's looking for you. Better not to look like you've disappeared."

They agree—reluctantly, but I don't care about shades of gray. We'll see them in the morning; they promise to bring more food, supplies. We watch them slip headphones over their ears and portable consoles in their pockets. They're not trying to keep the music in; they're trying to keep it out. It's everywhere, and none of it is safe.

The Corp never kills you. . . . Repeat, repeat. A horrible chorus, a horrible song.

Sabine emerges from Pixel's office, face puffy but dry. She looks cracked, not broken, and I wonder if maybe she's right.

If it would be more humane just to kill them, not make them live with everything they've done, the damage they've caused with bare hands or evil intent. Wraith, Omega, Jonas . . . all the way down a line that stretches far too long, from the North Edge to the South Shore.

None of us have slept since Central, or before. The old, remembered, invisible bruises on my throat throb again. Life, not letting go for a single beat. We share the food we brought with us, the last of what we have. Sabine kicks off her boots and curls on the couch farthest from me. Lynx and Spectrum some-how manage to fit themselves on one couch in the darkest cor-ner. Mage and I argue over who takes the one still on the dance floor from when we came here weeks ago. I let him win eventually; he grabs a gun and calls over his shoulder that I've already had my lucky shot.

Point. I still stick my tongue out at him, but he can't see. Phoenix hides a smile.

Several feet away, Ant shimmers on his viewer, and it feels like forever ago that the sight of it made me rage. Now sadness makes my muscles heavier than the exhaustion. With Haven gone, he's a boat on the river, its anchor snapped and lost. So much has changed. I've been wrong about so many other things. I came so close to losing both my brothers within weeks of each other, exactly as the Corp planned it years ago.

I'll never doubt Haven again. And now I just have to get the other one back.

"Hey." Ant's voice tugs me back to the present, and he cocks his head toward the nearest wall, lined with speakers. I move closer so we can talk without waking anyone. "This you?"

"Uh. Yeah, yes." There's not much we know is safe; this was recorded out at Central. No encoding, just me, Sabine, Lynx . . . and Fable. It's Fable I listen for now, playing with that crazy abandon he always had—for chasing girls or moving across the country or being onstage. I wonder whether he would've played any differently if he'd known he was recording the weapon that would kill him.

Yeah. He would've played harder.

With the strobes turned off, the music softened, Ant is the only real light, blue and undulating. "You okay?" I ask.

"Are you?"

He's right, it was a stupid question. Sure as I am that Omega won't hurt Haven, I'd never trust Wraith not to once she stops being useful to him. Only the knowledge that he worshipped her mother gives me the slightest bit of hope. I want to tell Ant that he'll get used to it, being away from her. That the pull lessons with every night spent alone. But it doesn't and I hope he doesn't learn that the hard way.

My hand hovers over the button that will temporarily turn him off, eyes on his. He nods, full darkness falling the instant after the *click*. Beyond the walls of the club I think I can feel the Web thrumming with its rhythmic pulse, but in here, now, is the closest I've come to being back on my beach. A wave of homesickness hits and I lie back on a hard, dusty couch with its years of silence stuffed into the cushions, staring at the ceiling until sleep comes.

It's early morning when I wake up, though the only way to tell is to look at a clock. No windows. It's always night in here. That used to be the point. A long, endless night, hot as summer even in January, the music just on the cusp of too loud, and after a few minutes nobody cared anyway. They were all too high, blissed out, alive with sweat and sound and glowing rainbows.

Sabine rolls over, feet kneading the end of her couch. On the dance floor, Mage snores, more at home than most of us here, but not as tempted by its whispers as I am. In the Web the walls have ears; they also have voices. Remember the stories of what happened here. Remember how good it was, how happy people were.

Quietly as I can, I gather the things I need, ears pricked for any sound. I carry my boots down the stairs, the metal too slick under my thick socks. Into the back room, closing the door behind me. Dust turns my fingers black as they feel along the top of the shelves, fold around a key. The chain rattles too loudly; the jump down into the tunnels sends my stomach lurching into my throat.

I dig a flashlight from my bag and start to walk, following the beam.

■

This is how I always imagined finding my cure.

Some of the details are wrong: the time, the place, and Fable's not beside me, helping. That's the most wrong of all. The others have their reasons. I knew I'd be doing this when I'd learned enough, and I have. Ant would appreciate the symmetry of the *where*, if he knew. Omega might, too, if he's still capable of thought at all.

Water drips down the slimy walls of a little hideaway I've only seen once before because I begged to.

I sit on the ground, two computers open in front of me. On one, another Corp drone drawls on the screen, monotonous and glassy-eyed. Ant on his viewer is more real, more of a person than this woman reminding all citizens that tracking is now required, to make their way to the nearest console or visit one of the clubs tonight.

I hope they do. All of them.

The screen changes. When I was a kid, President Z hid behind a black curtain, a disembodied voice. Apparently Wraith doesn't care if people know who he is, but then, why would he.

And it's not him I'm looking at.

Fire. They look like fire all lined up together, yellow, orange, red. Fitting. Perfect. I want to watch the whole city burn, the same white-hot as the woman beside Jonas, frighteningly beautiful, platinum-haired, lips and eyes and nails painted the color of snow.

My blue laces are untied, fraying.

Kill them all.

It's not really him. Any him.

This place, this city. Poisoned. Beautiful in the way only things damaged beyond repair can be. I ignore the sounds coming from outside. It's too quiet down here, I want music. Music. Cold sweat beads, making me shiver. When the flashback—or withdrawal—comes, I'm ready for it, let it take me completely. White rooms and red ones, flames and glittering ice.

The Corp is eternal. Yes. Yes, it is.

I come to flat on my back, every muscle locked, teeth clenched. Grime coats the ceiling and for too long I don't know where I am. When I remember, I don't know why I'm here. It comes back too slowly.

The news is still on; cameras pan across Seattle, Los Angeles. I can't watch. I'm sorry for what I'm about to do to all the cities that were strong enough to survive countless wars, countless bombs.

Mostly sorry.

I type on the other keyboard, stopping, starting. Closing my eyes and remembering everything I saw Lynx and Mage do out at Central.

Pieces of code fit together, a puzzle never meant to be assembled. Squinting gives me a headache, sparking behind my eyes. The chill down here joins the pain that crackles over my skin, every cell trying to stretch to the nearest console station.

I can't test this one. Even if I could, I wouldn't. A green bar stretches across the monitor.

Almost.

Almost.

Done.

I slam the computers closed, shove everything but the flashlight back in my bag, run through the tunnels. My tablet goes off a few minutes from the trapdoor; I tab Lynx back. Might as well use him if he's awake. Purple spikes appear first, the rest of his head, an arm reaching down to help me up. Half the old crates down here aren't safe to stand on anymore.

"Where the fuck were you?" he asks as I wind the chain back in place.

"You really want to know?"

"Tell me you weren't—"

"I wasn't."

He shakes his head. "Then nope."

"Anyone else awake?"

"Just Spectrum. C'mon."

We sit in Pixel's office until sounds reach us from beyond. Phoenix opens the door, Sabine behind her, and I slip out, heading for the balcony. Stop with my foot on the bottom step.

". . . you did more than anyone ever should've asked, man. I mean, we all did, but it was you. No one forgets that."

"No one asked."

Mage. And Ant. I consider leaving them to it, but Mage calls my name, gives me no choice but to go up. It doesn't seem like they've been arguing, or if they have, it's over for now. Again, Ant is the only thing lighting the room. Mage is on a chair near the makeshift viewer, relaxed, maybe more than I've seen him in a long time, the knot of secrets gone from between his shoulders. When I step closer, he yawns, stands, kisses my forehead.

"You guys okay now?" I ask Ant when Mage is gone.

"Will be. We've known each other a long time, and I think we have enough enemies already. You pick your battles, I guess."

Pain grips my chest. Enemies. My brother—Ant's brother—

and someone I chose to love. That's who he's talking about.

Enemy. It's an ugly word. A word with cruel edges.

"I didn't know." It's the truth, but I'm glad he won't ask me whether I would have told him Wraith was still alive if I *had* known. Not sure I have an answer to that.

"I know you didn't."

"Okay."

I've gotten so used to him that I catch myself nearly offering him a bottle of water when I get one for myself. Shaking my head, I fall into Mage's chair, swipe the blue strands from my eyes.

"Unplug me."

The room goes very quiet. Airless. Ant's projection shimmers, my eyes refocusing so I can't see *him*, just a mass of light. Something hums but I think it's inside my own head.

"What?" I heard Anthem, and he knows it.

"Delete me."

"Why?" It's a better question, a more honest one.

"Because I can't watch this happen again, Al, and even if I get her back, I can't really be with her, which is almost everything I've ever wanted. And if I don't get her back . . . there's so much I haven't said to her. How can a person ever be finished with that? I don't want to float here, having those conversations with myself. I'm done. I'm so tired. Omega. I just"—Ant puts his head in one translucent hand—"I can't."

Anger, quick and hot and entirely unfair rises in my throat. "But *I'm* supposed to? He's my brother, too. He's my fucking twin. I'm supposed to sit back and watch this, or join him, or fight him. Those are my only choices and they all suck, so doing something is better than doing nothing, and I'm sure as hell not going to go become the Corp's little mascot."

"I took my turn." Ant glares at me, eyes so bright they're

painful to look at. "I tried. I failed, obviously."

So that's what this is about. I wish I could fault him, but I can't, and it makes the anger flare hotter. "You bought us all eight years."

"Yeah." He scoffs. "Eight years of what? The one thing I was sure of was that we'd put an end to them; only they're back, and we didn't get rid of everyone we thought we did. All this time, I at least thought Scope died for something. Doing something. Instead, I lost my best friend and that yellow-wearing asshole has been wandering around, and now he has Omega."

"Scope did die for something." I stand, the chair suddenly uncomfortable. Ant flinches at the name. "He died for all of us. Mage and Phoenix did what they thought was right at the time—what else could they have done? Seriously? Haven needed you. Omega and I needed you."

The questions, pleas are all there in my head, but I can't make them come out, I don't know how. I need him to teach me what he knows, the things he learned. I know Omega and Jonas—maybe—but Ant will make the best guesses about Wraith, what he'll do. We need his link into the system, too, but most of all I need one of my brothers on my side or there's no point. That easy surrender will slide over my skin, pull me under, and I'll welcome it when it comes.

"Al—"

"No." I kick the chair. "No, Ant. I needed you then, and I need you now. You know Omega and I had a fight just before all this happened?" I wipe my eyes. "He called me a hypocrite, and yeah, maybe. But I'm not an idiot. All that stuff we did at Central"—all the stuff I just did down in the tunnels—"it's a guess. A theory. An experiment that I might've severely fucked up. What if I have to . . ."

254

"You won't."

"You can't say that. I have an idea, yeah, and maybe it'll work, but there've been plans before." I kick myself. Shit. Proving his point won't get me anywhere. I take a breath, try to find a hidden reserve of calm, and meet his eyes. "This could all go totally wrong. And I can't kill you both."

27

Hours drag. We have to wait until dark, when people are awake, out, tracking or at one of the clubs, ready again after last night's binge. Pixel and Isis arrive, their faces erasing the fear that caught our breath when the door opened, replacing it with a new kind.

Guards outside their apartment, uniforms climbing from the pod, giving them just enough time to sneak out the back door.

We don't have long. Withdrawal stabs at me—nails on my skin. I breathe, try to push it away.

"I need to talk to you guys," I say to Lynx, Spectrum, and Sabine, jerking my head toward the back room. Eyes follow us down the stairs, and I know they want to know what I'm up to.

We don't go down into the tunnels, but we're as far as we can get from everyone else and still be in the club. "Okay," I say, closing the door. Sabine watches me, her face a softer mask than it's been in days. Lynx and Spectrum are more curious, edgy, fidgeting. Spectrum wipes a crumb of black eyeliner from his cheek, and I nearly laugh that he bothered with it today. I pull a tiny black chip from my pocket, identical to the others we've made in appearance if not content. "I did something this morning."

"We about to find out what you were up to down there?" Lynx asks, flicking his gaze to the trapdoor.

"Yes." I tell them what it is.

A risk, that's what it is, and it makes me no better than Wraith or Omega.

"You know what you're asking," Spectrum says. I stand up straighter.

"I know I'm not asking."

It's the wrong thing to do, as bad as what the Corp has already done, but in another way. The same melody in a different key.

Sometimes that's the only way to make the music work.

"Let me get this straight," Sabine says. I wait, she walks in a small circle, footprints in the dust, faces me again. "You haven't tested this?"

"How can I? But it'll work."

Belief and doubt weigh back and forth in her hands. "Things are going to get crazy out there," she says finally.

"I know." I feel bad about that, but better about the relief that she's agreed to it.

"So we need to use this one first," Lynx says. "We'll have time to set up the one for Los Angeles and Seattle after."

"Yes." The track I made this morning is only for the Web, the last time I'll choose it over my beach. A special for the Citizens. An absurd memory returns of being in the living room of our apartment down in Two, my father dying on the couch, a bright-faced woman on TV reporting that new tracks had been released, everyone should go to the clubs to sample them.

Yes, go. Everybody go.

"You guys can get into headquarters without being seen?" I know, but I need to check.

"Oh, like it'd be the first time," Spectrum says. I've never known anyone who can roll his eyes like he can. "Challenge us, would you?"

I see the sarcasm for what it is, think about their faces in the pod on the way to Central.

We head back out, join the others. Lynx and Spectrum start to get ready, hands slow and methodical as they change into uniforms, pack bags, tuck guns into waistbands. I won't ask them again if they're sure they can do this, I know what they'll say. They'll never break a law bigger than this one, and they're always up for a new adventure.

"Good luck," I say. Lynx nods, eyes intense. Mage hands him a black chip, this one shaped a little differently, its edges crusted with blood. I hear the splash of bodies again, falling into the river. Mage's knuckles are bruised, blue. He gives another to Spectrum. Two more taken from the guards at Central to Sabine and me. The last one he keeps.

Just in case.

Only Lynx and Spectrum leave, but the club is even quieter after the chain rattles; the trapdoor slams. An awful, sucking silence, barely filled by Pixel turning the music up. I pace the dance floor, climb and descend the stairs a dozen times. They have to get all the way from here to the Vortex on foot, through dark tunnels.

Every second feels like an hour. The neon lights blur again; the ache turns to pain and screams along my nerves. This time when Isis knocks on the door of the hygiene cube, I wipe my mouth and tell her she can come in.

"Are you sure you're up to this?" she asks.

"I know what I'm doing."

"That wasn't the question."

"I think it worked," I whisper, afraid to say it too loud, make it too real in case I'm wrong. "I haven't had one in two days." Not a flashback, anyway. The withdrawal still bites at me, sharp-toothed, insistent.

"Oh, Al. You did it."

Yeah. And all I had to do was come back here, watch my brother resurrect the Corp, lose my boyfriend to the evil that has consumed half my life, and kill my best friend with my attempts to stop it.

"I'll want to check you out later."

"Sure. Okay." I don't really want to know what she'll find. What my brain looks like now. I think I'm finally myself and I don't want her to tell me otherwise.

Lines of code fall around Ant on the balcony. "They're in," he says, tracing their path through Corp headquarters, stolen chips opening forbidden doors. Sabine takes a bundle of clothes and disappears. I'm not changing. I'm going as myself or not at all.

Timing is everything. I need Omega, Wraith, and Jonas shut away in a windowless room, cut off, where they can't see what's happening outside, where no one can tell them. It's tempting to use the white one, but I have a different kind of chorus in mind.

As soon as I give them the word, Lynx and Spectrum will load the track I made in the tunnels into the system, send it playing across consoles and through club speakers. Over radio waves and out into the air, drowning the Web in sound. We'll take care of the rest . . . after. Send a different track out to save the people in Los Angeles, Seattle.

Save me. Save all of us.

"Guys, give us a minute?" Ant asks. Everyone gets up from the couches, files past me. Pixel gives me a long look; Phoenix kisses my cheek on her way. I face Ant, hope that he isn't going to say what I might in his shoes. I'm not saying good-bye to him, to anyone here. I am coming back. They have to believe that so I can believe it.

He waits for the door to Pixel's office to close. Another minute. A minute after that. I will back my annoyance. Fuck, just spit it out already.

"If I haven't said it before—" He stops, starts again. "Fuck, this is going to sound patronizing. I just mean, I'm proud of you. I swear, Al, back then . . . I thought I'd done enough. I really thought I stopped it, saved you guys. I had no idea I'd just made it worse."

Relief. Irritation. No. Enough. I stand, face him as squarely as I can. He's taller than I am anyway, and the viewer raises him several inches off the floor. "You did *everything*," I insist. "You bought us so much time. Can you imagine what life would've been like if you hadn't?" I can, too clearly. I've seen it now. "We all would've been brainwashed years ago. I wouldn't have learned to play, or gone to Los Angeles, or met Jonas. You bought me more of a lifetime than you ever had, Ant."

"Yeah?"

His uncertainty makes my eyes burn. "Yeah," I say. "And even if you hadn't, you loved us enough to try. There isn't anyone else in the Web who can say that."

It's time. I take out my tablet, stare for a minute at the black screen until it comes into focus. Touch the screen, bring it to life. I have choices here, who I send the message to. My fingers trace over the last message Jonas sent me, over Omega's name, ready to reply.

I can give you everything you want._

Okay, I type back to Wraith, an answer to messages sent weeks ago. I surrender._

■

"I'm coming with you," Pixel says, voice full of a quiet determination I've never heard from him. "That fucker's mine."

Arguments ricochet around my head. I don't want any of them to come, that's the point, but he's not doing it to help me, or take over because he thinks I can't handle what's about to come. This is him, his own revenge, and I can't deny him the chance.

"Fine." I turn to Ant. "Where are they?" I ask. My footfalls echo around the club as I pace.

"Wraith is at headquarters. Looks like Omega and Jonas are on their way back there."

Where I told Wraith I wanted all of them to meet me. I don't ask if *she's* with them, the girl with the white hair and the lips that have touched Jonas in the same places mine have, and he doesn't tell me. It won't make a difference, anyway. Inhale. Force away the image, that kiss.

It's not him in there, inside his own head. It's not any of them. This is going to work, has to work.

And I need to see his eyes, to watch my brother come back to me. I don't think about the alternative again, I've done that enough.

Pixel and Isis brought more guns, bullets. Lynx told them where to find his and Spectrum's stash. Our own contingency plan.

And headphones, consoles we've loaded with music we know is safe.

Okay.

"I'll get Haven back," I promise Ant. I'll get all of the ones who matter, and Wraith is Pixel's job now. He nods. Phoenix and Isis hold each other, watching me. Mage curls his beaten hands around the balcony railing. "You all have to promise me you'll stay here." Here, in this old building that so cleverly keeps sound in—and out. Thanks, Corp. "Stay here and don't listen to anything except the safe stuff."

One by one, they promise. "Al—" Ant begins. I walk right up to him.

"My turn," I tell him. "You'll see her soon."

And I switch him off.

"Okay," I say.

There's no reason to take the tunnels now and sneak toward headquarters, ducking into alcoves and holding our breath while disembodied flashlights bob past. They know we're coming. This is my Web as much as Omega's, Anthem saw to that, and I'm taking it back.

"I'm driving," Sabine says.

Good. We could use a little lunacy.

Outside, I see what I need to. Feet moving in unison. Choreographed, but this is not dancing. There is no joy here, no light, no euphoria. What they have been subjected to isn't music, just sound drawn from strings and keys by the long, cruel fingers of the Corp, stretching through the years since the rebellion to grasp their throats.

Omega, too. Jonas.

Wraith . . . well, Pixel has plans for him and none of us are standing in his way. We could break him, I think, if we had to. Fuck knows that's what the Corp would do.

But sometimes you just have to kill.

Sabine swerves the pod out into traffic, north, up through the Web that was my first home. The Web that created me, taught me what I needed to know to survive. In the opposite seat Pixel stares out the window, lips thin, angry and worried. My tablet buzzes.

They're ready.

One minute._

"Headphones on," Pixel says, leaning forward with a pair to cover Sabine's ears while the tires screech. I slip mine onto my head, turn up the volume on the portable console hooked to my belt.

One, two, one two three four . . .

And the music is everywhere.

I press the headphones tighter, because I promised.

Protection. The world has turned inside out, and out there is my voice, blasting from radios, speakers in clubs, consoles at packed stations. Stretching further than I would be able to hear even if my ears weren't covered, all the way to Los Angeles, Seattle, over radio waves and through communications systems.

Come on.

There. Across the street.

I only see it because I'm watching for it, eyes flicking back and forth, searching for any sign, however small. And it is small, just one footstep out of time, out of sync. Its owner jolts, stops, surprise twisting heavily painted features. I squint and it's like watching someone wake up, which I guess is exactly what it is. The blinks, the tentative stocktaking of surroundings, the familiar made strange, tainted by the fog not yet cleared from his brain.

He takes another step against the tide, the coordinated onrush like the water racing up the sand on my beach.

I keep watching. That one guy is just a spark, useless unless everything else catches fire.

Come on, come on.

We need the chaos. It's probably wrong of me to think of these people—my people, my fellow citizens—as kindling, but I do. This is what will burn the Corp to the ground for good.

There, and there, and there. The shackles are invisible, the chains inside their minds, but I can still see them being thrown off, torn away by the music playing everywhere. My finger catches on my headphones, meant to block it out. If I take them off I'll get a tiny hit. It's not encoded to be addictive, this track we made, but there will be something . . . other. For a few seconds, I wouldn't have to be me.

"Don't you dare," Pixel says. I don't understand the movement of his lips, but the meaning in him hitting my hand is pretty clear. Sure. *Now* he's paying attention.

Fine.

When we light our bonfires in the sand, there's always a point, my favorite instant, the second when licks of flame flash over into something crazed and uncontrollable. It happens in the crowd at Mage and Phoenix's club when the music is just right, too, the moment you know you have everyone's attention for as long as you ask for it. The moment they start to feel.

On the street, the fire ignites. The formation breaks completely.

Here we go.

People come from everywhere, streaming from apartment buildings and stores, disoriented and frightened. *I'm sorry we have to do this to you*, I want to yell, but they wouldn't hear me over the instructions planted in their brains. Instructions I put there, coded just this morning.

Windows smash. A fight breaks out over a pod and the winner climbs behind the wheel. The loser looks left, right, begins to run.

That's it. Run.

Toward the bridge. Get out of here. Go west to my ocean, let it save you as it saved me. We'll fix things there, too.

Light dawns behind Pixel's eyes, realization. I haven't wiped their brains clean, like I said I would. This is the choice Ant never would've made, but I'm not him. The timing is almost perfect, if accidental since Pixel wasn't supposed to be in the pod with me. He can't argue, stop it. I can almost see him trying to decide whether he would if it were possible.

Sabine punches the dashboard, foot twitching above the accelerator. I close my eyes and try to picture this scene in Los Angeles. That will be next, the people there taking their city back from an enemy they never asked for. My city.

From an enemy we took to them.

My fingers curl around my console. The glass spider looms ahead. I jump out as soon as Sabine stops, push my way through the crowd that is thick enough to crush me, squeeze the air from my lungs. My tablet flashes and the information it gives me makes the most twisted kind of sense I can think of.

Poetry. Symmetry.

Like the tunnel, I wonder if Omega will ever appreciate the elegance.

Pixel crashes into my back. Together we watch a cluster of guards desert their posts and climb into their pods, headphones still in their ears, playing our tracks now, not the ones Wraith forced on them.

I know where they are_ I type quickly and show Pixel the screen. He nods. From the corner of my eye I see Sabine disappearing around the corner, going to help Lynx and Spectrum save her city as she's helped me save mine.

The gun weighs heavy in my pocket. Time to see my brother.

28

I walk into the soundproof room alone, Pixel hiding, a button push away. It's a special kind of loud in here when I pull off my headphones, a silence so ringing and absolute it engulfs my ears. My heart stops.

"Welcome home, Alpha."

Omega sits on a stool, the same one Ant used while the red light blinked, recording his music and later mine. Anger seethes. How dare he smile, here of all places. But he knows what he's doing—or at least, the monster inside of him created by the Corp is enjoying this. And I am the one who told him to be here.

I used to think we told each other everything, but now I see how he's spent a long time looking at me and seeing someone who is almost a stranger. It's not him in there. I don't owe him all of the explanations that bubble at the back of my throat. Not yet. I owe him only a few.

"Where are they?" I ask instead.

"Coming, they had to get something. They'll be here in a sec. It's good to see you."

I don't answer. Wraith is Pixel's problem, but Jonas . . . Jonas is here somewhere.

"You're not really surrendering, are you?"

I lift my arm a few inches higher. My finger twitches against the trigger, a spasm for all the things he's forced me to do. I wonder if this is how it felt when he raised the gun to me in that hospital room. I doubt it. No fear tinges the eyes I know like my own. No remorse.

"It's over," I say. "I figured out the cure for me, for everyone. They're all leaving. You made it easy." A lie, but a satisfying one. I want to see that flinch. Later, I'll want him to know what I've done to myself to make this happen. What I've done to people I love. A console blinks on the wall and fuck, even now . . . but some of that will have to wait until he's Omega again.

"They had to keep listening so you could keep controlling them. That's an old Corp trick, but I guess you needed to stick with what works, right?"

He just looks at me, a pointed stare that pierces, deflates me. "It's over," I say again. "Come back to me. *Omega.* Come back."

There it is, that same flash of recognition I saw just before we left for Central. The crush of the crowd outside is long gone but again I can't breathe, a hand clenching my heart as tightly as the tracks held on to everyone's minds. I still don't know exactly why the Corp's plan worked on him and not me. *They're twins, not clones*, Isis repeats in my memories, and my skin grows cold at the thought of what might have happened if that weren't true.

We wouldn't be here, that's for sure.

I click a few buttons on my portable console and take a step toward him. "You just need to listen to this."

His hand jerks and drops back by his side.

"Please, Omega."

Jerk.

The gun is cold against my palm. Now, now is when I have to decide how far I'll go. Letting him walk away isn't an option, everything else is open, my choice. This has always been about choice, all of it.

But he stops me.

"I need to show you something first," he says, and his voice doesn't quite sound like his own. I would know. I search his eyes. Nothing. No hint. "Let me show you, and then I'll listen."

"What?" Hairs raise on my arms.

"Just wait."

In his lap, a tablet flashes. I'm too far to read the screen and it's too quiet in here.

The moment my heart speeds up is way too loud.

And it's that second which makes me realize this was a mistake—on my part, not his. I can't hear any of what's going on outside. My tablet hasn't gone off in ten minutes. I have no fucking idea where my friends are.

I'm not even sure I can bet on *who* they are. And they could be anywhere.

He wasn't just being clever, waiting for me in this room, or not only for the reason I thought.

"What am I waiting for?" I ask. The shake in my voice, I can hear that, and it's not comforting.

"You should have kept running," he says flatly. The hints of orange in his hair and clothes and makeup catch the lights, vivid as a warning. "I told you I wouldn't try to stop you if you did. You should've kept going, Alpha."

Maybe. But if he were the brother I'd known and loved for so long, he would have known why I couldn't.

The door opens. I press the button on my tablet.

Yellow, red. The fire complete.

Jonas.

And pink. Long streaks of it pouring out from underneath a blindfold. Taking away another of her senses. I run to her, tear it off, and her eyes blink at painful light.

"You can have her back," Wraith says to me. Omega shrugs. She was only used to hurt Ant, and doesn't matter anymore. Jonas was to hurt me, and that still matters.

Fear turns my mouth dry. Where the fuck is Pixel? He insisted on coming, now I'm counting on it.

"I cut the power to all the floors below this one," Wraith says, like he's the one who could read my mind if he tried, like he isn't the person in this room who knows me the least. "Locked all the doors, elevators aren't working. Anthem did that the last time, and hey, why screw with what works? They'll figure it out, but we've got a few minutes."

Jonas's eyes are blank, no sign of recognition. I don't know what the hell they've done to him, but I force that pain away, there are so many others that need my attention first.

"Now," Wraith continues. "What are we going to do with you? What punishment could possibly be good enough?"

I step back against the wall. A violin string twangs against my shoulder.

"You've done well," he says. "So what if you've sent everyone out west? I mean, good trick, but you know Los Angeles and Seattle are ours, too. Long as the mainframe here keeps running, who cares? This place is old anyway. I like the idea of living by the ocean."

Anger simmers. He's not getting my ocean.

"Do whatever you want to me," I snarl. "You can't stop what we've already done." I'm not completely sure that's true, but it sounds good. Like the kind of thing a person's supposed to say in this situation.

"I can do whatever I want." He looks at Omega, at Jonas, turns a mock-pitying expression on me. "It's adorable that you think you could stop me, just like Ant did, back in the day. No one can; no one will even try. Especially not these two."

I'm absolutely sure *that's* true.

My friends are trapped downstairs. Anthem's on his viewer at the club. No one in this room will help me, except Haven, and she can't. I can't ask her to.

"Maybe I'll show some mercy." He reaches into a pocket and pulls out a gun, identical to the one hanging limp and useless from my hand because I'd forgotten it was there. "Make it quick. Sound good?"

Sound. There's no sound here.

And everything happens at once.

The door opens again. Omega jumps to his feet. A flash of pink crosses my vision and strong, long-nailed hands shove me out of the way as my eardrums explode from the sound of the bullet in this room designed for noise. A bullet meant for me.

Green, purple, white. I see them all, but only for a second. Another shot rings out and Wraith falls over a drum kit, the cymbals crashing. But it's too late.

"Haven!" I scream. She's right in front of me, right where I was a second ago. I throw my arms out, try to catch her, but she sinks in slow motion, wordless as she hits the floor, blood blooming just above her heart.

■

The Web speeds past, unseen as I rehearse words that don't make sense, tears burning into the cracks in my lips. I tab Mage. Tell him where to meet me.

"She's—"

"I—"

"Haven—"

No. The unmistakable whistle is still loud, ringing, drowning out all the noise around us as the bullet slices over and over through the air. Her handprints are still seared into my skin, aching like bruises. Actual bruises on my knees throb from where I slammed into the floor.

Crunch. A wet, sickening kind of crunch. She didn't scream, but then, Haven's always been the strongest by far. Maybe—definitely—the best of us.

Jagged words cut my throat again and my teeth chatter. Every breath feels wrong, undeserved, stolen. I'm cheating; I shouldn't be here in this pod, racing away from headquarters.

Spectrum slams the brakes. I lurch forward, practically fall out the door, and I laugh. Like that could hurt me. I should be dead right now.

Nothing makes sense.

"Do you need me?" Spectrum asks. My knees knock together and I can't talk but I shake my head because no, I have to do this alone. Almost.

It takes too long for Mage to arrive, coming from farther away. I pace the floor, stare down at blood glowing on my hands under the lights.

"Al! Kiddo?" His voice is simultaneously panicked and relieved and curious, somehow all crammed into that one tiny syllable. "What's going on? Did it work? Is everything okay?"

I want to laugh again, except, no, I don't. Nothing's okay. Nothing is going to be okay. Omega and Jonas might recover; the others are taking care of what we went to the glass spider to do. The Web and Los Angeles and Seattle might recover, but things are as far from okay as I can remember them being.

"Al? What's wrong?"

And then his voice changes. My adopted uncle knows me well. "Who."

"Wraith tried to shoot me." The bullet screams through the

air again, a trail of heat close enough to burn. Whistle. *Crunch.* My knees throb harder. Mage is so relieved he laughs, the sound bubbling from the speaker. "Oh, thank fuck. Is everyone else—"

"She pushed me out of the way."

Silence. Deafening, dead silence, the complete absence of sound and motion. "Sabine?"

I shake my head. "Haven."

Fresh tears boil over, soaking my face. "I didn't know! They had her and then she was behind me and I didn't know, I swear, and now she's . . . she's . . ."

"Is she dead?" he asks, cold and clipped and clinical. For the first time, he sounds like a machine instead of like *him*. "Is she dead?"

"She isn't now." Pain stabs my lungs. "But she was when I took this." I hold out her memory chip, dripping, full of her crazy lifetime. "Mage, I promised him I'd bring her back."

He's not easily surprised, but he knows how I felt after Haven brought Ant to this very building, put him on the viewer six feet away from where I am now. Most of her stuff is still here; Pixel and Isis didn't move everything out after Wraith took her. Computers sit, humming and waiting, behind a desk.

"Please," I say. "This will kill him if we don't." Ant is alive now. I don't know when I started thinking of him like that. Figures I'd realize it in the last few minutes I have. He asked me to unplug him, delete him, and if I go back and tell him now that she's dead, he'll ask me again.

This way, they can be together. The forever they fought so hard for. I think of all the things I still have to say to Jonas, years worth, and finally understand why Haven made her choice, worked so hard to figure out how to do it.

"Can you?"

Slowly, he nods. "Think so. I helped her with a lot of the stuff downstairs. If her code's on here . . ." He moves over to the computers and I follow, put the chip down beside his hand.

"You have to hurry. Mage." My voice cracks, shatters. "I promised I'd bring her back."

■

We've learned enough lessons from the Corp. Right. Wrong. What works and what doesn't.

Eight years ago, Anthem broke them, and they came back.

For too many years before that, they ruled over us with their drugs and their guns, keeping the population down, at levels just right for their grand experiments.

I almost want to laugh. Pod after pod passes over the bridge, a smooth stream of headlights pointing west.

"They'll all get out?" Phoenix asks.

"Hope so. Lynx and Spectrum are getting Ant and everything from the club, they'll meet us on the way. You help Isis? I have to—"

Go back to Mage.

"We'll take care of them," Phoenix promises, tucking a strand of blue hair behind my ear. "Go."

Where are you?_

At the CRC. Nearly done installing.
Don't worry, kiddo._

Kiddo. He'll pay for that later. That there'll be a *later*, one without the Corp, sinks in so abruptly it steals my breath. For the very last time, I stand outside the black glass spider trying to catch it.

It's time to go home.

Traffic is hell getting up to Mage, a problem so ordinary it borders on ridiculous. I let the other pods go by, each one turning toward the mainland.

It's not safe for them here anymore, not safe for anyone. Los Angeles will take care of them, where sunlight chases away what might lurk in the shadows, or Seattle, where rain washes away the grime. Not here, this nothing-place that had to create its own light in shades of neon and only managed to highlight the darkness.

At the CRC, Mage is closing half a dozen computers when I open the door. He gives one to me, tucks a small black box into my pocket. "Anything else you want to take?" he asks. "We got time to go get your parents."

"No." I'm sure of it now—the secret to never coming back is to pretend that I can, that I will. "We good here?"

"Almost. Just the one last thing."

We shut the doors of the CRC a few minutes later, load up the pod with armfuls of electronics and climb in. Back down to headquarters, where Isis, Phoenix, and Pixel wait with Omega and Jonas, Sabine behind the wheel of a pod big enough to hold their stretchers in the back.

He looks so pale. They both do, but I stand beside Jonas, my hand twisting in the sheet pulled over him, fingers creeping until I finally link them with his. Warm, strong. I know these hands.

It takes hours for the Web to clear out, the citizens responding to a message in their heads they can't explain, not the first one that's been put there, but the last if I have anything to say about it. Everything else has been scrubbed clean, and here, in the empty lobby of headquarters, the whole place is hollow, sad, almost pathetic. Filled with memories, sure, but we can take the ones we want with us and leave the rest behind. Downstairs is the site of the old Energy Farm that sucked so much of the life from Ant, upstairs the office where Omega took the freedom from so many.

"Time?" Phoenix asks.

"Yep."

We push the stretchers out onto near-empty streets, the silence so absolute it's scary. Around us, the multicolored lights of the Vortex, flickering and pointless, paint the sidewalks and the sky.

But not for much longer.

"Keep them asleep?" I ask. Isis nods. She and Pixel take the pod with Sabine. Phoenix and Mage and I climb into the other, arranging ourselves around piles of metal, plastic, and wire. There's not much to say here, but then, we're not going far. Mage lets the others take the lead. We coast in the trails of their taillights over the bridge and stop just on the other side.

The roar of the river is loud after the disturbing quiet on the island. My eyes strain for any last pods winking among the buildings, but there's nothing. I walk right to the edge of the water, as close as I can get to the Web, as close as I'll ever get again.

"Haven should be here to see this," I say. "Ant, too." And all the others we've lost. But at least we'll be able to tell Ant and Haven about it, what the moment looked like, the held breath before it happened. Phoenix puts her arm around me.

I'm not sure when it all became less about getting my brother back, or Jonas, or getting rid of Wraith, and more about this moment. About making the choices Anthem never would have, but that I know are right. But the moment's here now, hovering, inching closer second by second.

Sometimes you have to kill.

And the Web goes . . .

Dark.

29

The room is white, bright white, lights exploding like miniature suns even when I close my eyes. Something *clicks*, a hand pats my shoulder.

"All done."

An image of my brain repeats across half a dozen monitors. I know more about what I'm looking at than I did a few months ago, though not as much as Isis beside me.

"Have you had any more?"

I shake my head. No, and the withdrawal is getting better, too. Some of that might be the knowledge that I'm not going through it alone, the way I was with my flashbacks and Omega across the country. Everyone here, Los Angeles people and Web citizens alike, is suffering the same insidious itch. An itch that will slowly fade.

More people than I'm used to fill the streets around the hospital, still a little dazed, blinded by the sun which will never feel like the same one that shone on the Web. Still getting their bearings, finding their way around a city that sprawls like the Web never did. I wave at some of them, see the flicker of recognition for who I am, but almost none of them know what I did—that it was me. I'm content never to have anyone visit me on my deathbed and call me a hero.

I feel the sun on my face, sinking lower and lower in the sky as I walk toward home, the beach. I've had enough of racing around in pods for a while. A ball of red fire in a sky free of clouds, no storms on the horizon, falling away to darkness.

■

The ocean glows blue.

Anthem blue. I dyed my hair back to its wild rainbow and the shades catch the firelight as I hide behind the strands. I almost miss the blue, but this is better because sometimes you have to say good-bye. He and Haven are safe, together in a room above Mage and Phoenix's club.

Omega sits on the sand a little way down the beach, out of the glow, moving every few minutes to toss a pebble into the waves. Small, harmless gestures, doing no damage, forgotten by the water as soon as it closes over the stone.

"It felt like a dream," Jonas says, inches away, too far and too close.

"A nightmare."

"Or that."

Splash. Another pebble, and the water bubbles up the shoreline. Jonas leans in; I turn my head so his lips land at the corner of my mouth. Disappointment crackles like the fire and I squeeze his fingers before standing, brushing the sand from my legs.

"We should go; we're going to be late," I say to Omega. He doesn't answer, but he follows, the three of us making our way back to the pod.

I drive, peering through the windshield at my city, the obvious marks of the short time the Corp had control here. It hurts to admit that some good things happened. The brainwashed population cleaned the streets, repaired buildings long left to ruin. Made everything slick and shiny, just like the Vortex. Somehow, it fits, looks even more like it belongs on this spread out to the hills and the mountains beyond. Jonas and Omega sit in the back, silent, still working at banishing the demons that took over them.

"Hey, Al," Phoenix calls from behind the bar as we walk in the club. Mage is in the DJ booth. I can't see Sabine, but she's here somewhere, and I'll find her in a minute. We'll go talk about Fable some more, because there's time now and it's the only thing that makes it hurt less. Lynx and Spectrum are on the dance floor, twined together, a sculpture of life carved from a single piece of stone.

Lights whirl. So much light, and I think of the dark, shadowy hulk of the Web in the rearview mirror.

"Do you think it will stay like that?" Jonas asks, reading my thoughts on my face. Another tiny part of me relaxes.

"No." Someone will come along and resurrect it, but it will never be what it was. Wraith is dead—Pixel checked. Twice.

In the crowd, I see faces I recognize. A guard, a guy who cleaned the studios at headquarters, a woman who ran one of the Sky-Clubs. Their eyes are clear, lips turned up in smiles not fake or forced.

"Dance with me?" I take Jonas's hand. I have everything I want.

Maybe the Web will rise again. Repeat itself. A chorus.

But not tonight.

Acknowledgments

The trouble with writing a sequel (other than that sequels are *really hard*, as I've now learned) is that you wind up thanking most of the same people. For anyone who read the *Coda* acknowledgments, I apologize for the repetition, but it must be done. *Chorus* exists because of:

My editor, Lisa Cheng, to whom these characters are as real as they are to me. Her understanding, encouragement, and saint-like patience turned this book into the story I wanted to tell. She is also just awesome in all the ways a person and friend can be.

The team at Running Press Kids: thanks to Teresa Bonaddio for the amazing cover and interior design. Marlo, Elenita, and Allison for holding my hand at ALA. Gigi Lamm and Val Howlett, publicists past and present, who both absolutely rock.

My agent, Brooks Sherman, who shares a lot of my weirder musical tastes and all of my literary interests. B, you're an incredible agent and one hell of a friend. Thanks for both.

Meredith Barnes, who hit play. Mer, if Alpha is one-tenth as kick-ass as you, I'm happy.

All the bands I listed in the first set of acknowledgments—and then some—for soundtracking my days and more than a few late nights, whether I'm writing or not. Special mention to The Limousines, Robert DeLong, and more eighties synthpop than I should probably admit.

My family, who know when to ask how things are going and when to just mail me chocolate.

The people who put up with me when I go all writing-weird, when I can't think or talk about anything else, or when I want to talk about everything *but* the book. Britt and Brie, yes, always.

Tonya, Caren, Melissa, Leiah, Jenny, and countless others, I love you all more than I love cake. Claire, Katherine, and Stefan, thanks for giving me a place to escape so that I remember why I want to return to these crazy novel things. Sam, thanks for the cocktails, and Heidi, thanks for the cheerleading.

And finally, *Chorus* wouldn't exist without you, the readers. To everyone who read *Coda* and blogged about it, reviewed it, or got in touch by email, tweet, Facebook, or carrier pigeon (sadly there were no carrier pigeons) I am speechlessly grateful. You kept me going during the challenging process of writing *Chorus* in ways I can't even describe. Please consider this book a thank you.

See where it all began . . .

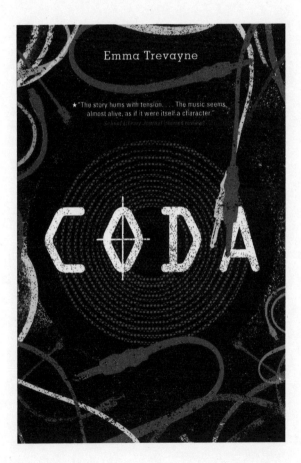

Emma Trevayne is a full-time writer and the author of *Coda* (a nominee for both the YALSA Best Fiction for Young Adults and ALA Rainbow Book lists) and *Flights and Chimes and Mysterious Times*, as well as a co-author of *The Cabinet of Curiosities*. She lives in London. You can visit her online at emmatrevayne.com or via Twitter @EMentior.